Doing Wrong

H. R. F. Keating is one of Britain's most highly acclaimed crime novelists. He has twice won the Crime Writers Association's Gold Dagger Award for best novel of the year, with *The Murder of the Maharajah* and *The Perfect Murder*, which was also made into a film by Merchant Ivory. In addition to his novels, H. R. F. Keating has also written non-fiction and edited numerous books in the crime field, including most recently *The Man Who . . . Anthology*, a tribute to Julian Symons.

Having served as Chairman of the Crime Writers Association and of the Society of Authors, H. R. F. Keating was elected President of the Detection Club in 1987. He is married to the actress Sheila Mitchell and lives in London.

'The Indianness of it all is conveyed with utmost skill'

EVENING STANDARD

'H. R. F. Keating's Inspector Ghote is a man much like ourselves only more so: diffident, misdoubting his own powers, often sadly muddled by the unaccountable happenings assailing him . . . Comedy of the international situation such as might have won the admiration of Henry James himself'

J. I. M. STEWART, TIMES LITERARY SUPPLEMENT

'Mr Keating has a long-established winner in his sympathetic and lively hero'

THE TIMES

'H. R. F. Keating breathes new life into the classic detective story'

REGINALD HILL

Doing Wrong

H. R. F. Keating

PAN

IN ASSOCIATION WITH MACMILLAN LONDON

First published 1994 by Macmillan London Limited

This edition published 1995 by Pan Books
an imprint of Macmillan General Books
Cavaye Place London SW10 9PG
and Basingstoke
in association with Macmillan London Limited

Associated companies throughout the world

ISBN 0 330 34004 2

1 3 5 7 9 8 6 4 2

A CIP catalogue record for this book is available from
the British Library

Phototypeset by Intype, London
Printed and bound in Great Britain by
Cox & Wyman Ltd, Reading, Berkshire

1

What have I done wrong, Inspector Ghote thought, climbing the stone stairs on his way to report to the Assistant Commissioner. Nothing. Truly nothing. I am right. Inspector Wagh is wrong.

Once again he saw the body in his mind's eye. Mrs Shoba Popatkar, veteran freedom fighter, former Minister, upholder of a hundred good causes. Her plain blue-check cotton sari flung out in a wide arc on the bare stone floor of her little flat. Her spectacles lying upside-down beside her. The time-sharpened old woman's face with its unmissable faint grey moustache, and the bruises in the fleshless throat where the murderer's thumbs had dug deep.

No, out there at Dadar, Wagh had got it wrong. Despite the way her purse was ripped open, that half-wit servant of hers did not arrange with some goonda to come and rob his employer. Why should he have? For years he has been her faithful employee. Oh, Wagh is saying it is always the servant one must first surmise on. True enough when nothing else is looking at all likely. But he should not have ignored and ignored every word of protest the fellow was babbling out when he arrested him. Just only because he is simple-minded.

And there are other things. Little things only. So little that Wagh made nothing of them. But there nevertheless. The small green uncollected return half of a rail ticket to Banares I was finding in that big leather handbag. No money in that, true. Something in Wagh's favour. But then what about the fellow I was just now questioning in the bazaar there? Fellow stating a man who asked him where Mrs Popatkar stayed had a Banares accent?

Yet not so much to set against Wagh's quick arrest. Will ACP sahib think I am making a fool of myself only to want to go to Banares?

What have I done wrong, H. K. Verma asked almost aloud to the dawn Banares sky as he climbed out of the wide flooded Ganges, the water from his soul-cleansing bathe streaming off his broad back.

Yes, I killed her. But I had to do it. It was right to do it. Right. God Krishna himself is saying it. In holy Geeta when he is telling Arjuna it is his duty to fight. To kill, if need be, each and every man in the army opposite.

Negotiating the last of the slippery, silted-over steps, nevertheless a huge groan escaped him.

But to have killed her . . . Strangled her . . .

When I was always wanting to do right. Always from boyhood days. Never have I so much as once thought of taking the life of any man, woman or child. But . . . But if I had not done that . . . And I was asking her not to tell the world what she had read in that confession of lost faith KK was making. I was asking and asking. I was begging her. And she would not listen. *No, no, truth must come out. It is what I have always fought for.* The obstinate old woman. When that truth will make so much of difference. Not to me alone, but to all I would be able to help in India. When I am, after so many years, having in my grasp one Cabinet seat. Minister for Social Upliftment. Yes, I will get that. It is all but arranged. I know it will come. I know.

No, no. I was right to do it. Right.

'Well, Inspector,' the Assistant Commissioner said, 'I expect, of course, when on an important case a Crime Branch officer is sent to keep an eye on the local fellows that he may find all is not up to the mark.'

Then a look of sharp doubt flicked on to his face.

'But I am well knowing Inspector Wagh out at Dadar,' he added. 'A first-class officer.'

'Oh, yes, sir. Yes. But, sir, I am thinking this time he is going too much by the rules in arresting the servant there. Altogether correct procedure, sir, and quick work also. But, sir, that fellow, Tantya by name, is truly half-witted. I am believing Mrs Popatkar was employing him out of kindness itself. She was having that reputation. So, sir, Inspector Wagh was not listening to all the jabber the fellow was uttering.'

'If it was half-witted nonsense only, Inspector, Wagh was quite right not to waste time with it.'

'Yes, sir. But, sir, Tantya was saying and repeating that Mrs Popatkar had suddenly decided to visit Banares and had given him some leave. He was to come back today only, before she herself thought she would be here in Bombay again. Sir, her killer must have come just only after she had arrived back earlier than she had thought. Her suitcase itself had not been unpacked even. Tantya is claiming, as far as I was able to make it out, that when he was coming back at the time she had told he was just only finding her dead. He was after all reporting crime, sir.'

'And you believe the fellow when Wagh does not?'

'Sir, it is not that only. Sir, I was finding in Mrs Popatkar's purse her rail ticket from Banares.'

'So the lady did visit Banares. Well, we are all meant to do that at some time or another. Stand in the Ganges, wash away the sins and so forth. That's no reason for her to have been murdered here in Bombay.'

Slowly H. K. Verma picked up his dhoti from the pile of clothes he had left at his usual place on the ghat steps.

But what if I was seen and remembered, there in Bombay, he asked himself, a quiver of fear running through the swell of his belly. What if I was seen in Dadar itself? Somewhere beside one of those decayed old houses

3

and the shops selling everything cheap that could be wanted? Or in that bazaar with those women in greasy saris squatting there with their newspaper sheets of wilting vegetables, and with those shapeless creatures in the doorways, those cripples and lepers lying wheresoever they could? Among the bargainings, the shoutings, the quarrellings?

Investigation must have already begun down there also. Questions already must be being asked. It will be a top-notch investigation too. Shoba Popatkar was a famed lady. Freedom fighter. Railways Minister in early Independence days. And resigning also when there was that train disaster: 200 killed. Who would do the same now?

But I will. If there is some altogether equal disaster in my department when I am a Minister in my turn, I would . . . If I am ever made Minister now. If police inquiries are not leading to me myself . . .

But they cannot. No inquiries can show I was there. Not howeversomuch of a first-class officer they are putting on to the case.

'But, sir,' Ghote said, aware that for some urgent inner reason he was perhaps pleading more than a self-respecting officer should. 'Sir, there is more itself. I was asking myself out there if it was truly likely that some small-time goonda would rob a lady known to all as doing so much of right thing. And, sir, I was also wondering whether in her hundred per cent bare flat there would be very much of anything to rob.'

'And where did all this wondering get you, Inspector?'

'Sir, I am believing the murder may be the work of some person wishing crime to be seen as a pure and simple housebreaking which was going wrong when Mrs Popatkar unexpectedly returned back.'

'And on the strength of this guess-guessing, Inspector, you are wanting to take permission to go all the way to Banares?'

'But, sir, one other thing also. I was making some

4

inquiries in the bazaar near Mrs Popatkar's flat. Sir, to find out if any stranger had been seen in vicinity itself. And, just only before coming to report, I was discovering one fellow who had been asked where Mrs Popatkar stayed. And, sir, this fellow was from UP-side himself, and he was recognizing the Hindi the man was speaking. Sir, it was very much of Bhojpuri, and, sir, you must be knowing that is the dialect they speak in that part of Uttar Pradesh.'

'Is it, Inspector? And is this expert in regional speech prepared to identify your mysterious visitor from Banares?'

'Sir, unfortunately he is not able. The man had gone before my witness had fully taken in what sort of Hindi he had been hearing. The fellow was altogether lost in the crowd in one half-minute only. You are knowing what like it is at that time of evening out in Dadar.'

'Yes, Inspector, that I do know.'

'But, sir, nevertheless, I may go to Banares? Sir, it is utter disgrace that a lady like Mrs Shoba Popatkar has been murdered itself.'

The ACP heaved a sigh.

H. K. Verma stood waiting for the new-risen sun to dry more of the wet off his body before beginning to wind his dhoti round his waist. Mother Ganga now was streaked in pink and yellow light when not ten minutes before, as he had clambered down at last into her sin-freeing water, her whole wide, floods-swollen expanse had been one mist-veiled grey sheet, the Sandbank on the far side altogether lost to sight.

For a moment he felt something of his old God-given morning tranquillity as his eyes followed a solitary boat in the distance, gliding in silence through the unruffled waters, the splash of its oars too far off to be heard. Then a burst of shouting brought him back to reality. A daring boy had succeeded in diving far out into the fast-flowing stream from the very top of the half-drowned temple at the foot of the next-door Dasawamedh Ghat. The triumphant yells of his friends broke clamorously into the soft murmur of prayers and early morning talk from the few worshippers at his own less frequented, semi-ruined bathing-place.

But what if someone who knew him among those people – the noises of garglings, nose-rinsing and body-scrubbing down at the water's edge came jarringly to him now – what if one of them was to greet him? Would it be noticed that he did not have his customary pile of fresh clothes? Be remembered? Mentioned later to some hunting panther of a police officer from Bombay-side?

But, no. No. Now that he had shiveringly immersed himself in the dawn-chill waters of the Ganga he was freed from that sin. If sin it had been. And freed surely – he must be – from its consequences. Surely, now, all of that had been wiped away. As if it had never happened. As if it had been someone else, someone altogether different, who in a sudden blur of rage had reached out to the old woman's scrawny neck and choked her into silence. Everlasting silence.

And he had taken some precautions. From the moment he had realized she lay dead at his feet his brain had become ice-clear. In an instant he had reviewed everything he had done coming to the flat. He had known for certain no one had seen him go inside. He had remembered that the questions he had asked finding his way had been no more than a few quick words. Encounters that among the jammed and jostling, shouting and arguing crowds there – a mercy that the old lady had chosen to live among the poors – could not have left any recollection. And then . . .

Then what cool, calculating voice within him had seen how easy it would be to make it all look like the work of some goonda? How easy to tear open that big, ugly handbag of hers? To snatch the few notes inside? He had even remembered fingerprints and had covered his bare hands with a corner of his dhoti. So, yes, it must look for all the world as if some good-for-nothing had killed Shoba Popatkar for what he could get.

He began pleating the travel-stained dhoti round himself, letting it fall down his still not wholly dry legs. Then the kurta, tugged over his head in one swift movement, and last his damp feet pushed into the socks and shoes he had been wearing the day before.

Shoes. Shoes, what a give-away they could be. Always, going down to the ghat, he slipped into a pair of chappals. Anyone who had seen him here would know it. It would be ridiculous to wear anything else going to the river. But at last the shoes were on and he could make his way back to the house.

No. Stop. Teeth. No toothbrush. Impossible to clean them. And he had done so morning after morning, never missing, year after year here at the ghat. Would failing to do it now somehow take away from his sin-lifting holy dip? No. Nonsense.

Nonsense. I must not give way to absurd superstitions. It is the going-down into the sacred water that washes sins away. No need for anything more than that. They even say – not that I can altogether believe it – it is enough simply to enter holy Banares for sins heaped up over a thousand lifetimes to be consumed by her fire as if they were just only tufts of cotton.

No, teeth brushed or not, I have been freed from that sin now. I am safe. I am.

The ACP heaved a sigh.

'Well,' he said, 'I've little doubt that before long Inspector Wagh will get hold of the culprit that servant is in league with.'

'But—'

'But, Inspector, I suppose there may be something in what you are saying. So go off to Benares, if you must. Only, do not get it into your head you may air-dash there like some filmi hero. There are perfectly good trains.'

'But, sir . . . Sir, by air it must be just only two–three

hours, and the train is taking more than twenty-four.'

'Then, you will have plenty of time to think, Inspector, yes? Time to dream up some reasonable idea of why anybody should want to come all the way from Banares just to kill a poor old former freedom fighter here in Bombay.'

2

H. K. Verma, approached by no friend, political client or acquaintance, plunged into the maze of narrow lanes that led from the Man Mandir Ghat to his house almost in the shadow of the gold-gleaming spires and dome of the Vishwanath Temple. By this route, at this early hour, he could count on hardly meeting a soul. Bathers going down to the Ganges or returning from it would almost all be taking the broad road to the Dasawamedh Ghat, most popular in the sacred city.

Hurrying between the tall old buildings with the sky now a thin strip of pale blue above, he began to feel luck must be with him. The little shops to either side still had their shutters down. At this hour there were no jostling passers-by to obscure the black, greasy marks rickshaw wallas' hands had left on the walls as they squeezed and fought their way along the narrow crowded gallis. No one was here to take note of his stained and wrinkled kurta. No one to wonder why, coming back from his sunrise dip, he was wearing shoes. Why his every step was ringing hideously out on the time-worn paving stones.

He came to the last corner before his house, where once on the wall some impudent jackal had painted in red *Please to Vote for Communist Party (Marxist)*. He turned, still blessing his luck, and saw that Karim, his Pathan watchman, was standing outside the gate. His long wooden staff, as on every morning when he expected his master back, was twirling with demonstrative vigour. His face with its massive curling moustache radiated unceasing vigilance.

For a moment H. K. Verma felt in his throat a lump of fear.

What if today Karim has noticed I did not leave the house earlier?

It took an upthrust of effort to bring out the jocular remark he produced almost every day. 'Ha, Karim, I was not spotting you when I was going out. Sleeping-sleeping, is it?'

But all was as usual. Karim gave him his leering smile and said, as always, 'Oh, huzoor, in the darkness you were not seeing. But every moment of the night I was awake, awake like a tiger only.'

The lump of fear dissolved altogether with the thought that now, if it should ever prove necessary, he had an alibi. Karim would have to swear after this, however contrary to the actual truth, that he had seen him leaving for his sunrise dip. If it should ever prove necessary. But it would not be necessary. It could not be. There was nothing to connect him in any way with that bare flat in that poor quarter of Bombay.

Slipping up the stairs, with shoes removed at the door clasped in his hand, he began finally to feel out of danger. And when he saw his fresh clothes, there on the chair just as they had been laid out the night before for him to take down to the ghat, he shook off the last clinging spider-webs of anxiety.

Only, moments later as he stripped off his soiled kurta and pulled away the scarcely less stained dhoti, to find his new optimism seeming to descend with them to the floor at his feet. His whole desperate attempt to get to Bombay in time to persuade the old woman not to spill out that fatal secret unrolled remorselessly in his mind.

Why did I need at the start of it all to telephone that idiot Srivastava at his library? Cannot at all remember. But what a state I found the old fool in. And, then, when he at last stammered out that Mrs Shoba Popatkar had insisted on seeing Krishnan Kalgutkar's *Recollections* . . .

'But, Srivastava sahib, that manuscript was deposited

in your library under strict instructions it was not to be read for one hundred and one years.'

'Sir, sir, I am knowing it. But, sir, perhaps you are not knowing Mrs Popatkar. Sir, she is not a person it is possible to refuse.'

And on the old idiot had babbled. Until, in exasperation, he had cut in.

'Srivastava sahib, when was Mrs Popatkar seeing? Was she having enough time to peruse the whole?'

'Oh, sir. She was leaving only ten–fifteen minutes past. And, yes, sir, she had read it all, she was saying *I know everything now.*'

'Leaving? Leaving for Bombay? Just now?'

'Yes, sir, yes. Bombay she was saying also.'

He had slammed the receiver down then, run out of the house just as he was, looked up and down the lane for an autorickshaw, a bicycle rickshaw, an ekka even with some broken-winded horse, anything. Because he knew, from all he had ever heard about Mrs Popatkar, she would be going to Bombay by train. She always made a point of travelling that way. And in lowest class. He had read it in the newspapers a hundred times.

But it had taken him ten minutes or more to find that cycle-rickshaw walla. Then in the press of the day in galli after galli, all crammed with pilgrims, shoppers, beggars, sadhus, wandering cows, dogs, goats, not till they were nearly half-way to the Cantonment Station had the fellow been able to pedal at more than walking speed.

And the Rajdani Express had left on time. To the second. When they had arrived just two minutes afterwards.

Then he had conceived the notion of getting to Bombay by air while high-principled Mrs Popatkar was slowly chugged over the many miles in her third-class bogie.

There had been the taxi he had taken from the station out along the twenty-odd kilometres to the Babatpur Airport. Would its driver remember him? He had not been able to prevent himself every few minutes shouting at the

11

fellow to go faster. But, if he did remember, would that journey itself betray him? Surely not. He had the right to make some inquiries at the airport rather than going to the Indian Airlines office near the Nadesar Palace. But at the airport ... In his agitation he had altogether lost his temper when the girl at the facilities desk had said the flight to Bombay was full house. He had shouted and stormed. He had made much of being a member of the Lok Sabha. To no avail. And then the stuck-up brat had rejected the bribe he offered. Probably too junior to be able to get anyone on to a fully booked flight.

She certainly would be bound to remember all that. So if some Bombay police officer came asking ... But no one would. There was nothing, nothing, to make any police officer think of coming to Banares simply because Mrs Popatkar had been killed.

Thank God, he had been more discreet next day. But no more successful. Whether others had offered bigger bribes or whether they were civil service high-ups or other MPs with more influence, there was not a seat to be had.

So then he had thought of Vikram. Vikram and his Flying Club. How often had he said to the boy's father that it was wrong for a grandson of his to belong to such a rich young men's club. To be flagrantly wasting so much of time and money. But then he had rejoiced in the thought that the boy might be able to fly him down to Bombay.

In time. And, yes, he had been in time to reach that flat just after Mrs Popatkar herself had arrived. And then ...

No. I will not think of it any more. I must blot it all out as if it had never happened.

It had never happened. I am here in Banares now. Sacred, safe Banares where I was born, where I married, where I watched over my wife's body on the funeral pyre at the Manikarnika Ghat. And where I absolutely intend to die myself. All has been forgiven, blotted out. It has been. It has.

He seized his fresh dhoti, wound it round.

12

How clean it smells. How smooth the starched cotton. And now the kurta. How pleasant it feels. How nice. Now to peel off those sweat-sticky socks, to slip into cool chappals.

Another man. My own man again. The man who soon, once all those last-minute details have been dealt with when Jagmohan Nagpal comes from Delhi, will be none other than Minister for Social Upliftment.

And a good Minister too. Not one of your bribes-takers, your money-makers. No, someone of integrity. There in his seat to do good to the common man. To do the right thing.

Twenty-eight hours in the Rajdani Express had not given Inspector Ghote any clearer idea what in Banares could have brought someone to Bombay to strangle respected, aged Mrs Shoba Popatkar. Spotting the red headcloth of a porter, he called to him to take the railway bed-roll he had hired for the journey. As he followed the man, he could not prevent himself uttering a little groan of misery.

His time in the train had not been pleasant. A swami, going to Banares for a meeting of the All-India Union of Saints and Holy Persons, had come on board at Nasik with a bevy of disciples who had stayed awake all night singing bhajans. And in the morning, bemused by lack of sleep, he had failed, out of his familiar morning routine, to brush his teeth. Now his mouth felt like the floor of an opium den, and, worse, he was possessed by a dim, uncomfortable feeling of a duty omitted. There was going to be some penalty somehow to be paid. The thought filled his mind now with smog-layers of pessimism.

Had he been stupid to have gone on and on trying to persuade the ACP to let him go to Banares? Stupid in that if he failed it would be a heavy black mark against him. Stupid but not wrong. Not wrong. Despite the scanty evidence he had, he was still sure the murder must have its source outside Dadar where Mrs Popatkar was such a loved and admired figure.

Of course it was possible the crime had been committed by a goonda from some other part of Bombay, or from anywhere. But only remotely possible. Why should anyone take it into their head to go to Dadar and rob that particular flat? On the other hand there was evidence, however scanty, pointing clearly to Banares. Including the one item he had thought it wise not to expose to the ACP's scorn.

But there had been the black much-worn address book he had taken from Mrs Popatkar's handbag when he had found her rail ticket. In it there was just a single Banares address. That of one Manzoor Syed.

And Manzoor Syed – the name had rung a faint bell – had proved to be, when he had telephoned a long-standing acquaintance, the crime reporter of the *Free Press Journal*, an industrialist with a somewhat doubtful reputation. He had half-remembered reading about him, the owner of factories all over India making office furniture, accessories for rail carriages, any number of similar things. Thanks to a certain unscrupulousness, generally unspecified, his enterprise had reached its present size from small beginnings in his native place, Banares.

It was possible, then, that Mrs Popatkar had come here to see him. Certainly there had been nothing else to indicate why she had made her sudden visit. Dull-brained Tantya had had no idea at all. So could it be – a scuttling shadow of doubt crossed his mind – that something arising from what she had said to Manzoor Syed here had made him, almost at once, follow her to Bombay? Or, perhaps more likely, made him send some goonda to do his dirty works for him?

In any case this was the only slight thread he had. Unless when he reported to the Senior Superintendent of Police some other line came up. That might happen. Banares, sacred city though it was, could not be without its wrong-doers.

A dart of memory brought back his encounter, as he had left Headquarters, with burly, guffawing Inspector

14

Tarlok Singh. He had received a ferocious dig in the ribs accompanied by the old warning, 'You are going to Banares, beware of whores, bulls, steps and holymen.' Then an equally ferocious handshake and 'That is not so wrong, you know. I have been to that place, and I can tell you – personal experience, bhai – very much beware of one of those things.' A mighty booming laugh.

Ahead, his porter contrived, despite the bulky roll on his head, to make a swift namaskar to a naked sadhu, marching down the platform towards them, body from head to foot burnt dark by the sun, brass-tipped danda staff held high, even a little threateningly. He hurried past, wondering whether he, too, ought to have greeted the holyman. Or was this one of the ones to be wary of, together with the whores – no sign of any here – the sacred bulls and the many steps leading down to the sin-cleansing Ganges?

Gritty with tiredness, doing all he could to keep down his swelling heaves of depression, he waited until the sole clerk with authority, it seemed, to receive his bed-roll had come back to his place. Then he waited yet longer while the fellow looked high and low for the Bed-roll Register. And then he waited again while the necessary carbons were hunted out. And finally waited once more while, with tongue moving carefully over his lips, the fellow laboriously entered each item in the register. One pillow, one pillow case, two sheets, one and a half towels . . .

Ticketless Traveller Is A Social Evil. A tattered poster on the wall of the booking office caught his eye.

And there, in a far corner, was a white hippy of some sort, looking at him over the discarded newspaper he was making a show of reading. Was even that boy, coming from the West and acting like a beggar itself, taking in at this moment a news item about the Popatkar murder?

He felt a new sliding of despondency. Had he been utterly foolish in insisting on coming to the sacred city?

Out in the forecourt at last, he saw that at least the city provided plenty of transport. He made his way over to the lines of waiting vehicles, opting for a modest auto-rickshaw rather than a taxi. If his visit turned out to be pointless, at least he would not have incurred more expenses than strictly necessary.

Then, as his driver trod again and again on the starting lever of the frail vehicle's motor-cycle, a face was thrust in under the tattered black plastic hood. A lean, eager-eyed face above a naked torso with a gamcha scarf across one bony shoulder.

'Gentleman, have you come to Holy Banares before?'

He was tempted to say he had not. It would avoid complicated explanations. But the truth was that for one day, years before, he had brought his wife here when she had begged him to make the pilgrimage. Duty at the time had limited their stay. But telling all this to this fellow, now loping along beside the autorickshaw as they slowly set off, would probably mean going on to say that he was a police officer. Perhaps even saying why he had come here, or avoiding saying it with difficulty. He might even feel obliged to state that he himself had not at all wanted to make that pilgrimage with Protima. Yet somehow he felt it would be wrong to begin his time in the city with anything of a lie.

'No, no, I was here before. But for one day only.'

Further explanation, mercifully, did not seem to be wanted.

'Then you cannot have done all that any person coming here should do. Were you even taking one dip in Mother Ganga herself?'

Should he lie now?

'No. No, I was not. That is— You see, I was not able to remain.'

'But even then you should have carried out your duties.'

The face of the man trotting beside him was fiercely stern, for all the sweat now glistening on it. And, abruptly, he knew what the fellow must be. A panda. One of those brahmins versed in all the complex rituals considered necessary to lead the sacred city's pilgrims through the proper discharge of their religious duties.

'Where is your native place?'

Inflexible inquiry.

'Er— Er— I am coming from Bombay.'

Not the whole truth now, but the easiest answer.

'Then it is at Rama Ghat or the Panchganga that you must be carrying out the rituals. I will tell the driver to go there.'

'No.'

He had shouted. But a shout seemed necessary.

'No, I have very urgent business. I would go to these ghats at some other time.'

He must not say that he was going directly to the Senior Superintendent's office.

'No business can be more urgent than performing the rituals beside Mother Ganga. It is your duty as a Hindu. Your duty to complete the rituals under a brahmin's guidance, and to pay also for this boon. I will tell your driver to change direction. Where is he taking you now? I will ask him.'

They had been forced to a temporary halt. A train of four or five camels, loads swinging bumpily across their backs, had blocked their path in picking their way round the mountainous shape of a sacred bull seated in deep contemplation in the roadway.

Ghote leant out and faced the panda eye to eye before he had a chance to get hold of the driver.

'I am not going to the ghats. I am going to the office of the Senior Superintendent of Police, Cornwallis Lines. On urgent and confidential police business.'

It was enough. The panda stepped back, glaring with affronted displeasure. Ahead, the last of the camels swayed past the great purply body of the bull.

3

Ghote had hardly been speaking to the Senior Superintendent for two minutes before he realized he was not going to get any suggestions for new lines to investigate. In fact, it was all too clear that an officer from elsewhere creating complications was highly unwelcome.

'No, Inspector, I am very much of opinion that you would not find any clue whatsoever here in Banares. You would do very much better to approach the case from Bombay itself.'

Flawless uniform behind a desk dotted with neatly piled papers, each under its heavy little round silvery paperweight. Leather-covered swagger-stick lined up in exact parallel with the desk's edge, precisely six inches in.

'First of all, you are not at all knowing Banares, isn't it?'

Ghote would have liked to have replied that he knew quite enough of the city. But truth must prevail.

'No, sir. I am not knowing.'

'Yes, well, in that case you would have great difficulties working here. This is a city of almost one million inhabitants, and they are not at all like the riff-raffs of Bombay. Here we have many, many respected pandits, teaching religion itself. Also perhaps as many as one lakh of pujaris conducting worship at our more than two thousand temples. Then there are the ghatias at the side of Mother Ganga leading pilgrims through the rituals, and the pandas, worthy of respect at all times. You must also count the vyasas, tellers of holy tales. How can you break into the discourses of such persons with your questions?

18

Especially if there is, here itself, nothing any investigation is—'

Ghote interrupted.

It was hardly right to contradict a senior officer, especially when he had not finished what he was saying. But the exasperation he felt at being told once again he was wrong to see Banares as the source of Mrs Popatkar's murder was too much.

'Sir, it is up to you to provide assistance to any officer coming to investigate definitely suspicious circumstances. If I am needing some colleague to take me here and there, it is your bounden duty to provide.'

'Look here, Inspector, I am not going to be told by any Bombaywalla what is and is not my duty. You seem to forget you have come to a city that was here for thousands of years when Bombay was just only a string of swampy islands. To a city that was here in all the glory of civilization when no other city in the world was at all existing, not your Rome or your London, not your Jerusalem or Washington itself.'

'Nevertheless, sir, I am requiring your co-operation. One of India's great fighters of Independence days has been altogether done to death. In whatsoever part of the country there is one clue to who is her murderer, then at that place a full investigation must be carried out.'

Opposite, the Senior Superintendent reached out to his swagger-stick, lifted it, then banged it back on to the desk. It lay just three or four degrees out of true.

'Very well, Inspector,' he said through rage-stiffened lips. 'I will provide you your assistance. But kindly do not expect me to produce some officer out of my hat. The post-monsoon time is when pilgrims are coming here not by the thousand but by the hundreds of thousands. Each and every one of my officers is fully employed.'

But then a quickly-come, quickly-gone gleam came into his eyes.

'However, if you are coming in three–four hours I would see what I can do.'

19

Ghote had observed the expression under the peak of the Senior Superintendent's cap, the hat from which no assisting officer could be produced. And he guessed that some surprise, probably of an unpleasant sort, had just be devised for him. But he had, it seemed, won his battle. He would be content with that.

'Very well, sir,' he said, glancing at his watch, 'I will return at twelve-thirty precisely. Thank you for all your helps.'

After all, he thought, I have the address of Manzoor Syed, industrialist of doubtful reputation. However many times I am having to ask the way, surely I must be able to find his place on my own. And perhaps when I have tackled that fellow face to face there will be no more need for any assistance from Senior Superintendent sahib, offered in some decent manner or with snag concealed therein.

H. K. Verma began to feel the day was going well. He had been telephoned from Delhi with confirmation that Jagmohan Nagpal, deep in the counsels of the High Command, would be coming to Banares next day. He would arrive in time for a holy dip in the Ganges before lunch. It would be appreciated if a press photographer happened to be at the ghat.

That had been arranged. Not for nothing had the people at both the morninger *Aj* and the eveninger *Gandiva* been cultivated over the years. Then, too, the string of petitioners in the courtyard outside his office had been more rewarding than usual. Promises had been accepted with many a grateful salaam. Garlands, three or four, had been draped around his neck and after a minute laid aside.

Perhaps in a day or two, or a week or two at the most, he would be in a position, Minister for Social Upliftment, to fulfil some of those easily given pledges.

By then, too, perhaps some antisocial in Bombay would have been pulled in for the Shoba Popatkar murder. Some fellow just only a bandicoot to be skinned alive. A real history-sheeter with a list of crimes to his name as long as a fakir's beard. Some fellow put behind the bars, an under-trial to stay there until the crime itself had all but been forgotten. The whole business, with its overhanging threat like distant thunder, would then be safely laid to rest.

The Shoba Popatkar murder. For an instant, with those words, the thought of it, of what had actually happened – that bare room, the old woman's body, her sari flung wildly out on the stone floor – rose up like the hundred-headed snake Kaliya emerging from the blackened waters of the lake it had poisoned in the Forest of Brindaban. But at once he slew the demon, as God Krishna had slain Kaliya, before its presence in his mind began to infect his whole life. What had been done had been done. Standing in sin-lifting Mother Ganga, he had sought forgiveness for a necessary action. And now life must go on.

Where should he take Jagmohanji for lunch? It must be somewhere good. He must show full appreciation.

Suddenly there swept over him a longing for the old days when politics had not been all to do with keeping sweet those who might be of some advantage. When he had been young . . . Young and full of good ideals. When getting rid of the British had been the only thing that had to be thought about.

He brought his lips together in a hard, puffed line.

Those days were gone. Things were different now. Good had to be arrived at by whatever means were necessary. Toadying to those above, promising to those below, bribing your way to a little publicity for the party, writing letters to the press about nothing that mattered. Good had to be arrived at these days even by – Even by that. By what he had done. What he had been forced to do.

Tomorrow at sunrise, he thought, when the waters of Mother Ganga are lapping round me, I shall ask for something somehow to bring back for me the simple times. Those long-ago days when I had one good deed only before me.

The restaurant at the Hotel de Paris in the Mall? Yes, that should be just right. Not the height of luxury like the five-stars Taj Ganges or the refurbished Clark's or the Ashok. A mistake to look too much of a bootlicker. But a good place nevertheless. An air of Old Banares, dating with its solid pillared front from British days. Unchanging, the height of respectability. Just what should please Jagmohanji.

It took Ghote much longer than he had counted on to find Manzoor Syed's house. First a long, long autorickshaw ride brought him to an address which turned out to be completely wrong. Then a yet more wearisome, jostled and jangled trip took him back to the heart of the ancient, built-upon, ruined and rebuilt city. At last he was able to ring the bell beside an ancient door, its time-blistered panels framed by sombre brass studs, in a long windowless façade in a close-smelling galli.

The servant who agreed that 'Ji haan, sahib, this is the house of Mr Manzoor Syed' took his card and left him waiting in a sun-hammered, untended garden. Grey paving slates zigzagged with cracks. A waterless fountain. The long, rope-like roots of its sole tree, a twisted pipal, brown and dry. A pink-faced monkey eventually appearing on the top of the high wall, looking down at him, whisking away.

Then, just when he had begun to think that Manzoor Syed, alarmed at a Bombay CIDwalla's card, had left by some other door, the servant returned. He was hurried along ancient stone-walled passages hung with portraits of long-ago muslim taluqdars, courtiers and landowners, in and out of deserted rooms where nothing seemed ever to have happened, up sharp-twisting little flights of stairs.

Once, from the arch of a crumbling stone balcony, he caught a momentary view of the city, now far below. Jumbled roofs, a temple dome, a huge hoarding advertising a film – gun-waving police inspector, full-bosomed star – with below it, hardly glimpsed, another big painted poster. Stark words in English, *Don't Play With Fire Consequences Are Dire.*

At last, they came to a doorway with a bead-curtain in glowing coloured glass. The servant ushered him forward. Squaring his shoulders, he brushed through.

Facing him was a man in a long, beautifully cut black sherwani, a black muslim cap at a slight angle above a long, firm-set, narrow face set off by a thin moustache, its ends curling with an air of implacable disdain.

'Inspector Ghote,' he said, looking down at the pasteboard slip in his hand. 'All the way from Bombay. What can you be wanting to see me about? You are lucky, indeed, to find me. I returned only yesterday from America.'

'Sir,' Ghote said, suppressing the nervous cough that had risen up in his throat, 'I am here in connection with the death of Mrs Shoba Popatkar.'

They were the words he had prepared, as he had waited in the dry garden. Would the abrupt announcement produce a telltale reaction?

But the long, set face remained impassive.

At once Ghote knew why. Manzoor Syed must be speaking the truth in saying he had returned to India only the day before. If so, Mrs Popatkar could not have seen him when she had come to Benares. There could be nothing in her visit to cause this man to need to end her life. Or have it ended for him.

'You are knowing that Mrs Popatkar has been murdered?' he said, asking himself anxiously how he could get to see this cool, aristocratic Muslim's passport and check on his story.

'Yes. Yes, Inspector, I saw a newspaper when we landed in Calcutta. A tragic business. She and I were very old friends—'

He brought himself to a halt then, and smiled with a wry twist of his thin moustache.

'Well, perhaps I should say old enemies.'

Enemies? But then . . .

23

'But such old enemies,' Manzoor Syed went on, 'that in a way we had become friends. I encountered her first, you know, many years ago when she was Minister for Railways and I was at the very beginning of my career, if you can call a career the business I began when our family fortune appeared to have – well, disappeared.'

'Yes, sir?'

But the fellow's passport, can I just only demand to inspect? After all, if he is lying about the time he reached here, even by twenty-four hours, he could have seen her. And *enemies* . . . He did say that. But a person of as much influence as this man, how can I do it?

'Yes, Inspector.' Manzoor Syed smiled with a touch of ruefulness. 'Let me tell you what happened. There was I, a young man desperately in need of some capital, and, to tell the truth, not much worried about how I might get it. But I was still in those days innocent, or partially innocent, shall we say? And it never occurred to me that anyone would be proof against the offer of a bribe, provided only the bribe was big enough. Now, I knew the new Minister for Railways was a woman without resources, and so, when I wanted to secure a contract to provide seats for new rolling-stock the Ministry had sanctioned it seemed simple just to have what we call "a frank talk" with the Minister. And she rebuffed me, Inspector. In no uncertain terms. I can hear her words now. *Mr Syed, it is the duty of every man, woman and even child in this world to do right, and what you have proposed to me is nothing more than bare-faced doing wrong.'*

The eyes in the narrow face opposite lit up with what could only be delight.

'Yes, Inspector, I was given a fine shelling, I can tell you. Not that it did me any good. I have found, you know, ever since that bribery, combined with a certain ruthlessness, almost always works altogether admirably in business.'

'Yes, sir.'

What else to say?

'But then . . .' Manzoor Syed went on. 'Then, and this is the cream of it, Inspector, a few weeks after that terrible shelling I learnt my quotation for the seating, which was as a matter of face decently low, had been accepted. It was the beginning of such success as I have had.'

And then the happy light went out of his eyes.

'But why, Inspector, have you come all the way to Banares to see myself in connection with Shoba Popatkar's death?'

Ghote felt sweat spring up at his hairline.

'Sir,' he said, spinning out the words. 'First of all, I was finding your name in Mrs Popatkar's address book.'

'I am not surprised, Inspector. Mrs Popatkar did not hesitate to take advantage of the weak position I was in frequently to demand money from me. For the highest reasons, of course. She was president, you know, of a charity for blinded rail workers, and we Muslims have an obligation to help all unfortunates, particularly, I don't know why, the blind. So, over the years whenever she asked I have given. Quite generously I think.'

'I see, sir, yes.'

But he was not sure he did see, or not very clearly. How could it be that this man, not ashamed to admit he had bribed and browbeaten his way to fortune, could still be happy to answer charitable requests when long ago he must have become immune to Mrs Popatkar's mild moral blackmail?

'But the mere finding of my name in that address book, Inspector,' Manzoor Syed went on, 'can hardly have been reason to suspect me – because you do, don't you? – of killing Mrs Popatkar. Or, I suppose, of paying to have her killed?'

'No, sir, no. I am also having evidence of an individual speaking Hindi with many overtones of Bhojpuri seen in the vicinity of Mrs Popatkar's residence, and also I was learning Mrs Popatkar had made a sudden unexplained trip here to Benares just before her death.'

'Had she indeed, Inspector? Now I wonder why that can have been. It certainly was not to see me. I was on holiday in America. Oh, but wait—'

A smile.

'You will not have believed that, will you, Inspector? So, simple answer. Let me show you my passport.'

He turned to a tall, heavily carved almirah behind him and pulled open one of its doors.

'Oh, no, sir, no. Quite unnecessary I am assuring you.'

'No, Inspector. Absolutely necessary. When you are dealing with such an unscrupulous fellow as myself. Please look.'

He thrust the little green book forward. Ghote took it, flipped it open, saw what he knew must be there. The fresh, blotchy but plainly readable stamp making it clear that Manzoor Syed had returned to India only yesterday.

'Thank you, sir.'

'So, Inspector, your journey here has been fruitless. However, you are a good Hindu, no doubt. You can at least take the opportunity of disembarrassing yourself of any sins you may have committed with a plunge into the waters of the Ganges.'

And, as the heavy old door to the rambling house was swung to behind him, Ghote realized with dismay he was now going to be very much later than he had promised in learning from the Senior Superintendent what help he was to get in this altogether exasperating city.

4

H. K. Verma woke suddenly from his after-lunch nap.

I was dreaming of it, he thought. I was there in that horrible tiny plane Vikram was piloting. That dog he is taking everywhere with him – What he is calling it as? A German Shepherd – lying behind us, quiet like a lamb. But not always behaving so well. Not when Vikki, as he insists to call himself, is inciting and instigating it to chase the servants. Even to attack anyone coming into the compound not wearing decent clothes.

But did Vikki – no, Vikram, Vikram – believe it when I said I was having urgent secret political business in Bombay? He might have. He must know from what his father has said I am at last on verge of joining Government. Not that he takes any interest. Just only jumping at the chance to fly all the way to Bombay. With myself paying each and every cost.

'Broke, Grandfather. Broke as usual. Hundred per cent karka.'

'But your father makes you such a generous allowance. I am often telling him it is too much.'

'And I am often telling him it's not one half enough.'

'A college boy should not have so many needs.'

'Oh, Grandfather, you know perfectly well I have left college. What good is it to me to be a BAABF?'

And, in his urgency to get to Bombay he had foolishly humoured the boy by asking what the string of letters meant.

'Grandfather, don't you know that even? *BA Appeared But Failed.*'

At least he had had the sense not to rebuke the boy for his idleness then, provoking some endless argument. Instead, had just asked what the Bombay flight would cost. And had hurried to the bank, enormous though the sum seemed.

But what after all can the boy be doing with all the money Krishnakanta gives him? Running a posh sports car. And there was something the other day about some crash or accident. Something they were quick to hush up before me.

But at least the boy was there in Bombay waiting for me when I came back from— From that place. Where that happened. And he asked me nothing when I said I must return here at once. But he must have seen I was altogether agitated, if only because I had stopped berating.

Oh, if it truly had been somewhat of politics in Bombay. If that had not happened . . .

'Well, Inspector,' the Senior Superintendent said, 'you are later coming than you told.'

'Yes, sir. There was a gentleman I had to question, and I was having very much trouble finding his place.'

'But you were making an arrest?'

'No, sir. No. The gentleman in question was out of India itself until yesterday.'

'I see. And you believed what this gentleman, whoever he is, was telling you?'

'Sir, I was examining his passport.'

'Hm. Well, I am glad to find a Bombay CIDwalla knows his job. Now, despite your setback, you are still wanting to carry on investigations here in Banares?'

'Yes, sir.'

But the question had not been put with the plain hostility his earlier request for assistance had met. It seemed now, somehow, his determination to stay on in Banares was not as unwelcome as before.

What it is he has got in store for me?

28

'Well then, Inspector, let me tell you what I have been able to do by way of providing you full assistance. I cannot, of course, allocate you one of my regular officers. I was telling how much of pressure I am under at this post-monsoon period. Banares is getting up to one million pilgrims per year, you know, and the majority come just now.'

'Yes, sir.'

'But there is a former officer in my force who has agreed to help. One Inspector Mishra. A true Banarasi, born and bred. Knowing the city from top to bottom. Its history from the most early times. One mine of information only. He would be just the man for you. I have put him fully in the picture already.'

A sharp ping on the shiny domed bell beside the neat piles of papers on the desk.

'Send in Inspector Mishra.'

Ghote saw a man in his late fifties dressed in a brightly cheerful pink shirt, with a bold-featured round face, full-lipped and fleshy, his greying hair curling almost riotously down to his neck.

Smiling broadly, he thrust out a hand to shake.

'Welcome to Banares, city of light, city of temples, the Golden Temple, the Monkey Temple, the Tulsi Manas Temple, the—'

'Thank you, Inspector, thank you,' Ghote broke in.

Would this wide-smiling fellow want to take him into each and every one of those?

'Welcome, welcome.' Inspector Mishra still pumped enthusiastically the hand he held captive. 'Welcome to Banares, city of holy ghats from the Asi, where Goddess Durga dropped her sword after she was slaying the demons Shumba and Nishuma, past the Panchgama where there is meeting five holy rivers (four mystical), on to the Varuna, last of the sacred bathing spots.'

'Thank you,' Ghote said again, managing at last to slide his hand from the moist grasp.

'And not forgetting,' the Banarasi inspector swooshed

29

on, 'our five burning ghats where we are all hoping to end this life. Yes, welcome to the city of death.'

'That will do, Mishra,' the Senior Superintendent put in, not without a certain sharpness.

Outside, Ghote felt it was time to assert himself. He saw now why the Senior Superintendent had been so pleased with the assisting officer he had found for him. Evidently he saw Mishra as conveniently drowning this interloper in an ever-rolling muddy historical-geographical sea.

But history and geography were not what he had come to Banares for.

'Inspector,' he said, 'I have much to do in such time as I am able to be here. Already I have found one good lead exhausted. But, even while you were most kindly welcoming, I had thought of some other lines to take.'

Inspector Mishra's large and lazy eyes blinked up and down.

'Yes. Now, first of all, the unknown culprit I am suspecting when he came to Bombay was asking questions in Hindi very much tinged with Bhojpuri. So, one, we are looking for a Bhojpuri speaker.'

Inspector Mishra broke out into a laugh that was, plainly, rather more a giggle.

'Oh, Inspector,' he said, 'we are having, then, a marathon impossible task.'

He did not seem displeased at the prospect.

'What impossible?' Ghote snapped out. 'Inspector, there is not much that cannot be dealt with by plenty of hard work.'

'But finding one man with a Bhojpuri accent to his Hindi here in Banares,' Mishra replied, a little sobered, 'I am thinking that truly would be impossible. Half the inhabitants of the city will speak Bhojpuri. You can hardly arrest each and every one of them.'

Ghote pursed his lips in angry defeat.

'Very well,' he said. 'Nevertheless, Inspector, I am one hundred per cent convinced the key to the murder of Mrs

30

Shoba Popatkar must be found in the visit she made here immediately before her death. She was here, you know, just only for one day. Now, where exactly it was she was going? No clue at present existing.'

'Hopeless case,' Mishra said comfortably.

'No, no. What must be done is to trace so far as we are able every step she was taking in this city of yours.'

'But— But so many steps she could have taken. To any single one of the ghats, to perhaps her favourite temple of the two thousand, or even to buy some of our many world-famed handicrafts. We are having very good brass idols, you know, depicting almost each and every god. Also silks, shawls, brocades and embroideries. Perhaps she was coming for one of our famous saris, so fine you are able to pull the whole through a small gold ring.'

'No,' Ghote snapped, stemming the tide as best he could. 'Mrs Shoba Popatkar would not have made a twenty-eight hour rail journey just to be buying frivolities. She was not at all such a person. No, we must look altogether elsewhere.'

'But where?' Mishra asked, his round face still bearing the hurt look that had come on to it at the word *frivolities*.

'At the station, of course,' Ghote replied. 'She was starting her stay in Banares there. It is there we must start our following.'

'The station? The Cantonment Station? But that is not the most pleasant places in Banares for you.'

'That I am already knowing, Inspector. I had hardly left my train this morning when I was accosted by a so-called panda wanting money to lead me through rituals beside the Ganga, and I was seeing there also very many bad-looking characters, even one very much unsavoury white hippy fellow.'

'Oh, but it is not for the bad things I am saying Cantonment Station is not pleasant. It is that there you would find nothing of majaa, of fun, and especially nothing of our best Banares gift which is masti.'

'Masti? What masti?'

'Oh, hard to explain our Banares masti, Inspector. You must see for yourself. Experience for yourself. Best I can say is deep enjoyment of all that life is offering. Banares is famed for its masti. Even our goondas are undertaking their wicked doings with utmost enjoyment. Our whores also, in Dal Mandi, they are the most tickling in all India. And our paans. Oh, Inspector, not for nothing was the great film star Amitabh singing, *The sweet betel-leaf of Banares/Makes me want to set the world aright.*'

'Inspector,' Ghote said, suppressing the fury he felt at being saddled with this fellow, 'I see a taxi there. For God's sake, let's get over to the station.'

H. K. Verma felt tears of rage come into his eyes.

Would it all never go away? Simply waiting for the telephone to be answered at the Hotel de Paris, calling personally to make sure of the best table, the thought of old Srivastava in his musty library had leapt into his head. Electric-light bright. And how could such a petty detail as that phone call that had started it all be stuck so fast in his memory? A stone embedded in a tree. It was there, as if he had only just slammed down the receiver that day. This very receiver he was holding.

'Why? Why, Srivastava sahib?' he had shouted. 'Why was she getting hold of the *Recollections* now only?'

'Sir, she must have been hearing some rumours.'

He had cursed himself then. If, before the split in the ruling party and Government needing an injection of support, he had not had the idea of gaining some attention by putting it about that there was some juicy secret in the *Recollections*, all would have been well. But, no, he must go hinting at some sex scandal or something, and in no time everyone was wanting to go through the *Recollections*. And he had been so delighted with his chalak, and the way it had produced so many mentions of the party in the papers. All the speculations and gossips, Calcutta-side, Bombay-side, everywhere. Till Mrs Shoba Popatkar had got it into her head it would be the right thing simply to bring to light the truth.

And now, what if some CIDwalla from Bombay should find his way to Srivastava at the Banares Hindu University? Then . . . Then there would be a path open, if the investigator had the brain to see it, pointing like an arrow to himself.

But, no. No, that could not possibly happen. Why should the investigation of a murder in distant Bombay even bring a detective to Banares? Far away, holy Banares?

But if, somehow, it became possible . . .

His hand shaking, he put the receiver back before the hotel had answered.

Getting out of the taxi, the first person to catch Ghote's eye was the white hippy who had appeared to be watching him when he had been waiting to get rid of his bed-roll. The fellow was, he saw now, even more of a wretched specimen than he remembered. Thin to the point of starvation. Blond hair above his pinched and lined face a thickly dirt-clogged mass. Shirt ripped down one side and as dirt-encrusted as his hair. Grimy blue jeans ragged at the ends and gaping with holes at the knees.

With a bite of malice he pointed out this example of Banares squalor to Mishra.

But the Banares inspector was not at all put out.

'Oh, yes, I am knowing that boy. He has been in the city some time. You are often seeing here, and at Manikarnika Ghat also. He is said to be working for the Dom Raja.'

'The Dom Raja?'

'Ah, yes. You are not, of course, knowing who is that individual. A very-very Banarasi figure. I must tell you all about him.'

Inwardly Ghote cursed. It looked as if he had let himself in for a whole new spate of information. None of it ever to be of any use. But he had asked the question.

'Yes, you see, the Dom Raja is the hereditary in-charge of the Manikarnika Ghat, the most used of all our famed burning ghats. Long, long ago, in perhaps mythical times even, one Raja Harishchandra, a very-very truth-loving man, was asked by the great brahmin Vishvamitra for a fee we are calling *rajasuya dakshina*. In his hundred per cent wish to do right thing he was at once giving the said Vishvamitra no less than his whole kingdom. Then, when Vishvamitra was still asking and demanding, all that Raja Harishchandra could do was to come here to Banares and sell himself as slave to some brahmins to do the dirty works of the burning grounds. In the end, you know, Harishchandra was rewarded by the gods. They were restoring him his throne. And those brahmins, known by the name of Doms, were having to perform the cremation works. The head of their community is known as the Dom Raja.'

'Most interesting, but—'

'But I am sorry to say some of those Dom rajas have been very-very naughty fellows. Demanding too much of fees, selling for extortionate sums the wood for the pyres, and even the stones that are needed to sink in the Ganga the bodies of smallpox victims and the very young children. They have been drinking wines, taking drugs also. And that is what that junky fellow there is doing, we are believing. I think he is even staying in that man's house. The house that is looking out over the Ganges just by the Manikarnika Ghat. If you go by boat along the river you would see it. There are two tigers on the balcony there. Life-size plus, and full-colour painted. They remind how death can seize you at just only any moment.'

'Yes, yes,' Ghote persisted. 'But this boy?'

'Oh, he is just only selling some what they are calling brown sugar to tourists and hippies coming from the West. Not to worry.'

For a moment Ghote was tempted to ask if peddling crudely processed heroin to tourists was an example of Mishra's much praised masti in action. But, mountain of useless information though Mishra seemed to be, he might need his help later. And already his investigation had been delayed long enough. So he said nothing and looked round the forecourt wondering who might have remembered Mrs Shoba Popatkar from almost a week before. If anybody had.

'We should try those fellows with the autorickshaws,' he said. 'She must have taken some transport when she came.'

'Why not?' Mishra answered, ambling in the strong afternoon sun over to the line of little black-hooded yellow-bodied vehicles.

Yet none of the drivers seemed to be able to remember among the thousands of passengers coming and going an aged lady wearing a very plain sari with a suitcase and a stout leather handbag. The bag that, back in Bombay, had yielded a Banares rail ticket and an address book.

But then they had a lucky break. Their activities had aroused the suspicions of a young Railways Police constable. He came over. But, as soon as he recalled having once met Inspector Mishra, he broke into a wide grin.

'Mrs Shoba Popatkar you are asking,' he said. 'I was seeing just only last week. My father was in Railways Police before me, and he was often telling about her and all her good works. Showing us her picture in newspaper sometimes also. So when I was seeing, here itself, at once I was knowing who it was. Then I was requesting her if I could be of some helps, and she was saying she was wanting to go to the BHU.'

Ghote had to ask then what the letters stood for, and got from Mishra a longer history of Banares Hindu University than he at all wanted. Of how it was a huge seat of learning just beyond the boundary of the holy city. Of how it had been founded in 1904 by Mrs Annie Besant and Pandit Madan Malaviya. Of how once an American studying there had assured him that 'India's conscience is her greatest gift to the world'. Of how Pandit Malaviya had at the end of his life refused to spend his last days within holy Banares, where dying he would be guaranteed release from the cycle of birth and rebirth, because he had too much to do in a next life.

After failing more than once to break into this outflow, at last Ghote simply seized Mishra by the arm and tugged him away.

'We are going there,' he shouted at him. 'We are going to your BHU. Where it is? How do we reach?'

Mishra blinked and blinked.

'But I was telling you, Inspector. It is just outside the boundary of the city. We can go by taxi. It would not take too long. But, first, there is a place near here where you can get very excellent thandai, the most cooling drink existing. With a nice amount of bhang mixed in, and, perhaps better even for giving soul-cleansing blessing, one pinch of Ganges silt itself. You should try.'

'Inspector,' Ghote spat out, hardly checking his rage, 'let me say it once more. I am here in Banares for just only one thing. To find out what Mrs Shoba Popatkar came here for. What made some person unknown follow her all the way back to Bombay and strangle her. And this perhaps we will discover as soon as we are getting to your BHU. So, take me there. Now. Take, take, take.'

5

The peon from the office downstairs sidled in when H. K. Verma, in answer to a knock at the door that had been somehow both timid and urgent, called, 'Come.' There was a look of scared apology on his face.

'What is it, Raman? Do not stand there like a stupid owl only. What it is?'

'Oh, sahib, it is—'

'Speak up, speak up, man. What has got into you?'

'Sir, it is police. Sir, an inspector. From Bombay, sir.'

Raman thrust out the card he had been given. H. K. Verma ignored it. He hardly even saw it. A great frozen block seemed to have occupied his whole head, his whole body.

At last he heard Raman speak again.

'Sahib, he is wanting to see. Must I bring him upstairs, sahib?'

'No.'

It was all he could manage to utter.

But after a long moment, hearing inside himself now the tiny thunder of his heart, beating and knocking, he forced some more words out.

'No. No, say it is too late. I cannot see anybody just now. Say he is to come back. Tomorrow. Another day.'

Raman looked as if that was a message he could not see himself delivering. He made no effort to go.

H. K. Verma moved to give him a slap. But at once thought better of it.

His mind had abruptly become unlocked from its state

of ice-bound fear. Ideas, wild notions, absurd fantasies raced each other one after another.

He would prevent Raman going down and the fellow below would just turn tail and go away. Back to Bombay. Back to Bombay from where he should never have come. From where it was impossible that he had come.

He would get away himself, leap down into the galli below, somehow land on his feet like a cat, run and run and run. There must be somewhere to hide. To hide for ever. A temple? A math, where he could live out the life of a monk, one among a hundred anonymous orange-robed figures?

He would go down now, at once, and – and— And obliterate this Bombay fellow. Wipe him from the face of the earth. Never more to be heard of. They would forget all about him back where he had come from. The inquiry would disappear like dust blown away in the hot summer wind.

Mrs Popatkar had not been killed. She was alive. Alive again and well. But, no. No, she must not be alive. Not alive to tell the world what KK had believed before he died.

The thought brought back sobriety.

It would be no use sending away this fellow now, if even he would consent to go. No. No, he must be faced. The worst must be faced. And perhaps, after all, this was not the worst. How could this Bombay inspector, how could anybody, truly know what had happened in that bare little flat? No one could. This fellow must be just only guessing. If that.

'No, Raman,' he said, wondering at the simple calm in his voice. 'No, I might as well be seeing. Bring him up.'

'Ji haan, sahib.'

Ghote stepped in past the peon, a one-eyed fellow. For a moment, first seeing him, he had remembered the super-stition from his childhood: a one-eyed man means evil. But this man had seemed more scared than wicked.

The room was large and bare. Three or four narrow sofas covered in red rexine were pushed up against the walls. A table in one corner was just big enough for a TV set under its embroidered dust-cover and a cream-coloured telephone. From up near the ceiling a row of stained-glass ventilators sent light from the massive illuminations on the Vishwanath Temple, the Golden Temple, in multi-coloured rays sliding across the floor and the blue-painted walls. One, a reddish oblong, cut across a large framed photograph of a group of white-capped politicians, *Lucky Friends With Respected Party Leader H. K. Verma.*

Dominating the whole room, however, was the party leader himself, the man the librarian at Banares Hindu University had said it was necessary to see before anyone could inspect Krishnan Kalgutkar's *Recollections.* A commanding presence, seated in a massive woven-cane peacock-throne chair, its back widespread behind him, his hands firmly placed on its broad arms. A white kurta of homespun khadi fell from his broad shoulders. A dhoti in the same pure white lay draped in graceful folds from sail-swelling belly down over well-rounded knees.

A big well-fleshed face with dark, brooding eyes, deep-set under a wide brow. A faint, ambiguous smile on full orator's lips.

'Good evening, sir. I am by name Inspector Ghote, of the Bombay CID. I am sorry to have to trouble you at this hour. But I am in Banares to make inquiries concerning the death of Mrs Shoba Popatkar in Bombay. You are perhaps aware Mrs Popatkar, a lady well known in our history, has been murdered?'

A muscle in H. K. Verma's big, sad-eyed face flickered for an instant.

'Yes, yes. I was, of course, reading the obituary in *Times of India.* A very terrible business. Very terrible.'

'Yes, sir. And that is why we are pursuing each and every angle with all our efforts and energies. That is why I am here in Banares myself.'

'Yes, Inspector. But sit, sit. No formalities. Sit. But, tell me, how is it that inquiries into a murder in Bombay have brought you here, so many hundred miles distant?'

Ghote, perching himself on one of the narrow rexine sofas at a considerable distance from the party leader, gave a little cough.

'It is quite simple, sir. You see, we were learning from inquiries in Bombay that Mrs Popatkar had come here shortly before her death, without informing anyone of reason for her visit. And we have found also a witness, a fellow from the UP itself, who is stating that just only before the time she was attacked – the culprit was strangling his victim, sir – a man speaking Hindi with what he was recognizing as very much of a Bhojpuri accent was asking where Mrs Popatkar is staying.'

H. K. Verma remained silent for so long that Ghote began to wonder whether his reasons for coming to Banares had appeared absurd.

But at last there came an answer.

'I see, Inspector. And— And do you have a good description of this UPite?'

'No, sir. I regret to say not. The witness was not at all realizing he had heard that familiar accent until the man had gone altogether out of sight.'

'I see. A great pity.'

H. K. Verma appeared to be pondering the implications.

'Otherwise,' he said at last, 'you might have already been able to lay hands on this – this murderer.'

'Yes, sir. But we are hopeful still. You see, it is our belief that the culprit went to Bombay because of something Mrs Popatkar must have learnt or discovered here itself. And, sir, today only I was finding what that might be.'

Again no response.

No wonder this fellow has not succeeded to lead his party to more than a handful of Lok Sabha members from up and down India, Ghote thought. For all the weight of his presence he is slow as a buffalo.

'Yes, Inspector, and what is that?'

The big, brown, deep-set eyes were fixed on him with sombre intentness, as if his answer was somehow of major importance.

'Oh, sir, it is quite simple. You see, I was able to trace Mrs Popatkar from the Cantonment Station where she was arriving— You know she is always travelling by train, not plane, and in lowest class also?'

'Yes, yes. I did not ever have the honour to meet Mrs Popatkar, but that is a well-known fact. A well-known fact, after all.'

'Well, sir, with the assistance of a former officer of the Banares police, a very helpful colleague for me, I was able to trace Mrs Popatkar's steps from the station to the Banares Hindu University, sir. The BHU, as it is known.'

'Yes, yes. And then?'

A spark of impatience.

Was he saying too much? Was he irritating this influential fellow?

'Oh, then, sir, I found she had gone to a small library at the BHU. A place that is devoted to preserving what they are calling contemporary documents, sir.'

'Is there such a—'

H. K. Verma abruptly stopped. A loud and prolonged cough followed.

'Ah, but, no,' he resumed eventually. 'No, I am well knowing the place you mean. Mr Srivastava, the librarian there, is a good friend of mine.'

'Yes, sir. He was the gentleman who was giving me your name. You see, sir, he was telling me that Mrs Popatkar had come to his library for the purposes of consulting one document only, the *Recollections* of Mr Krishnan Kalgutkar, sir, the founder of your party.'

Once again H. K. Verma was slow to react. But at last he answered.

'And it is because of that you have come to me?'

'Oh, yes, sir. You see, Mr Srivastava was stating no one

is permitted to see that document for one hundred and one years, sir. Even though Mrs Popatkar had insisted to do it, and he had not been able to prevent. So, sir, you see, I am thinking that what it was she read there may be a clue to why this person from Banares was needing to end her life. So, sir, I have come to you to take special permission to go through these *Recollections* myself. Mr Srivastava was saying there is no other way.'

'No, Inspector,' H. K. Verma brought himself to say.

Then blankness overwhelmed him. He could think of no possible reason to forbid this Bombay CIDwalla from poking his nose into the *Recollections*. And if he did, what would he find? The founder of our party believing at his life's end he had been wrong . . . That all we stood for in so many wilderness years was wrong . . . So we would be laughing-stocks only. The High Command never daring to take us in. Not however much they are needing the few of our votes block.

And the fellow must know already, or he would very soon read it in the papers, that the leader of the party had been asked to take his votes-bank into Government, and was to be given a Cabinet seat as Minister for Social Upliftment.

The finger will point to me only. And when more inquiries are made . . . So many weak points waiting. Things I thought would never come to light. The girl at Babatpur Airport I lost my temper with. All the other attempts I made to get a flight. The people who fuelled Vikram's plane. Vikram himself, even. The authorities in Bombay who must have logged his plane's arrival. A dozen lurking dangers. A hundred. Each one adding little by little to the case they will make against me.

'Sir, no?'

The fellow sounded mystified. Will my refusal alone be enough to confirm whatever suspicions he has? I must think of something more to say. Something to put the fellow off.

'No, Inspector. You will be disappointed I know. But it is not at all possible.'

Why would it not be possible? I must produce some better reason. Something altogether convincing.

'You see, Inspector, as Mr Srivastava was telling you, there is a strict embargo on anyone whosoever seeing those *Recollections*. For one hundred and one years after Krishnan Kalgutkar's death. So . . .'

Can I make some sort of a joke about it? Will that put this fellow off?

'So, Inspector, I am afraid you will have a very long stay here in Banares. Ninety-seven years, if I am getting right my sums.'

'Well, of course, I am not able to wait that long, sir. You see, what is in that document is perhaps vital evidence. And— And, sir, I must mention there is Section 186 of Indian Penal Code, *Obstructing a public servant in the discharge of public functions*, sir.'

The impertinent rat.

'I hope you are not threatening me, Inspector.'

'Oh, no, sir, no. No, I was mentioning only. Because, you see, sir, it is vital that I am seeing these *Recollections*.'

Time to make him altogether give this up. With one good lie, since it has to be.

'Inspector, I am not at all understanding why it is so vital. KK himself was speaking about the *Recollections* to me shortly before his sad demise. He died, I am happy to say, here in Banares itself, a part of his body immersed in the waters of Holy Ganges. Now I am able to assure you that, though he said there were personal matters there it would be better not to let come to the light for many years, there was nothing else that needed to be concealed. There is, therefore, nothing that could have caused anybody to murder Mrs Shoba Popatkar. Nothing that can have any possible bearing on your inquiries. Nothing.'

'Then, sir, excuse me.'

How the fellow was persisting and persisting.

'Then, sir, if these *Recollections* have in them nothing that needs to be concealed, why may I not see?'

'Inspector.'

Thunder here. Trumpet like an elephant in rage itself.

'Inspector, are you having no sense of decency whatsoever? The *Recollections* are under the ban of a dying man. Are you daring to defy his most sacred wishes?'

'No, sir. No. Not at all.'

Ha, I have done it. I have put this bandicoot in a cage where he belongs. Let him squeak there as long as he likes.

Yes, now the fellow was getting up from his seat. Looking disgraced and defeated. Well, good riddance only.

'Then I must accept that, sir. But— But I think I must say also that, if my inquiries do not produce any other reason for that man coming from here so soon after Mrs Popatkar had made her visit, then I may have to return and definitely take your permission.'

Well, let him. Let him return and return. So long as he is never getting to see the *Recollections* I am safe.

Ghote, lying on bedding whose cleanliness he did not feel altogether happy about, perhaps without good reason, realized that sleep was going to escape him. The clamour of the city all round, the clang-clang of bells as worshippers went into the temples, the rise and fall of bhajan singing, the grinding of traffic in the street outside, the shouts and yells of life going on far into the night, all had ceased some time before. But the thoughts churning in his head were keeping him awake just as effectively.

Had he been right to have left H. K. Verma without forcing out of him permission to inspect Krishnan Kalgutkar's *Recollections*? Then could he go to that library and insist, like Mrs Popatkar, on seeing the document, permission or no permission? No, Mr Srivastava had apparently already got into deep troubles over allowing it to be read once. He would never let it happen a second time.

And had he been right to have accepted H. K. Verma's

assurance that there was nothing in the *Recollections* that could have caused anybody to attempt to shut Mrs Popatkar's mouth? Was there, as he had self-thought at the time, something, somehow, a little wrong about the way that assurance had been given? What had it been? Nothing he could lay a finger on even now.

Or was that niggle of doubt no more than his imagination?

And then, damn it, there was the way he had been landed with camping in this hotel. That fool Mishra about to tell him, as they were going from the BHU to H. K. Verma's house, about some famous theft from the Golden Temple, had suddenly shouted to the driver to stop.

'Look, look. Here is the very place where you must put up, Inspector. Very good hotel. I am knowing it well. Hotel Relax. Relax by name, relax also by nature. It would begin to give you an idea of our Banarasi way of life, of our masti itself, happy relaxing.'

And before he had had time to object or even agree the fellow had stopped the autorickshaw, jumped down, run into the place. He had thought of protesting. But he had to stay somewhere. And in any case as soon as Mishra had returned he had plunged back into his story.

'You are knowing what is the Golden Yoni?'

He had felt obliged to answer.

'Yoni, yes, I am knowing. Everyone is knowing. Object of worship, the opposite of lingam, the female organ instead of the male. I suppose the Golden Yoni was stolen from this Golden Temple.'

'Yes, yes. From Golden Temple itself,' Mishra replied, eyes glowing with enjoyment. 'The greatest theft in the world. The lingam only those fellows were leaving. Even our stop-at-nothing goondas are knowing what is a hundred and one per cent sacred. And afterwards . . . You can imagine. Entire Banares was desolate. If those thieves had been found they would have been torn to pieces.'

'So you were never able to track down culprits? But I am supposing they were able to wash away that sin the next day even, going down at sunrise to the Ganges?'

He had felt entitled to that jibe. But Mishra had quickly got his own back. Shouting above the noise all round, the yammer of the motor-cycle engine in front, the incessant tonk-tonk of temple entrance bells, the jabber of voices, the bleatings of beggars, the bawling of hawkers, he had produced his answer.

'No, Inspector, you are altogether wrong if you are believing the Golden Yoni thieves were able to escape the outcome of their wrong-doings. You see, if you are committing a sin inside Banares itself it is what they are calling *vajralepa*, hard as rock. Not even Ganga jal can wash it away. No, no, those fellows are doomed to their next lives as the lowest of the low. As mosquitoes every one.'

And now, whining as if it was one of the Golden Yoni thieves in his next life itself, a mosquito had got into the room and seemed intent on landing anywhere it could on his hot and restless body.

Oh, and in his rush to leave for this place he had forgotten to pack sharp-smelling Odomos cream. Completely without any defence.

And completely, too, he thought with a heavy thump of dismay, without an idea of where to carry on his inquiries when morning came. If ever it did come in this cursed night.

6

H. K. Verma had slept badly. Try as he might he had not been able to stop the thoughts fighting each other in his head. This Inspector Ghote from Bombay, did he suspect something? Or was he just only in truth wanting to see KK's *Recollections*? But even if that was all he wanted, it was the path down, down, downwards to ruin only.

Yet how could he have stopped the fellow finding those terrible last words of KK's in any other way than he had? But that blank refusal – nothing, nothing else at all, had entered his head – could so easily have alerted him to the fact that the *Recollections* were a clue pointing simply to himself.

If the Bombaywalla was clever enough to see it . . . He had not seemed so. He seemed to have accepted that KK had discussed the *Recollections* and there was nothing in them that could have led to Mrs Popatkar being murdered. Feeble though that was. But would the fellow eventually have doubts? Would he ask himself, sooner or later, why the guardian of the *Recollections* had been so violent in refusing to let an officer of the law read them?

Then . . . A sudden, fearful, beguiling temptation.

Shall I let this prying Bombay mosquito learn everything? Read the *Recollections*? Let entire disaster come. The burden will be lifted. I would be confessing what I have done, even if not directly. I would be as much free from the weight of the sin as I felt when I was stepping out of the Ganga. Only to find relief draining from me drop by drop almost as the Ganga water drained from my back.

He lay there, his heart thumping and thumping.

But am I truly burdened with sin, he asked himself. Truly? Surely that – that unthinkable thing, after all was a real act of right-doing? The outcome will – it will, it will, it will – mean a better life for the downtrodden by the lakh, by the million, by the crore. Once Social Upliftment Ministry is in my hands.

So surely I was in the right then.

But if that was the right thing to do, equally as much stopping the act coming to light is a right thing also.

Then – a terrible idea – is there a way of preventing this Bombay intruder with his as yet unmade guesses . . .?

The thought was with him still, painful as a fragment of grit under an eyelid and as hard to get rid of, as he went to the Ganges for his sunrise dip. But the swirling water of the wide, soul-cleansing river failed now to give him the new-day, new-start feeling it had always done. Day after day, year after year, whenever he had been at home in Banares.

Ghote had not arranged to avail himself of Inspector Mishra's assistance after the first day. When with darkness rapidly coming on they had parted before he had gone in to see H. K. Verma he had imagined himself next morning setting forth, full of the fire of the chase. He would go back to that library tucked away among all the various learned institutions in the wide spaces of the Banares Hindu University. There, armed with H. K. Verma's authority – no reason for him not to give it? – he would plunge through the *Recollections*. Then, learning what it was Mrs Shoba Popatkar had found in them, he would know who in Banares had had reason to shut her mouth. And he would have brought the culprit in. Got the necessary assistance from the Senior Superintendent over the formalities, and taken his man back to Bombay. In handcuffs.

But now there seemed little he could do. Heavy with gloom and muzzy-headed after his wretched night, he had risen late and then after mooning long over his breakfast had sat reading the unfamiliar pages of the Banares paper *Aj*, vaguely hoping he might find in it something to give him an idea. At last with a groaning sigh he admitted to himself the only feeble thing left was to return to the Cantonment Station and see if he could trace Mrs Popatkar leaving Banares. She just might have spoken to somebody, said something. At least it would be better than going tamely back to Bombay.

It was with a sullen hatred for everything his eyes lit on that H. K. Verma set off soon after he had got back from the Ganges to see his son. He would have to get home again in plenty of time to receive Jagmohan Nagpal before the High Command walla took in his turn a Ganges dip, to the click-click-clicking of the photographers from the *Aj* and the *Gandiva*. But certain information had to be prized out of Krishnakanta.

He wanted it. Urgently. However much he kept telling himself he did not want it. That he ought not to want it. That he did not wish even to know it.

It was almost nine o'clock by the time he arrived at the big house on the outskirts of the city with its wide lawns and its high surrounding walls. But, to his disgust, he found no one in the family was yet up.

'I am having my holy dip at sunrise,' he said when he at last got hold of Krishnakanta. 'Three hours past already, more even. And you are not even starting your day.'

Krishnakanta leant forward and spooned English marmalade heavily on to the toast on his plate.

'But I am making damn good use of my day when I am up,' he said. 'Better than any politicking-molliticking.'

'Well, let me tell you that my politicking, as you are pleased to call it, is about to bring forth very much of fruit. Jagmohan Nagpal is coming today to see me.'

He glared at the loaded piece of toast Krishnakanta was now manoeuvring towards his mouth.

'And why cannot you eat proper food? What is wrong with good Indian khana?'

'Nothing, Pitaji. Nothing at all. If you are liking it. There is no question of wrong and right. I simply prefer what I am eating now.'

'And I suppose that boy of yours is the same? Or does he lie in bed all morning and eat nothing at all?'

He knew he ought not to be going on like this. But these businessman's Western ways of Krishnakanta's simply infuriated him. They were wrong. Wrong.

Or was it that complaining of marmalade and Vikki – no, Vikram – was simply a way of avoiding what he had come with such urgency to find out?

But Krishnakanta had become sharply alert.

'Nagpalji coming? Does this mean what one of my Delhi contactmen was saying . . .?'

'Yes, yes, of course. Strictly confidential for the moment, but it is going to be Minister for Social Upliftment.'

Now a quick scowl stopped the marmalade-dripping toast finding its destination.

'Social Upliftment, what good is that only?'

H. K. Verma almost jumped up from his chair.

'What good it is? What good it is? That is the seat in whole Government where a man of goodwill can do most for his downtrodden fellow citizens.'

'Pitaji, it is me, Krishnakanta, you are talking to. No point in hypocrisies with me. You know just as much as I do that one and all in this world are beasts of prey only. It is jungle we are in. Jungle. And the hardest hunters eat best.'

'No. No. That is not the way I was teaching you. Don't you remember as a boy coming with me, at this time of year itself, to the Ram Lila out at Ramnagar? How we discussed after each evening's play its example of goodness?'

Krishnakanta gave a snort of laughter.

'No, Pitaji, what I remember is asking and asking till you were buying me sweets.'

'Oh, yes, you were always greedy. I should have beaten you.'

'And that would not have made me less greedy, I promise you. Come, you know very well why Social Upliftment Ministry is no good. Precious little procurement in it. Not a damn thing for any factory of mine.'

H. K. Verma sat in glowering silence.

Why did the boy assume he would take the evil course? Using his office to line family pockets. He would not. He had never taken the evil course. He had—

Then, shrieking like a dust-storm at the height of summer, into his head rushed horribly vivid images straight from Bombay. The deep pits in the old woman's neck as his thumbs had found them. The sudden heavy limpness of her frail body sagging from his two clenched hands. And, last, the cheap blue-check cotton sari flung wide on the stone floor as he had thrown her aside. He had tripped on it as he had turned to get away. He could almost feel how it had tugged for one horrible clinging moment at his foot before he had kicked it clear.

Evil motives. Yes, I had them. That truly is what urged me on. Evil. No getting past that. What I did was evil. And what I came here intending to do, or have done for me, is evil also. Getting rid of that prying policewalla. Finding out from Krishnakanta, without if possible letting him know why, where to find some willing men from the wrestling pits. The goondas he used to beat up strike leaders. And worse than beat even, if the hints I would not let myself hear were true.

But no. No, I will not go down that path. I will not inside Banares itself commit a sin that would be rock-hard. Let the Bombay rat live. I am at least as good a man as that, whatever Krishnakanta is thinking of me. There are some things I would never do.

But should I have even thought of it? No. No, I never should have. But I did. I did.

When Jagmohanji takes his Ganga dip I will take also. To clear my soul.

But will Jagmohan object to any stealing of photo lime-light? He might. Almost certainly he will.

Better play safe.

At the Cantonment Station Ghote had some luck. Perhaps, he thought wryly, because no amount of luck was likely to do him any good now. But the first ticket examiner he approached had known Mrs Popatkar to talk to. She had come to Banares many times, he said, visiting the Northern Railway General Hospital. And he had seen her as she had left on the day before her death. She had arrived at the station in a great hurry and had only just caught the Rajdani Express. It had been one of the days when it had left exactly on time.

'She was not saying anything to you?'

'No, no. Too much of hurry. She was just only wishing me as she ran by.'

Checked. Nothing more to be learnt about what it was she had come to Banares for. No clue at all as to what it was she had read in Krishnan Kalgutkar's *Recollections.*

Turning away, yet more deep in despondency, his eye was caught by a familiar figure. The white hippy. Or, if what Inspector Mishra had said here at the station when he had noticed the fellow hovering as they had gone to question the autorickshaw drivers, the white junky, the hawker of brown sugar.

And the fellow, plainly, was watching him himself. He looked as if he was wanting to speak, and yet was hesitating to.

Did the riff-raff believe he was a customer for his crude heroin? He might. Yesterday morning he had seen him staring in the same way from behind the newspaper he was pretending to read. As if wondering what this person not behaving much like a pilgrim or a tourist had come to Banares for.

Right, let's catch the fellow. See what he is up to. At least something useful to do, here in this good-for-nothing city.

He put on an air of thoughtfulness, turned and began to walk wanderingly off in the direction of the forecourt.

And, yes, he was drawing the fellow along behind.

Slow the steps a little more. Hope to bring him nearer without him realizing. Slow yet again. Do not for anything look round. Just count on such a junky not being a hundred per cent alert. Slow again.

And whip round.

His outstretched hands came neatly first on to one elbow then on to the other of the boy's grimy, torn shirt. He gripped hard on the skeletal bones.

H. K. Verma went to seek guidance in just such an unthinking rush as, from the moment he banged down the telephone on Mr Srivastava, he had gone racing off after Mrs Popatkar. He was hardly aware what put the notion into his head.

He had been sitting in his office filling in the time before he was due to meet Jagmohan Nagpal by listening to some of the petitioners he had found waiting when he got back from Krishnakanta's. It had seemed no different from any other day. He had received garlands. He had made promises. He had avoided committing himself. He had brought out appropriate words. He had denounced the unjust. He had – he supposed – garnered a few more votes for any future election. He had even, once or twice, been able to give useful advice.

But his heart had been even less in it than usual. Two thoughts had swum up time and again into his mind. The promise, as soon as Jagmohanji arrived, of power at last. And the threat – push it down as he might, argue against it as he might – of disaster.

Suddenly he had been unable to endure it a moment longer. He had risen to his feet, plunged for the door, almost knocking over an aged former Class Four Government servant clutching his tattered bundle of testimonials, and sought the freedom of the fresh air.

The crowded galli outside had been as oppressive. But

there was a tall building near by whose roof looked out over the Ganges. He mounted its stone stairs in a bull-like run.

And on the parapet of the roof, an everyday enough sight, a man was sitting in meditation. Cross-legged, one arm resting flaccidly on a knee, the other passing through his fingers a long brown-beads rudraksha, he was looking sightlessly at the swift-flowing, mud-brown river far below. But seeing him caused the notion of seeking guidance to explode in his head in a shellburst of white light.

He knew at once, too, to whom he would go. To the Collector Swami.

He had as a boy known him when he had been Collector – that title dating from early British days when revenue collection was the principal task of any rural administrative officer – of Rajapur District where the family house had been. At retirement age, unexpectedly, this dry-as-dust official had taken sannyas, left family, home and wealth to live in a community in the holy city. Where now he was the spiritual leader. Collector Swami, so called.

'Collector Swami, it is good of you to see me at so short notice.'

'My son, what does notice, short or long, mean to one who sees the world of hours and minutes as no more than a cinema show?'

But now, suddenly, he found the thunderclap resolution he had come to at the sight of the meditating man had deserted him. All the while as he had stumbled down the long flights of stairs to ground level, almost run through the crowded gallis to the swami's big old nearby house, had hurried through its passageways, past a dozen bewildering turnings, up the old wooden stairs, their time-eroded steps powdering away, the desire to be told whether what he had done was right or wrong had throbbed in him like a quivering headache. But now as soon as he had come into the presence of the Collector Swami, seated in a red velvet armchair that was more a throne,

54

that pain-filled desire had left him. Only an empty blankness remained.

'My son, you are wishing for the life which is not life.'

Was that a statement? Or a question? And did he want that?

No. No, though dimly he could see the attraction of such a non-life life. But, no, he was too wedded to reality to go along that hard path. Now, especially, when what he had wanted, ever since as little more than a schoolboy he had joined the party, was at last within his grasp. The chance to do good to his fellow men.

Except there was just only that fly-speck in his vision.

However, he lowered himself cross-legged to the carpet in front of the Collector Swami's throne-chair. And, once down, he could not hold himself back from asking the direct question. Or asking it almost directly.

'Collector Swami, I— That is, Collector Swami, I have a good friend . . .'

He found he could go no further.

'Tell me about your good friend. He is in trouble, of course.'

'No. Yes. Yes, Collector Swami, perhaps he is in bad trouble.'

On the swami's face – head like a stone carving, rounded and massive – there played now the slightest of smiles.

'Collector Swami, what if a man – if my friend, my friend only – had taken the life of— Of someone? If he had done it, had had to do it, because that person was standing in the way of a great good. Collector Swami, can that deed have been a good deed also? Can it? Can it?'

Silence.

H. K. Verma searched for an answer in the brooding and baleful eyes under the cliff-jut of the forehead.

Or was he expected to find that answer in himself? But it was to be told, told the answer, told the truth, that he had come scurrying to the man in the old, rubbed velvet throne-chair. He had answers enough himself. But each contradicted the other. Sometimes it was the Geeta and God Krishna's charge to Arjun, *There is a war that opens the doors of Heaven, Arjuna. Happy the warriors whose fate is to fight such a war.* Sometimes it was the Indian Penal Code and the wiry little police officer who had travelled here all the way from Bombay.

He had to know which voice spoke right. Which of the many voices.

But now, without preliminary, Collector Swami spoke.

'In the cinema of the world, if you are determined to stay there, it is each man's duty to do what is right. To see this and to agree to it is easy. But, my son, that is not enough. The heart must feed upon that truth. It must feed as the insect feeds on the leaf. Until it has altogether taken up the green and it shows what food it has eaten in every smallest fibre of its body.'

Then silence. Brooding silence.

Infuriating silence. Deprived of the answer from outside, from above, H. K. Verma pushed himself to his feet, made a perfunctory namaskar, then trudged away.

The look of fear on the junky's pinched and twitching face was plain to see.

'Now, what it is you are wanting?' Ghote shot the words out like so many open-handed slaps.

'I— I—'

'Yes? Talk. Talk. I am a police officer. Talk.'

'Yeah. Know you are. Kinda heard you yesterday.'

The boy must be American. How did it happen that a young man from there could get into a state like this fellow? He smelt. The high, rotten smell of a long unwashed body. A boy from the land of hot showers in every home, of pools behind every house filled with twinkling bright blue water.

But something was wrong. The boy knew he was a police officer. He must have crept up when he had been talking to Mishra as they questioned the autorickshaw wallas. So he could not have been waiting to offer him brown sugar. No one would be that much of a fool.

'Very well, so you are knowing I am police officer. Why then are you wanting to say something to me? Do not pretend. I was seeing you and damn well knowing what you were trying to decide to do.'

'Okay, that's what I was doing. Making up my mind. You see, I guess I know something you want to know.'

'What? What it is?'

'About . . .'

The boy gave him a cautious sideways look.

'About someone you're maybe interested in.'

'Who is that?'

Could it be Mrs Popatkar? But how should this boy know what he had come to Banares to do? Yet perhaps it could be. He had been just on the other side of the line of autorickshaws. He could well have heard Mrs Popatkar's name.

'Well, who it is you think I am interested in?'

'Come on, Inspector, you know. Well as I do.'

The boy was losing his fright more and more with every passing second. A growing slackness in the arms he still gripped.

He must have overheard a good deal, too. Even to know my rank. So how much more?

'All right. You are knowing I have come to Banares because of the murder of a lady by the name of Mrs Shoba Popatkar. Very well. You have something to tell about her?'

'Could have. If it's worth my while.'

'Now you are asking for money?'

'Heck, no. I'd want more than a guy like you could find.'

So, he has come to impudence. But all the same he is knowing I am investigating Shoba Popatkar murder, and he is believing at least he has something to tell I would want to hear. Pay no attention, then, to any of his cheeks.

'Well, if you are not asking for money – and do not expect to get from me in any case – what it is you are asking?'

'Just a little something you could find out for me, if you wanted.'

'Yes?'

'The fuzz here are kinda planning some sort of raid on the house of the guy I work for.'

'And who is that?'

'Guy called the Dom Raja. Know who I mean?'

So Mishra's unending historical outpourings had been some use after all.

'Yes, I am knowing. He is the in-charge at the big burning ghat, yes?'

'That's him. Dom Raja of the Manikarnika Ghat. You find out for me just when they plan to raid his house. I'll tell you what someone here in Banares did the day of your murder. Deal?'

Ghote felt an uprising of outrage. Did this little American riff-raff – only he was not in fact so little, half a head taller than himself – did he think he was going to tell him when a drugs raid was going to take place just in exchange for something he had most probably altogether made up?

'You come with me,' he snapped. 'I think what you are daring to call the fuzz would want one word with you.'

And the boy slipped from his grasp.

A single quick ducking motion and the thin elbows he had been keeping a grip on – only it had been a grip that had gradually relaxed – had slipped from under his hands. Then the boy was running hard away.

He felt a complete fool. Was he no longer capable of bringing in a little miscreant like this?

The boy was dodging and dipping through the dozens of waiting passengers, the family parties squatting in sprawling circles, the sleepers flat on their backs, the vendors of cold drinks, of plaster idols of the gods, of things to eat, of bright-coloured magazines.

Round the boy went, as Ghote followed, through the patient lines waiting to buy tickets, to make reservations, to hire bed-rolls. Once he almost sent flying a bereaved new arrival holding in front of himself a roses-draped urn of ashes ready to immerse in the waiting Ganges.

But almost at once Ghote realized he stood no chance. He was in strange territory while the boy would know the station and its twists and turns back-to-front. He stopped, panting for breath, and stood cursing himself.

If he had had the sense to keep a better grip on the damn riff-raff he could have slapped the answer out of him in two–three minutes.

What someone here in Banares did the day of your murder. Which someone? And what had they done? On the day of the murder? So it had not been a matter of following Mrs Popatkar on to the Rajdani Express, trailing her in Bombay, waiting for the opportunity. But could it be someone who had gone to Bombay by air? That way, although there was no direct flight and you had to go to Calcutta first, you could easily arrive before the train. You could lie in wait.

But who could it have been who had done that? The man with the Bhojpuri accent. Almost certainly. Confirmation at least that he himself was in the right place now. In sacred Banares, where you had to beware of whores and holymen, let alone those slimy steps to the ghats and the holy bulls sitting sullenly everywhere.

No, now the more he thought about it the more he felt the American boy did really know something worth hearing. He had had something to offer. Someone even.

But what? Who?

7

It came to H. K. Verma almost as a death blow.

Jagmohan Nagpal's dip in the Ganges had been a complete success. The photographers had clicked and clicked. Jagmohanji descending the steps of the Dasawamedh Ghat among all the crowds, his hand thrust out giving to a decent-looking beggar. None of your repellent sores-covered creatures. Click, click. Jagmohanji sitting cross-legged under the wide, rattan-covered umbrella of one of the pandas – those big umbrellas always looking good in a photo – listening with inclined head to the holy words. Click, click, click. Jagmohanji, divested of his clothes, all but enough to conceal his lank old man's middle, about to enter the river, a woman in a green sari squatting at just the right spot in the background, hands clasped in prayer. Click, click, click, click. Jagmohanji in the river gazing fixedly out towards the far bank. Click, click, click, click, click.

Only what had he been thinking of then? Of his soul? Or of how he was to say what he had come to say?

Even the Hotel de Paris lunch had been a success, the table he had eventually reserved, all ready despite the earliness of the hour, the setting perfect, the waiters assiduous. 'Yes, yes, I am always liking this place. I am often coming when I am in your ages-old city.' Generous amounts of political gossip as they had eaten. How tickling to hear such scandalous snippets about people soon to be Cabinet colleagues. And how much Jagmohanji had enjoyed the food, as if eating and eating only was what he had come all the way from Delhi to do. Nothing could have gone better.

Then, afterwards, sitting in two long chairs outside looking on to the gardens, altogether safe from being overheard. Some excellent sweetmeats in a basket on the table between them, Banares specialities, squares of pista barfi with silver top and bottom, crisp bars of nuts-rich chikky, creamy coconut chumchum. Now, he had thought, now at any moment it will come. The formal offer from the High Command Minister for Social Upliftment.

And what had Jagmohan said?

'But I must be telling you the good news. Yes, we have succeeded after all to resolve our differences with those fellows. They are not going to cross the floor. Our troubles are all ended.'

'Not going to cross the floor?'

He had barely been able to get the words out.

'And— And, Jagmohanji, this is meaning that you— That High Command is no longer needing . . .'

He had come to a halt then. Some things were too terrible to be uttered aloud.

'Well, yes, of course, my friend. That is the situation. Actually. Please remember, though, we will always be most grateful for your good offer. But it is quite unnecessary now, Bhagwan be thanked.'

It seemed as if the whole world had, in a moment, lost all its colour.

Gone. Gone his one chance of joining Government. Gone all that he had hoped for over so many years. Gone the Ministry, and all he had seen himself doing there. Social Upliftment. He had had hopes, true hopes, high hopes. They had been a distant shining before him all through the wilderness years. From his young manhood when his father had proudly presented him to KK till today.

Gone. Gone. All gone.

And so – it had been some time before the thought had come to him, stupefied as he was – so he had done that for nothing. He had done what he had done in Bombay for nothing. There had been no need. None at all. None.

The realization, creeping up to him like a soft-footed thug, had made him clutch suddenly at the thick wooden sides of his chair and hold tight with abruptly sweat-slippery palms. Otherwise, he felt, he might have toppled to the paving-stones.

There it was. The fact. He had not needed to have done that, to have gone like a madman to Bombay and . . . and done what he had done.

What would it matter now if Mrs Popatkar had broadcast to the highest heavens that KK had lost faith in what the party had stood for? Had lost the faith proclaimed ever since, as long ago as 1934 when Gandhiji had failed to persuade his fellow Congress leaders to prefer the method of truth and non-violence to so-called legitimate means, he had set up his own breakaway party.

That secret buried in the *Recollections* might be all but forgotten in five–ten years when perhaps his next chance might come. If he was here in this life to take it. But at this time, at this time as it seemed until just a minute ago, it would have blasted all his hopes into nothing.

Yes, he had committed a murder for nothing. Nothing. Nothing. Nothing.

Jagmohan was still speaking, but he paid no heed. He hardly realized the malicious devil – he cares just only for his own enjoyments – had been adding something more. Some more platitudes.

What was he to do? Everything had changed. The world had changed. He was no longer living the same life as he had been till only a minute ago. The life where he had gone to Bombay, battling past each and every difficulty, fixedly set on one thing only. On not letting Mrs Shoba Popatkar tell what it was she had read in the *Recollections*. The life where, tracking her down at last in all the hulla-gulla of that appalling Dadar, he had argued with her, had pleaded, had at last reached out with rage-impelled hands and squeezed and squeezed at her throat until she shut up. Until she had been shut up. For ever. The life in which he had killed Mrs Shoba Popatkar, freedom fighter, former Minister for Railways, shouter-out aloud of each and every truth she had come to know.

Only one thing to do, Ghote thought. Just one thing only. Get hold of Mishra and ask him where the white junky he knows so much about is likely to be found. Because whatever the boy has got hold of – if he has got hold of anything – it is my only hope of learning who in Banares went to Bombay and strangled Mrs Shoba Popatkar. If I cannot find the boy before another day or two at the most I will have to go back myself. Bloody Banares with its whores, its bulls, its steps and its holymen will have beaten me. I will find myself slinking home like a kicked dog only.

But at least Mishra, in the course of heaping on to him every possible fact and fancy about the city of his birth, had mentioned where he lived. He hurried out into the station forecourt and grabbed a taxi.

It was, at it turned out, Mishra's granddaughter, a tiny three-year-old slip of a thing clinging to her mother's sari but bright-eyed as a little nut-nibbling, tree-scrambling gilhari, who answered his request.

'No, no, Dadaji is at Sandbank.'

'At the Sandbank?'

What on earth could Mishra be doing out there on the other side of the river? It was surely an altogether desolate spot.

'Yes, yes. He is going in the morning every day now. He is retired, you see. Dada was a big-big inspector, but now he stays at home, and – and he is being very nice to me. Are you retired also? Do you have a little girl like me?'

The tiny thing's mother succeeded in breaking into the prattle long enough to explain. Her father-in-law went almost every morning over to the Sandbank to join the exercisers there.

Ghote thanked her and hastily left. He had wanted to ask who or what the exercisers were, but he suspected he would get in reply a whole spate of information, from either mother or daughter, he by no means needed. Like father-in-law, like daughter. Like grandfather, like grand-daughter.

The taxi driver, however, supplied him with the answer, shouted across his shoulder. Crossing the Ganga to the wide stretch of smooth sand on the far side to bathe, to perform exercises, or just to walk about in the open away from the narrow gallis of the city was the favourite pastime of every true Banarasi.

'You must go also, sahib. I will take you to a very good friend of mine who will row you there. Almost nothing to pay.'

There was rather more than 'almost nothing' to pay the taxi walla's good friend. But as the man took his boat further and further out into the wide river with mild, unhurried creaking strokes of his long bamboo oars, Ghote began to think that what he had had to pay was not bad value. It was wonderfully pleasant and cool on the water, and the leisurely style of their progress was little by little filling him with a sense of relaxation.

Idly he watched the shore they had left gradually recede. Yes, there was what must be the Dom Raja's house, with those two larger-than-life, bright-painted tigers on the parapet, tails twisting high as if they had scented prey. The souls of sinners passing by? His soul even?

He refused to let himself think about it.

The great tall ghats clustered with temples rose up and up behind in intricate towers of red and yellow, with the gold of the dome of the Vishwanath Temple dazzling among them and the minarets of the mosque built long ago by Moslem invaders still dominating the skyline. Soon everything seemed to become hazed. The masses of bathers and pilgrims, tourists and touts, melted into one dust-lost shimmer of humanity.

He felt the lassitude of the softly lapping water seeping into every corner of his mind. The Banarasi life.

If any one individual there among those hazy crowds was by some chance the murderer he had come here to find, so be it. He would come to light later, or he would not. The itch of duty, the incessant inner demand to be doing the right thing, had fallen away from him with each soft splash of the boatman's oars as he slowly lifted their heart-shaped blades from the water, slowly dipped them again.

A larger craft made its way past, the rows of tourists in it, American, French, German – who could tell? – staring dutifully at the ghats and their crowds. A boat no bigger than their own crossed just in front of them with at its narrow stern the lonely figure of a father holding the wrapped body of an infant below the age of being committed to the fire at the burning ghats. The boatman gave a signal and the wretched father rose to his feet, stood for a moment swaying in the gentle movement of the river and then let the little body with its stone weight fall into the water.

Now they were nearing the far bank. His melancholy calm began to leave him.

Mishra, would he manage to find him out here? And if he did would he be able to help? Or would he be willing to do no more than narrate the history of his city till he had exhausted every temple and palace in it? And the junky, even if they were finding him, would he really have something to tell that would lead to the strangler who had gone to Bombay from here? Might that man himself even be over here on the Sandbank in the way that so many Banarasis came day by day?

The boat nosed its way into the waterlogged sand at the river's edge. He jumped out and looked around.

There were certainly plenty of men about taking exercise, most of them naked all but for gaudy cotton shorts or a little pouch round their private parts. Some stood energetically touching their toes, left then right, left then right. Others were pitting themselves in friendly wrestling matches, head to head, shoulder to shoulder, straining at each other minute after minute in widespread inverted Vs. With, he could not help noting, a simple joyousness shining in their eyes. Banarasi masti.

He began climbing the gentle incline, feet sinking into the soft sand, looking at each step this way and that in the hope of spotting Mishra. A man passed, coming down carefully dabbing at his wrists with a little cotton pad. He caught the swooning smell of the perfume he was applying, and shook his head in rejection. Too much of masti.

Now, further from the river where it was drier, there were parties of card-players, planking the cards down on the sand. Others were strolling idly here and there or sitting in happy parties passing from one to another brass tumblers, which from the gentle giggling laughter that rose up were doubtless filled with bhang-laced thandai such as Mishra had tried to make him drink at the Cantonment Station. Massage wallas were carefully anointing reclining bodies with odoriferous sandalwood paste.

Down at the water's edge behind him there were people – almost all men – dipping garments into the stream to wash and holding them high while the water ran out of them. Near by, on flimsy improvised lines more garments hung drying.

And it was partly hidden by one of these lines of gaily multi-coloured clothes that he eventually spotted Mishra. He ran over.

Mishra, naked all bar his shorts, was sitting idly combing his hair, his stout body still wet from bathing in the river. He looked up in mild surprise.

'Ah, Inspector, so you have begun to learn our Banares way. You have come to the Sandbank to enjoy. But how did you know I would be here?'

'It was your daughter-in-law— Or, rather, your little granddaughter who was telling me. That and other things also.'

66

'Yes, yes. She is an altogether clever little creature. Just only three and one half years and talking, talking. She could read also, but for some reason she does not want.'

'Oh, yes,' Ghote found himself replying, 'that was just the case with my son, Ved. When he was that age also. We knew he was able to read but he would not do it before us. He was afraid to do it wrong, you know.'

'Ah, that must be the case with little Rukmini. She is always so concerned to be doing what is right. I am thinking she will end up as a member of judiciary itself.'

Ghote was put out by this friendly chat Mishra had somehow succeeded in luring him into. He would have liked to have barked out at once an urgent request for assistance. But it was only right to tell the fellow what a bright little grandchild he had.

'But sit, sit,' Mishra said now. 'Take off your shirt and pant, let the breeze tickle you only.'

The fellow would keep him here all the rest of the day if he was not careful.

'Inspector,' he said sharply, 'you were allocated to me for my assistance by the Senior Superintendent himself, and it is that assistance I am here now to require.'

Mishra's big eyes blinked up at him.

'Oh, you Bombayman,' he said. 'Never stopping. Never enjoying.'

Ghote drew in a tense breath.

'Let me tell you what is situation.'

'Please, please. But at least be seated first. Sand just here is dry and very soft. You will be comfortable.'

Grudgingly Ghote lowered himself. He would have to do whatever was necessary to make use of this lazy chap. No point in antagonizing. And, true, the sand made a comfortable sitting place.

He explained, rapidly and concisely as he could, what he had learnt, or almost learnt, from the junky.

'Ah, yes,' said Mishra when he had finished. 'I would not at all be surprised if that young man is knowing something. Rick. His name is Rick. He goes about everywhere, and he has the ears of a cockroach. Definitely.'

'Yes, he certainly heard almost all we were saying when we were questioning those autorickshaw fellows. He is damn well knowing why I am here.'

'Then we had better find.'

To Ghote's surprise the full-bellied Banarasi jumped to his feet and began hooking a shirt, bright yellow today rather than pink, off the line that had hidden him from view.

'Yes,' he said once he was dressed, 'there are a good many places where I have seen that boy. He would not be at Cantonment Station now. That is one certain thing. But where else is likely? Not at this time of day at the Manikarnika Ghat. His dealings there are night-time matters only when the real badmashes are roaming. Fellows, I regret to inform, who would murder you for just only two rupees. I tell you, when I had to go there late at night on duty I would feel my knees were made of butter only.'

He gave a little shudder. Then pulled himself together.

'So where to go to find this cockroach?'

He lowered himself again on to the soft, footmark crisscrossed sand.

'Now let me see. Thatheri Bazaar, I have noticed him there often. It is where they are selling very much of our fine Banares brassware. You know we—'

Mishra checked himself, and produced a brilliant, apologetic smile.

This was better, Ghote thought. The fellow is after all the police officer I had begun to doubt had ever existed. Police ways did not drop off from him when he retired, to be utterly replaced with Banarasi living, Banares praising. Banares narrating to whatsoever strangers come his way. Now we may get somewhere.

'No, perhaps not Thatheri. If he is there we would hardly find. Too much of crowds. No, first, I think, the Chowk. Plenty of tourists there. What he is liking for his nefarious purposes. Then perhaps some of the ghats, the most easy to reach.'

He looked up.

'But, you know, it is getting on in time. Have you eaten since the start of the day?'

'Well, no. No, I have not. But I do not think this is the moment to be time-wasting with any meals. We should go to the Chowk straightaway.'

'No, Inspector. Take some good advice. We may be having a long day in front of us. I cannot be guaranteeing we shall find our fellow just as soon as we look. But no need to take you to any of our fine Banares restaurants. We have Chinese, you know, even Continental, but best of all are our vegetarian. I wish you would come with me to the Solty in Godaulia or the Tulsi in Lohurabir.'

He put up a fending-off hand as Ghote drew himself up to speak.

'No, no. I know we have no time now for such pleasures. Perhaps before you go ... But just now what have I got with me?'

From a little hollow in the sand just beside where he had been sitting he produced, with a flourish he could not prevent himself making, a solidly large tiffin carrier.

'Plenty here for two. I am always taking too much. Now, sit again and eat. We would not be too long.'

Ghote sat. Ate. Acknowledged that he was hungry, and would have grown very bad-tempered and impatient if he had attempted to go for the rest of the day without some food. Acknowledged that what he was eating was delicious.

Trust masti-loving Mishra.

And in a very short time they were climbing into one of the boats waiting to take people across again to the swarming city opposite. The craft slid rapidly backwards into the water, their boatman running at the prow and leaping nimbly aboard.

Off. Off on the hunt.

And, as the boatman with one lunged-at stroke of an oar swirled them round till they were pointing arrow-poised at the city itself, something just caught Ghote's eye.

'Mishra bhai,' he said, 'did you see who that was, just only getting out of a boat and striding away up the Sand-bank. It was that fellow H. K. Verma I went to see last night. His face was like thunder itself. I wonder what was upsetting.'

8

H. K. Verma had been unable to endure the closeness of
the city as, almost unseeing, he left the Hotel de Paris –
Where had Jagmohan Nagpal gone? He could not remember – and told an autorickshaw walla to take him to his
house. But, suddenly glimpsing a sort of salvation, he had
re-directed the man to the Dasawamedh Ghat. Descending its steps in a series of heavy lurches this way and that,
he had staggered into the first boat he came across. With
a lumbering gesture rather than any words he had indicated the Sandbank.

The same black, bleak thoughts surged onwards in his
head as he strode away after landing, blindly seeking some
solitude. Murder. Murder. He had committed a murder.
A murder. He had committed a murder for no reason
whatsoever. Murder. Murder.

Everything in front of him seemed smashed to ruins.
He had had till now a reason for living. This life at least
had seemed to be mapped out for him. In the last few
weeks the map had been brilliant with the promise of
high, sunlit uplands ahead. All the good that he had tried
to live by, ever since he had been able to know right from
wrong, seemed to be coming to flower. Everything from
the time he had begun to grasp what would earn a smile,
what a slap. The best days lay in front, the days of justice,
of doing good. And in one short jab of speech, there in
the quiet garden at the Hotel de Paris, it had been shat-
tered into fragments.

Yes, only one thing to be done now. To surrender himself to the law.

Unseeingly he strode over the yielding sand, careless of whom he brushed against, where he went.

A line of drying clothes, precariously supported from two lengths of bamboo, swung crazily to the ground as his onward-thrusting weight struck it. He failed even to notice, to hear the shouts of protest from behind.

How was he to set about it? About lifting from his shoulders the burden of his crime? Should he get hold of that Bombay CIDwalla and confess to him? But how could he find him among the crammed-thick gallis and streets and lanes of the city? The fellow might not even still be here. He might have given up his hunt. He might have thought it was useless.

So, go to the police thana at the Chowk? Go up to one of the constables lounging about there and say, *I have committed a murder*?

No. There were limits. He could not abase himself before a fellow of that sort, a man like those he had ordered about without a thought until today. Until today when the Lok Sabha member, the party leader, the person of influence, had been transformed, in a single instant, into a paltry murderer. Then go in through the thana's great gate and seek out the duty inspector behind his desk? Or, better, report to the Senior Superintendent of Police out at Cornwallis Lines? He had met the fellow. A gentleman. He would understand.

But would he? How could anyone understand what had happened to him? What had entered into Shri H. K. Verma, Member of Parliament? How could anyone understand that he, H. K. Verma, had in a moment of blotting-out rage become a killer?

No. Certainly not the Senior Superintendent.

But who else? Even if he went back again to Bombay and sought out whoever was in charge of criminal investigations there, some Assistant Commissioner or other, even then what he had done would look just as ridiculous. To have killed for what had turned out to be no reason at all.

A laughing-stock. Better to be a murderer who had tried to get away with it than to be such a stupid, pathetic figure.

But why should he not get away with it? Get away with it still, despite there having been no reason to have done it. Despite what he had told himself and told himself again and again when at last after that night he had stepped down into the merciful waters of Mother Ganga. That his action was right-doing. That he had been taking up arms as God Krishna had advised Arjun was his duty before the great battle of Kurukshetra.

Well, that had gone. The belief, if he had ever truly had it, that it had been a good action to end Mrs Shoba Popatkar's life. But let it go. He would strike out for himself now. It was time. For too long, for all his life, he had acted so as to bring good to others. He had tried to do right. Well, now it was time to do whatever had to be done for himself alone.

There was, after all, still nothing to link him to those disgusting few minutes in that bare little flat in Bombay. So why should anyone make the link? Why should anyone think that a man of his sort would do a thing like that? Very well, the little detective from Bombay had come to see him. But that had been for a reason that had nothing to do with a murder so many hundreds of miles away. Oh, yes, the man was investigating the case, and had even realized that there was some link to Banares. But he was still far, far from knowing anything that mattered.

And if the fellow did get some inkling ... Well then, there had been what he had contemplated when he had gone to talk with Krishnakanta. That could still be done. If necessary.

Ghote, standing up high, clutching one of the pillars of the lace-like yellowy ironwork of the shopping arcade in front of the Satyanarayan Temple in the Chowk, peered hard into the mass of people going past. Mishra's suggested starting point for their hunt had at first seemed a

73

good choice. Tourists, foreign or Indian, crammed every yard of its pavements. The brown-sugar vendor Rick was as likely to be at work there as anywhere in the city.

But in the mass of people moving from little shop to little shop or emerging from the flower market with long brilliant fat orange marigold garlands or baskets of multi-coloured rose petals for worship at the city's innumerable temples what hope, he thought now, was there of spotting that dirty white face? That clotted mass of blond hair? The traffic in the roadway in front of him passed in a dust-clouded, jammed, slow-moving blur.

Rick could have gone by opposite concealed by that couple in the overloaded cycle rickshaw, each clutching hard at a small scrambling son. Or he could, even at this very moment, be standing somewhere in the dark interior of the next-door shop, the one selling luggage, satchels and little rubber cushions. He could be there, peering out waiting to pounce, terrifying the shopkeeper with his wild looks.

He glanced at his watch.

At least it was almost the time Mishra, patrolling further along the busy road, had agreed to rendezvous with him. They were not going to have any luck here. If they had, surely it would have been when they had first arrived, sweaty and a little puffed after climbing the steep hill from the Ganges. Mishra had led him straight to the imposing State Bank of India building, with its two rifle-armed guards outside, one so fat his jacket gaped wide under his bandolier, the other comically so lean that his neck protruded from his jacket like a tortoise's. With all the tourists going in and out changing traveller's cheques it ought to have been the very place for Rick. But though they had waited for almost half an hour there had been no sign of the boy. Perhaps the big police station there with its looming ancient-looking walls and its mass-ive gate and lounging constables kept him away.

Mishra had gone in and had had a word with the duty inspector. But, emerging at last – How much idle talking had gone on, Ghote asked himself – he said nothing had been seen of Rick in the area for some days.

It was then, optimism leaking away, that they had decided to split up. They would give the boy thirty minutes more, just in case, before moving on to—

And then Ghote saw him.

Just as he had feared, the boy was on the far side of the traffic-thick road. It had been the merest piece of luck that a cow, a ribbon of marigold garland hanging from its munching jaw, had decided to wander into the roadway. It created a break in the endless line of rickshaws. In it Rick had been for a moment clear to see.

Ghote looked wildly round in case Mishra was within sight.

He was. He was walking along quite slowly on the same side of the road as Rick, with a look – Ghote felt a jet of acrid fury – of altogether happy indolence.

'Mishra,' he yelled. 'Mishra.'

He had hardly hoped to be heard above the clashing of the traffic and the clatter of high-pitched talk and shouts everywhere. But he was. He saw Mishra come out of his softly contented daze with a jerk.

And he actually looked across the road in his direction.

'There. There.'

He shouted with all the force of his lungs, pointing ferociously.

Mishra caught on. He looked in the right direction. And suddenly became galvanized.

Ghote set off on his side of the road. Alternately he glanced at the distant sight of Rick's greasy blond head, mercifully bobbing above the sea of black and sari-covered ones all around and at the jostling vehicles beside him, hoping for enough of a gap to dart across.

It came.

On the far side he pushed and shoved until he caught up with Mishra.

'We have got him,' he shouted. 'Got him.'

Mishra, turning, gave him one of his lazy, spreadingly benign smiles.

'Not yet, altogether. But we will. If not now, tomorrow. Or soon.'

With difficulty Ghote suppressed the rebuke that had come, a ready-made little block of fury, into his mind. This was not the right way to chase a wrong-doer.

He attempted to shorten the distance between them and the blond, bobbing head, leaving Mishra to come on or not as he would. Without much success. For all that he was able to go much faster on the steeply downward hill, ahead Rick had precisely the same advantage.

And, irritatingly, it was Mishra who spotted some six or seven minutes later, that the boy ahead had abruptly taken a turn to the left.

'Bans Phatak,' he called out cheerfully. 'He has gone down there.'

Strugglingly they made their way onwards, turned the same corner, saw the dirty blond head as much in advance as before.

'Come on.'

The words escaped Ghote in a squawk of frustration.

But still the blond head was as far off as ever. There was a crossroads at the end of the downwards-sloping lane with a temple – yet another – at one corner.

'Yes, look,' Mishra said, 'he has turned into Vishwanath Lane. Very many interesting sights for you, if we are unable to catch him.'

Ghote succeeded in saying nothing.

But here there were – it hardly seemed possible – even more people. The whole narrow lane appeared to be devoted to shops selling every possible sort of religious object. 'It is for all these worshippers coming towards,' Mishra said. 'They are going to our very-very famed Vishwanath Temple.'

Pushing onwards, Ghote did his best to ignore the piled-high sweetmeats designed for offerings, the careful stacks of upjutting miniature lingams stamped out in a dozen different materials, the swathes of long dangling beads, the sealed vessels of Ganges water, the heaps of different incenses – each sweet odour from the burning samples catching at his nostrils as he forced his way forwards.

And ahead that tousled blond hair seemed never to get any nearer.

With sudden recklessness, he plunged onwards yet more furiously. And his foot just tipped one of the little miniatures of God Ganesha in the front rank of a crowded display. Sending the whole row skittering over, row after row behind tumbling in turn.

For a moment he thought of stopping, attempting to put things right, or even simply thrusting a little money at the solemn boy vendor sitting with out-thrust legs beside his bright-painted wares,

But no time for niceties. And in any case the solemn urchin was spattering out a great stream of abuse. 'May the vultures eat your eyes. Donkey from anywhere. Off-spring of an owl.'

Damn city. Was no one in it a decent, ordinary person, wanting to live a decent life? Not even the children?

'Yes,' said Mishra, catching up, 'first words a Banarasi child learns are curses.'

His round face wore an expression of pride.

'Where has he gone?' Ghote shouted. 'Where has that Rick gone?'

'There. There. You can see him ahead. Next to that tall fellow in the orange Rajasthani turban.'

True enough, Rick was not out of sight. But they had still hardly gained on him, for all Ghote's shoving and pushing. Nor had Mishra been cured of his determination to show off his city, however hot the chase.

'Look, Inspector. Dandapani, an altogether Banarasi idol. In that niche in the wall there. Police officer, you may say, of Kashi, as our city is called in its holy aspect. With his two assistant officers, Udbhrama, who is Doubt, and Sambhrama, Confusion, he is making sure the really great sinner is never dying inside the city. Somehow he is externing them. On some visit to family, or for business only. You should have made a namaskar to him.'

Ghote, pressing onwards, thought with inner savagery that he was glad his palms had remained unjoined.

He attempted to run. Was halted once more after just three or four strides by the people surging up towards him.

They reached a wide, intersecting road. Rick had turned to the left again, downhill.

'He must be making for Dasawamedh Ghat,' Mishra said, panting now. 'Where most pilgrims go. Shrine of Sitala, goddess of smallpox also.'

But they still were far from being able to grab the American when at last they reached the great sweep of steps at the ghat and the wide Ganges at their foot.

At first Ghote thought that they had utterly lost him. Here he was by no means the only white face or blond head to be seen. As the heat of the afternoon had begun to lessen, from big tourist bus after big tourist bus flocks of Westerners were descending, cameras at the ready, faces avid with curiosity and soon blinking in bewilderment. Some already were climbing wearily back, discussing, flipping the pages of guide-books. Loud voices mangled horribly the names of gods, goddesses and benefactors from ages past.

'I will go along towards the Man Mandir Ghat,' Mishra said. 'Best to split up again. If I see him I will come back for you.'

'Very good, Inspector.'

Almost at once he saw the blond head of the junky. The boy was down by the edge of the river. He was talking, as animatedly as any of the hectoring pandas, to a tall Western tourist in a dull-coloured safari suit, fat guide book open in his hands.

Was he trying to persuade the scholarly-looking fellow to buy brown sugar or bhang? Perhaps he was simply telling him things about Banares, whether true or false, to induce him in gratitude to hand over some money.

But – troubles never over – it would be almost imposs-ible to approach without being seen. Down at the river's edge the American boy was far too isolated.

Fetch Mishra? Make a two-pronged attack?

No, by the time he had found him Rick could have moved on anywhere. Taken this tourist to see something else. Or abandoned him as unprofitable.

So, circle round. Take what cover I can. Get as near as possible. Keep my eyes on the fellow every instant. And then ... A dash for it. Never mind the foreigner. Grab hard, keep hold, march the fellow away.

And then get out of him that name.

He set off down the wide steps, making himself walk idly, head lowered to avoid attention.

And, a piece of luck. As he neared the water he realized he could put between himself and Rick a panda under his rattan umbrella with a plump woman in a silk sari intently listening to his discourse.

The panda looked a good deal less impressive than most of them with their white dhotis tucked round their waists as they sat pronouncing instructions, bare-chested all but for their sacred threads. 'Put a flower in the pot', 'No, not that way', 'Rub in a circle', 'Sprinkle Ganga water'. This fellow wore a stained singlet and a pair of check shorts and was badly in need of a shave. Neverthe-less he must have some special power because the woman sitting cross-legged in front of him was deep in con-centration.

Which was just what he wanted. He could get quite close behind the panda's back and wait till Rick, some twenty yards away, turned for long enough in the opposite direction. Then, up on the feet, the swift dash, the grab.

Soon he realized what the plump woman was consulting the panda about. She had failed to conceive, and it seemed she had heard that this holyman among all the others had some secret that would bring her what she wanted.

'You understand,' the panda had said, 'that nothing any doctor whatsoever can do will cure sterility.'

'Ji, maharaj,' had come the respectful answer.

'It is your karma. That is all.'

'Yes, maharaj. God has blessed my husband with all he could want, except only a son.'

'Ah, your husband? What is he?'

'He is Purchasing Officer for a big corporation in Calcutta. He was trying to get leave to come here just now, maharaj, but they would not let him have.'

'Yes. So what is he pulling down?'

'His per annum is five lakhs, maharaj.'

The panda sat in deep thoughtful silence.

'Maharaj,' there came at last the timid suggested inquiry, 'is it possible to counteract the effects of bad karma?'

'Sometimes. Yes, sometimes that is possible. There is a yojana in the scriptures that can bring such a miracle.'

'Maharaj, what must I do?'

'It is I who must do everything, with God's help.'

The merest flick of a gesture towards the mat he was sitting on indicated that more help than God's was also necessary.

The woman drew a fat cloth purse from under her sari, tugged its cords open. Banknotes landed in a soft pile on the mat. When they had mounted to a certain point the panda began to chant.

After a little he looked across at his client.

'Tomorrow you must fast,' he said. 'From dawn to sunset. Then two hours after sunset you must come to this ghat once more. My hut is just here. I will chant some other secret mantras there.'

So that is the sterility cure. I might have known. Banares, city of light, city of the right way, city of the wrong way. Beware of holymen.

He looked over to where wrong-way Rick was working his way into the good graces of the innocent Western tourist with the big guide book.

There was no sign of either of them.

Cursing, he ran all the way along the ghat, turned, ran

80

back in the other direction, forced himself to take the steps to the top at a run, dodging pandas' umbrellas, knocking into descending pilgrims intent on reaching the holy river, pushing aside bemused tourists.

Nowhere.

Not Rick. Not his tall Western acquaintance.

Feeling all the good drained out of him, he let himself at last descend the steps again and made his way to where Mishra had left him. He spotted him soon enough, standing looking meditatively out at the Ganges, its slowly moving boats, its waters darkening now as the sun at last dipped towards the horizon.

He told him what had happened. A full confession.

It made him feel no better.

'What a pity, Inspector. What a pity. When you were so near. But tomorrow I am sure we would find the chap. Or the next day. Or later.'

'Inspector, if I do not make any progress I will be called back to Bombay.'

'Oh, but, no. No, you must not go. You have yet to see one tenth, one hundredth, of all there is in Banares.'

'I dare say, Inspector. But I am not here for seeing.'

'But while you are investigating you could also see. And learn. Banares has much to teach.'

Mishra looked out at the river, up to the tall temples behind.

'However, Inspector, it would be dark in just only some minutes. So nothing to be done tonight.'

His round face took on a look of redoubled cheerfulness.

'So perhaps you would like to come with me to Ramnagar where the Ram Lila plays are taking place. Very very instructive, the life of Rama. And very good spectacle also.'

'No, Inspector.'

'No? Then do you like films? We have some very fine cinemas in Banares. They are showing latest Bombay films.'

'No, Inspector.'

Ghote thought of the *latest Bombay film* his son had been rattling on and on about just before the Popatkar case had broken. Ved had conceived a tremendous admiration for Gulshan Gover's portrayal of the villain. 'Pitaji, that man was so good. He was stopping at nothing to get his way. I think in true life he would have won every time against the hero they had.'

But outside the ridiculous world of film surely no one was quite like that. Surely no one could overcome his natural instincts and take the evil path on every occasion.

Or could they?

'Good night, Mishra,' he said. 'I will perhaps call at your home tomorrow.'

Utterly weary he climbed back up towards the Hotel Relax, a bath, something to eat and an early bed.

And, just as he came into sight of the hotel, a shrill whistle from somewhere just above his head caused him to turn, startled. And there was Rick.

9

'At last.' Ghote found he was being made to feel as if he had arrived late at a long-agreed rendezvous with the American junky. Rick was perched on the high, lime-washed, slogan-daubed compound wall of the UP Road Transport Corporation. The pale glow from a distant security light-post just lit up his taut, pinched face.

But, expected or not, would it be possible now to get out of the boy what he knew? Or did he in fact know anything? Had that business at the Cantonment Station been no more than a half-hearted attempt to extract information about an expected raid on the Dom Raja's house? A clever lie based on his overheard talk with Mishra?

Could he grab hold of the fellow? Slap what he wanted out of him? At least now he knew what a twisting monkey he was.

But, up on the wall, a good two feet above his own head, legs dangling not on this side but the other, he was almost impossible to get at. No doubt why he had chosen just this spot.

'What it is you are wanting?' he growled at him, hoping to conceal the thoughts passing through his mind. 'You were very-very ready to run off when I was last seeing.'

'Yeah. Thought you'd give me a hard time. Know you Indian fuzz. Bastards. No exceptions.'

Not the moment to challenge that.

'I am asking what it is you are wanting.'

'Same as before, man. You tell me when your pals here are going to raid my boss's place, I'll tell you what somebody did the day your Mrs Pop-whatever was killed.'

'But I am not at all knowing police plans here in Banares. I hail from Bombay itself. As you were hearing, isn't it?'

'Okay, okay. You don't know now, but don't tell me you can't find out. Tell the guys here it's your opinion they never get anywhere, then one of them'll spill all right.'

Probably true. Have a Bombay officer saying and stating the local fellows are no good, they will at once boast of their each and every success and plan. But if he is believing I would do a thing like that, he is hundred per cent in error.

'And what if I am doing just only that? How should I be knowing you had anything whatsoever to give in exchange? I do not even know if you are truly belonging to the Dom Raja. An American boy itself.'

Can I, if I shift round a little, get to where I can reach up and grab?

'Oh, I belong to the Dom Raja all right,' Rick answered. 'I'm all his now.'

His face twisted in what looked in the pale light like a wry smile.

'You know I came here to Banares to study Hindu religion? Wanted to get my life right, all that crap. Thought the answer must be here, Banares Hindu University. And I worked there all right. Read the Vedas. Knew the whole Bhagavad Geeta by heart. Then I thought maybe I'd better try bhang. And other stuff.'

He fell silent, looking back it seemed on the life he had led.

The moment to try for him? While he is thinking of how once he was altogether set on right-doing?

But, at just the instant he was going to launch himself, the boy began again.

'So who did I have to go to to get the stuff? The Doms, who else? And after a while I just became one of them. Learnt to bargain over wood for the pyres, over the price of a bundle of dry grass to touch to the sacred fire. Yeah, and now I take the hot ashes to cook on, and damn it, I've had my share, come night, of meat from those fires.'

Ghote could not check an expression of instant profound disgust.

'Come on,' Rick said. 'Why look like that? What's wrong? It's meat, right? Just meat. Can be good, too.'

But, as if he knew in himself why his interrogator had not been able to disguise his revulsion, he hurried on.

'Yeah, so I've got to be buddy-buddy with the Dom Raja. Heck, no one else'll talk to him, only the Doms. He likes new company.'

Now, Ghote thought. Now, again, while he is thoughtful only.

He took a small step back as if he needed to be able to see the boy's face better, and then a good half-step forward.

'Oh, no. You stay just where you are, mister. I said all you fuzz were two-timing bastards.'

Ghote registered a defeat. Even a just rebuke.

'And you are stating you yourself are not at all two-timing?' he replied.

Rick grinned.

'Guess you'll just have to trust me.'

'So you are cent per cent trustworthy, yes?'

A wider grin in the pallid light.

'Okay, point taken.'

For a moment or two Rick thought. Then he spoke again.

'Right, tell you what I'll do. I'll let you have a sample. It's real good of me, more than you deserve. But it'll give you some incentive, your side of the bargain.'

Now Ghote put on an equal show of considering, though he had no intention of asking Inspector Mishra or anyone else what plans there were to raid the Dom Raja's house.

Then he spoke in his turn.

'Very well. It is not very much of loyal to my Banares colleagues. But after all what am I owing fellows here?

Nothing. And I am very much needing to know each thing I can about the killing of Mrs Shoba Popatkar.'

'Deal.'

'So what is it you can tell?'

'Oh, no. First we fix a time and a place for you to give me the dope on the raid.'

'Very well.'

Will the boy even give me the taste he has promised, once a new meeting is arranged? Well, he will or he will not. Nothing to be done about it.

He waited.

'Yeah, let's say tomorrow night. They won't come before that. So, midnight tomorrow. Right?'

'Yes, midnight itself. But where?'

'You know the Manikarnika Ghat? Seen it yet? Everybody comes to Banares wants to see that.'

The Manikarnika Ghat. And what had Mishra said about being on duty there at night? *I tell you, my knees were made of butter only.*

He swallowed.

'Yes, I am knowing where is that ghat. I have not seen, but everyone in India is knowing the burning ghats of Banares, and hoping to die at same.'

'Yeah, well, when and where you die's your business. But just you be there tomorrow midnight. With what I need to hear.'

'But I myself, what am I to hear now only?'

'A name. I'll give you a name. Guy that's maybe involved.'

In the darkness under the shadow of the high compound wall he strained to hear, to see that ill-lit face.

'Right. How about a well-known guy in this city? Name of H. K. Verma?'

And in an instant the boy tumbled out of sight.

Grimly H. K. Verma approached his familiar bathing place at the Man Mandir Ghat. Waking at his usual hour, he had thought of not going. What point was there in a sunrise dip if he had no intention of abandoning his sin? He had committed it. Killed the old woman. Strangled her. Thumbs in the pits in her neck. So no onion tears now. He had decided to escape the consequences of that act. And to do whatever proved necessary to make sure of it.

Very well, the business in Bombay had turned out, bitterly, to have been utterly pointless. But at least he was determined not to suffer for it if it could in any way be avoided. He was set now on a course of look after Number Ek. He had given up doing good to others. He had given up striving and striving to do the right thing. So why parade down to the Ganga, take off his clothes, shiver in its waters?

They were anyhow not only cold at this time of year but unpleasant. No, worse than unpleasant. Why now pretend anything else? Everything they had always said about the never-ending purity of the running river was nowadays a lie. The sometimes only half-burnt bodies of the dead floating in it were no longer made safe. The smallpox victims, the corpses of babies, the dead sacred cows all now added their putrefaction to the damage done by huge quantities of human excrement and industrial poisons that in these days cascaded into the water. Ganga jal no longer automatically neutralized them.

Any more than it neutralized your sin.

But, lying in bed with these thoughts marching through his head, he had soon enough realized that after all he did have to go down to the ghat. It was what he did every morning. It was what he had done for years, every day he had been here at home in sacred Banares. Suddenly to stop would draw attention to himself.

With set features, at the spot where he always left his fresh clothes he peeled off yesterday's kurta, tugged yesterday's dhoti from his waist, kicked off his chappals.

That morning when, back from Bombay, after half a night of skulking here and there in the city avoiding being seen, he had come at last to Ganga Ma, had taken off that other creased and grimy kurta and travel-stained dhoti and had stepped down with such relief into the chill just-at-sunrise water. He had felt his sin being washed away then. He had truly felt it.

What mockeries.

He planked down the stone steps, heavy-footed, and waded in. Stood then with arms lifted to greet the new-risen sun just lipping, a red ball, over the Sandbank opposite.

Go through it all. Leave out nothing. Not one customary action, not one customary word of prayer. However hollow.

Perhaps if he kept to it all with absolute strictness, perhaps it would at least bring him luck. Perhaps he already had been lucky. Perhaps that mosquito of a Bombay CIDwalla had been convinced there was nothing here in Banares for him. Even at this moment he could be flying back to Bombay.

No, all that he needed now was no ill-luck. Nothing to happen that he had not counted on. If he could have that, he was safe. Truly. He had been clever, after all. Once that appalling moment was past. Once he had let that suddenly limp, not very heavy body fall.

And he had been lucky then also. Flying with young Vikki had in the end been altogether the best way of getting to Bombay. The boy would never give him away. He probably still had not the least notion why actually he had been asked to go there at such short notice. And Vikki was the only link that could altogether betray him.

He was safe. Safe. Surely he was safe.

'Arise! Life's breath has returned,' he spouted out to the wide dawn-grey stretch of the unresponsive river. 'Darkness has fled, light comes! Now is the path opened for our Lord, the Sun. Now our days will stretch out before us.'

Ash in the mouth. Unnourishing, grating ash.

*

Ghote woke after a night of turmoiling thoughts knowing what he would have to do. He had even asked himself the moment Rick had vanished as if he was not a creature of flesh and blood at all – dried-out flesh, thin, fevered blood – if he should go straight down to H. K. Verma's house near the Golden Temple and confront him there and then.

But, he had thought at once, Rick had not actually claimed H. K. Verma was Mrs Popatkar's murderer. All he had said was that he was 'maybe involved'.

And what reason could a man like H. K. Verma have for killing Mrs Popatkar? What could possibly drive such a respectable figure to go all the way from Banares to Bombay, strangle someone they had probably never even met and then return? No, it was absurd. Absurd.

And certainly if he was to go as far as questioning a man of so much influence he would have to be very clear about what he was going to say. He could scarcely march in and state that a witness had named him, Shri H. K. Verma, party leader, as being involved in murder. All he would get would be a scornful denial. And then H. K. Verma would start pulling his strings, telephoning Delhi, using his contacts. In no time he would find himself ordered back to Bombay. To get such a firing from the Assistant Commissioner as he had never had before.

So he had plodded heavily back to the Hotel Relax, had taken a shower but felt no relief. He had succeeded then in getting Inspector Wagh in Dadar on the phone. Only to find his faint hope the case had been solved in Bombay met with a furious 'No bloody progress, Inspector'. At dinner he had hardly eaten a thing and in bed he had been unable to sleep. His thoughts had whined at him as insistently as the mosquitoes that made him at last wrap the sheet round body and head as if he was a corpse on a litter on its way to the burning ghat, jogging bearers chanting and chanting, *Rama namu, satya hai, Rama nama, satya hai*. Rama name, truth is.

Was it possible that a man like H. K. Verma had even

gone so far as to order Mrs Popatkar's murder? Send some hired fellow from the holy Banares? No doubt there were such men. The two-rupee murderers Mishra spoke about. Or someone from the city's wrestling pits. Mishra had swerved away from saying very much about those. Not wanting to spoil his picture of happy, masti-filled Banares.

But, even supposing H. K. Verma had had Mrs Popatkar killed or even had actually killed her himself, why would he have wanted it done? Very hard to see.

What if – this was a possibility, just – Mrs Popatkar had gone to H. K. Verma requesting permission to read the *Recollections* when she was first refused? And something had passed between them then that made it imperative for her to be silenced? Mr Srivastava at the library had said nothing about her going, but what if she had tried to take H. K. Verma's permission?

But, no. No, it was ridiculously unlikely that anything said between them, if they had ever even met, could have been so loaded with vital consequences.

Yet Rick, pale-faced Rick in the thin light on top of the compound wall, had given him H. K. Verma's name. Why? Of course Rick could have been selling him dummy goods. He could have simply hit on H. K. Verma, for some reason, for no reason, and made use of the name as bait to get the information he wanted. But why should he have picked on H. K. Verma unless . . .

With the first white glimmer of the new day he knew beyond argument he would have to go and see the man again. Right or wrong, Rick's hinted accusation had to be put to the test.

He would go at once. No doubt the fellow was one of the holy dip at sunrise brigade. The pious smirk on his face when he had talked about KK having died by the side of the Ganges was evidence enough of that. But, as soon as he was back from whichever ghat he went to, he would see him and get at the truth.

*

90

Turning the corner of the lane just by that impudent wall-slogan *Please to Vote for Communist Party (Marxist)*, H. K. Verma saw Karim. Standing proudly, as ever at this particular time of the morning, legs astride, twirling his lathi as if about to repel a whole army of rioters.

He felt a little upwards bounce of satisfaction. At least he had contrived, when he had returned from his holy dip that terrible morning, to trick the stupid Pathan into having to swear he had seen him leaving earlier to go down to the Ganges. In all probability such a small piece of false alibi would never be needed. Impossible to imagine any circumstances where a police investigator, the little runt from Bombay for instance, would question Karim. But all the same one dangling end neatly tucked away.

'Ha, Karim, I was not spotting you when I was going out. Was it sleep–sleeping, eh?'

But now there came no instant *Every moment of the night I was awake, awake like a tiger only*. Instead a more than usually cunning leer came on to the Pathan's narrow face behind the massively curling moustache.

'What is it, Karim?'

A cold finger of doubt suddenly touched him.

'Huzoor, a watchman as never-sleeping as I, he is deserving more of pay than you are giving.'

'What? What nonsense only. You are damn well paid, Karim, considering how you spend most of the night sound asleep, as I very well know.'

'Ah, no, huzoor. Sometimes I am damn awake. Like on the morning, early, when you were coming back wearing dirty clothes only.'

A chill spread all through him.

What could Karim know? How could he possibly know he been in Bombay the night before? That he had hidden here and there in the city after Vikki had brought him back, waiting till he could pretend to have gone for his holy dip?

'Oh, huzoor, very well I am knowing, when at last I am

thinking, that I was not at all seeing you come out that day just before the sun was rising. Huzoor, if you are wanting to spend night at Dal Mandi, you should be giving Karim one damn good tip first.'

'Dal Mandi, but I was not—'

He stopped himself.

What madness. He had been on the very point of denying it was at the prostitute quarter he had spent that night.

'Very well, Karim, and what if I was at Dal Mandi? I dare say you yourself have been there many, many times.'

He felt relief pouring down on to him like a blessing.

'Oh, yes, huzoor, but I am not a man that is having his name in the *Aj* and the *Gandiva*.'

'What do you know about that, you fool? Since when have you been able to read?'

'No, huzoor, I am not able, true. But all the more, huzoor, I am keeping open my ears. I am knowing what they are putting in those papers. And what in their gossips and rumours they would like to put.'

What to do? Pay the rogue?

And let him think what he knows is worth money because it would hurt my name and fame? No, too dangerous. Somehow he may learn one day how much more valuable is his little piece of knowledge.

'So it is blackmail you are trying, no? Well, you have tried it with the wrong man. Out. Out of my house this moment. Take your possessions and get back to your native place, damn you. And think yourself lucky it is not the jail you find yourself inside.'

It worked. As he had guessed it would. Only shout loud enough.

The leering smile went from Karim's face like the lights being extinguished at the end of each Ram Lila play out at Ramnagar. He dropped his now useless lathi with a rattling clatter. Left it lying on the stones of the lane and slunk off like a jackal towards his quarter.

Good riddance. Very good riddance.

With a last contemptuous glare at the fellow's back, he stepped in at the gate.

'Mr Verma! Mr H. K. Verma, can I be having just only one word?'

He turned.

It was the Bombay detective.

10

'Well, Inspector – Inspector – I have forgotten what is your good name.'

'It is Ghote, sir. Inspector Ghote.'

'Well, Inspector Ghote, what can I be doing for you?'

H. K. Verma heard the note of frank calmness in his voice with a surge of pleasure. Mounting the stairs in front of this unexpected apparition, he had felt nervousness running up and down inside him like so many gecko lizards on a wall. He had let himself believe the man must have gone back to Bombay. So at once, under the shock of turning at the gate to see him there, the temptation had come flooding back. To stop as soon as he reached the head of the stairs, to draw himself up and . . . confess.

But, as quickly, the resolve he had arrived at out at the Sandbank had come back to him. No, he was not going to suffer twice for his defeat at Jagmohan Nagpal's hands. If he had gained nothing by what he had done there in that little flat in Bombay, he was not going to lose his liberty, his life, because of it.

What could this sneaking fellow following him possibly know? Nothing. No doubt all he had come for was to beg once more to go through the *Recollections*. Well, he would get the same answer as before. This time in terms to make him really go whistling back.

But the man's demand when it was made – the fellow seemed to be in some difficulty about what he was going to say – was not what he had expected.

'Sir, you were explaining . . . Sir, when I was here before

you were stating that the *Recollections* of the late Krishnan Kalgutkar were not to be made public for one hundred and one years after his decease. You were saying, sir, that it would be ninety-seven years more before I could see and examine same. But, sir, I am not hundred per cent clear. Did you yourself ever go through those *Recollections*?'

What to answer? When the fellow was here before I succeeded to give the impression I had not read the *Recollections*. That I had only just spoken about them once with KK. I remember I was doing that. So has the fellow been digging and pigging and found out something? Perhaps that chatterbox Srivastava believes I must be well acquainted with every word KK left behind.

Or does this fellow know that it was I myself and not KK who made that stipulation of one hundred and one years? Is he attempting to catch me out in a lie? Is he convinced now I am a liar altogether? That I am the murderer of Mrs Shoba Popatkar?

But, no, surely he cannot be. I am too far separated from that woman. No, it will be safe to repeat my denial. Altogether safe.

'Inspector, that ban which the late Krishnan Kalgutkar was imposing is applying, naturally, to myself. Absolutely to the same extent as to any other person.'

Hah. That seems to have dealt with him. His face has fallen one mile.

'I see, sir. And that is definite?'

'Definite, Inspector.'

'Then . . . Then, sir, there is something else also I must be asking. Sir, is it that— Sir, were you yourself meeting Mrs Shoba Popatkar when she was here in Banares? Was she coming here to your house?'

'No, no, Inspector. Mrs Popatkar was never inside this house. You may ask anybody. Ask my peon. By the name of Raman. Ask Raman. He would tell you. Mrs Popatkar has never been here.'

The little mongoose is standing there thinking and

thinking. I can see it, as if I was inside his head only. He is going over and over in his mind for some way to be catching me out.

Speak, damn you. Speak.

Now a little cough. As if he is not sure whether he can say what he is going to say. But I am up to your each and every trickery, Mr Inspector. So speak. Let me hear it.

'And you were never – excuse me, sir, for asking – you were never meeting Mrs Popatkar somewhere else in Banares? Perhaps she was visiting some temple, and you were there also?'

Yes, once again he is trying his cunning ways. I had told him I had never met her. Definitely told. It is one more trick. But how to defeat him? Anger, perhaps. Yes, anger. Just as I was showing and displaying to that snake Karim.

'Inspector, the last time you were here I was stating altogether clearly that I had never met Mrs Popatkar. Are you calling me a liar? Let me tell you, and you had better remember: H. K. Verma is not in the habit of using lies. He has devoted his entire life to the truth. To the truth, Inspector. Understand?'

'Yes, sir, yes.'

Well, why is the fellow not going now? He has put his questions, and he has had his answers. So *Thank you, sahib. Thank you. Most grateful.* And off you go.

'But, sir, excuse me, can I ask also if you were ever having any sort of dealings whatsoever with Mrs Popatkar? By letter, sir? Or by any other means even?'

He suspects something. He must do. Why is he going on and on with these questions? Mrs Popatkar this, and Mrs Popatkar that? But what can he suspect exactly? Nothing. Nothing.

And if he has found an evidence, why is he not directly coming out with it? Why is he not asking whatever it is he thinks he knows? Why is he not accusing?

'Sir?'

'No. No, Inspector, I was never having any dealings of any sort with Mrs Shoba Popatkar. You say she was here in Banares. Very well, I must take your word for that. But, I tell you, I never saw her here. I had no idea she had come here. I really know nothing about her. Nothing.'

Was I overdoing it? But the little tick has to be made to get out. At once. Before I am making some mistake. Out.

'Very well, sir. I am sorry to have taken up your time, but you would understand that in a case of murder, and the murder of a lady with such a fine place in India's history, every nook and corner must be investigated.'

'Yes, yes.'

'Sir, no progress is being made in Bombay itself. I was telephoning officer in charge of case, and he was saying they are no more advanced since they were arresting a servant on suspicion only. I am feeling it is up to me now, sir. Up to myself alone. That is why I have been asking and asking these questions.'

'Very well, you are doing no more than your duty. I am quite understanding. But I am a busy man, Inspector, so if you would let me get on with my work . . .'

Make it look as if I truly am busy. What to do? Yes, go over to the table, pull out the chair, pick up a ballpoint from that jar. Let him see it. But I have nothing to write. Not even a piece-paper to write on.

Well, put the ballpoint back. I must have made him see now he is not wanted. And, yes, he is going. At last he is going.

'Thank you, sir. I would not keep you from your work any longer. Thank you.'

'No. Wait.'

'Yes, sir? What it is?'

What was it the poking, prying mongoose said? *It is up to myself alone.* If . . . If he is truly alone, then perhaps my idea before . . .

'Inspector, you are enjoying your stay in our beautiful city? You have been able to visit our temples? The Bharat Mata Temple is very interesting, with a relief map of our country carved in marble itself. Or the Tulsi Manas Temple, built in 1964 only. Its walls are inscribed with the verses of Sant Tulsidas himself. Very, very good.'

'No, sir, no. I am not able to see any such. I am here on duty only.'

On the little mongoose's face a look of disapproval. A dedicated fellow. But dedicated is dangerous. Dangerous. I must find out where he can be . . .

'Quite so, Inspector. On duty. Very very commendable. Doing the right thing. But you have at least some decent boarding and lodging here, I trust.'

'Oh, yes, sir. At a place called Hotel Relax. I was given its name by the former Banares officer who has been most helpful in assisting me to find my way about your city.'

'Ah. A former police officer? So you are . . . So you share your thoughts on this matter with him? Discuss your each and every suspicion, no?'

'Well, sir, I have not thought it proper to share my ideas about the case itself with an officer who is actually retired.'

'No. No, I see it would be wrong to do so. Quite wrong. Good. Excellent, Inspector. Hotel Relax, you were saying? Well, I must not be keeping you. Each to his own work, yes?'

'Yes, sir. And thank you again for your helps.'

So that badmash Rick was giving me one false clue. Nothing but deny and deny from Shri H. K. Verma. As clear as clear can be. Well, one good thing only. I will not have to go down to the Manikarnika Ghat tonight at midnight and risk my life and limb among those two-rupee killers who were turning to butter Inspector Mishra's knees.

Yet . . .

Yet, after all, the fellow just now was . . . Was what? Yes, somehow uneasy. Too much of protest. Too much of bluster. And when I was about to leave, keeping me back at last moment with those questions. As if to butter my chapattis only. But before that, yes, it had been just the opposite, displaying very much of impatience to see me go. The way he was picking up that ballpoint, as if he had some work to do, making sure I was seeing and then dropping same. Left-over election give-aways. *Vote for H. K. Verma Honesty Is Best Policy.*

But honesty was not his policy up there. Definitely not. And, when I was there before even, I was, just only a little, feeling something to be wrong also.

Yet at the worst would a man like H. K. Verma truly go all the way from Banares to Bombay and strangle someone? Well, influential people have committed murder before now. No one except a saint is so right-doing that, given some special circumstances, they will at least not want to commit murder.

On the other hand ... Perhaps after all that Rick was giving me H. K.'s name out of thin air only. It is as likely. More so even.

So – a tumbling of interior dismay – no way to get out of it. I must go to the Manikarnika Ghat tonight after all. I have to get hold of Rick once more, even if it is by offering some false informations about a raid on the Dom Raja's house. If I am to find out who was strangling Mrs Shoba Popatkar, that is all that is left to me. Otherwise I might as well go back to Bombay. Leave matters to that follow-the-rules fellow, Wagh.

But the Manikarnika Ghat. At midnight. Where Inspector Mishra had felt his knees turn to butter.

11

Ghote had spent most of the rest of the morning out at the Banares Hindu University once more. He had decided he ought to check the truth of H. K. Verma's statement that Mrs Popatkar had not gone to visit him by talking again to Mr Srivastava in his little, out-of-the-way library. Checking with H. K. Verma's one-eyed peon – what was his name? Raman – would be a waste of time. Of course the fellow would confirm Mrs Popatkar had never come to the house. If in fact she had not, he would simply be telling the truth. And if, despite what H. K. Verma had insisted, she had been there that day asking to go through the *Recollections*, Raman would have been instructed to lie and lie.

But with Mr Srivastava it would be different. Even if H. K. Verma had telephoned him with the same instruction he had given to Raman, it should not be difficult to get past his defences. He was the sort of well-wishing academic – like some he had known in his college days – it would be child's play to shake the truth out of.

It was. First, some casual questions. Then a few sharp words. And the old librarian was reduced to sheer willingness to babble out everything he knew. But from all his gabblings it was simply clear that Mrs Popatkar had not gone from the university to H. K. Verma. He was certain about the hour she had arrived at the library. It had been only a few minutes after he had got there himself, and he made a point of never being even five minutes late. And, yes, she had stayed, head deep in the *Recollections*, until she had jumped up – 'Looking altogether triumphant, my dear sir' – handed back the manuscript, taken a quick look at her watch and hurried off, saying she could just catch the Rajdani Express.

So, Ghote thought to himself, mooching dispiritedly past the Armed Police constable at the tall archway entrance to the university, there is one thing more only to be done. The Manikarnika Ghat. At midnight.

But, first, look at the place under the bright light of the sun.

At some distance from the ghat – he could see the haze of smoke from the pyres rising up against the sky beyond the river – he abandoned his autorickshaw to make his way down on foot. The better he knew the surroundings the better the chances in the dark of night of escaping any pursuing goondas.

But, as he paid off the rickshaw walla something just caught his eye. It was, he thought with a jolt of super-stitious fear, as if he was being given a warning.

Buttoning his wallet carefully back into his trouser pocket, he read to himself the lines of poetry he had glimpsed boldly painted on the wall just beside him. Lines he had half-noticed more than once on walls in Banares.

Seeing the grinding-stone turning, turning,
Kabir began to weep.
Between the two stones, not a single grain saved.

And beside them a picture. Banarasis seemed to delight in daubing their walls with these. This was of a woman working a grinding-stone, such as he had known as a boy in his village. But she was throwing into it, not grains of wheat but little human beings.

Yes, death, he thought. It comes to us all. But to some sooner than they expect. He felt in his knees something of the butter-soft feeling Mishra had spoken about.

But – he straightened his shoulders – down at the burn-ing ghat at midnight Rick would be waiting. And in his head there might be the answer to what connection there was between H. K. Verma and Mrs Shoba Popatkar. Only through him could he hope to learn why Mrs Popatkar had died.

He marched through the busy narrow lane down towards the river and the ghat.

Still with every step death seemed to flaunt itself in his face. The goods-crammed shops to either side offered scarcely anything but the necessities of the death ceremonies. Great rolls of white cloth to be cut into the fifteen-feet lengths specified for wrapping the corpse of a man, of coloured cloth for that of a woman. Sweetmeats for the mourners. Powdered sandalwood to scatter on the pyres. Clay water-pots for the chief mourner at last to break in the fire. Long brilliant chains of marigolds for garlands, with beside them piles of sacred lotus flowers. Huge pyramids of vermilion powder for marking the forehead of the dead. Candles in little dishes to float out into the sacred river.

Then a big abandoned temple – a faded notice still saying *Gentlemen Not Belonging to Hindu Religion Are Requested Not To Enter* – used for the storage of stack upon stack of wood for the fires, twisted like the limbs of innumerable interlocked wrestling animals. Up on its roof coolies were loading a huge weighing-machine with more timber, pausing every now and again to see what point the big black needle on its battered old dial had reached.

He remembered something Mishra had told him, a passing particle of his outpouring of information. The standard weight of wood for an ordinary body was two hundred kilogrammes. For a fat body it was three hundred. He looked down at his own wiry form. Yes, a two-hundred kilo fellow, definitely.

His mouth tightened.

As soon as the Bombay detective had left, H. K. Verma telephoned his son. It was not an easy call to make. He was still not even sure he wanted to make it. Or needed to make it.

But best to be on the safe side.

So, first, some pleasantries.

'You are well?'

'Yes, yes, Pitaji. Just as well as I was when you were here yesterday itself.'

'Yes. Well, yes. And Vikram – Vikki as he is liking to be called. That little trouble you were almost mentioning, it is all settled now?'

'Oh, yes. Yes. No problem. Or if not quite no problem, I do not expect trouble to last too long.'

'Good, good. Well, I am liking to know all is going well. So . . . Well . . . Ah, yes, there was one thing I had wanted to ask.'

Oh, too direct altogether. Why can I not manage the way I am able to in negotiating for the party? With Jagmohan— No, not with Jagmohan. Forget Jagmohan.

'Yes, Pitaji?'

Impatience coming over the line as if the boy is in the room and tap-tap-tapping his foot only. The boy. He must be more than forty now, and not at all a boy.

'Oh, I was just only wondering how you are managing at one of your mills when you are having a long-running strike.'

'Oh, yes? And why is that interesting you just now? You were talking and talking about social upliftment when you were here. About helping the downtrodden and what-all.'

Has the boy heard something? Is it common gup in Delhi that my votes block is worthless only now? With all his contactmen there, has he learnt what has happened?

'I am always wanting to help the downtrodden. But just now, well, I am interested in what happened when you had that strike at the Azamgarh mill last year.'

'When we had to send in some musclemen? It had to be done, you know. No use to be a straw-wrestler only. You are not blaming me now?'

A straw-wrestler. Has he guessed already?

'No, no. Why should I blame? I know that there are

times and places when something of force is necessary. In fact . . .'

Now I will have to say it.

'What in fact, Pitaji? I must leave for office, you know. Business does not run itself.'

'Yes, yes, I understand. Well, tell me then. If I . . . If I was wanting some – what did you say? – some musclemen myself, where should I be going?'

'Oh, Pitaji, too good. You are joining the real world at last.'

'Never mind the joking. Can you tell me some names, yes or no?'

'Oh, yes, Pitaji. If you are ready to dirty your hands. There is a wrestling pit near the Serpent Well. It goes by that name also, the Nag Kuan pit. Tell them there that you are coming from me. They will give you what-all help you are wanting. But do not be going just now. Those fellows are sleeping in the morning, not taking any of your sunrise immersions. They are not at all holy dip goers, I can tell you.'

Yet another litter going by on its way to the ghat and its ever-smoking fires, from the red shroud on it that of a woman still married. *Rama nama, satya hai, Rama nama, satya hai.* On and on went the hoarsely shouted chant as the bearers padded past.

It was only the sight of a Western tourist, stepping with comic haste into a doorway and standing there rigid until the funeral had gone by, that brought Ghote back to the everyday. No need to be as scared as that fellow by the fate that awaited him. Every grain, white, brown or black, must go some day between Kabir's millstones. To nothingness. Or the next spoke on the wheel of existence. Whichever you believed. Whichever you hoped. So accept. Do not even weep like Kabir.

He stepped out, and in a minute or so was descending the wide steep steps to the Manikarnika Ghat itself. There at the steps' foot were – he counted – three, four, five pyres. Four heaps of smouldering ash, one still brightly burning fire, flames spluttering with their anointing of ghee.

Into his mind came words he had read in his first hours in Banares. On the hoarding glimpsed from Manzoor Syed's maze-like halevi. *Don't Play With Fire Consequences Are Dire.* What was he contemplating now? Nothing else than playing with fire of the worst kind.

But, no, no going back. Dire or no dire, I must be here again at midnight. Rick will be waiting. My only hope.

He surveyed the scene.

The wide sweep of the steps and the platforms here and there on them were dotted with the big brownish rattan umbrellas of the ghatia priests. White-clad mourners sat cross-legged in front of them, receiving instruction in the rules and regulations of the funeral ceremonies. Running and dodging between, urchins chased each other, their shouts rising up. Down by the river itself ragged, white-headclothed Doms were going from pyre to pyre poking and prodding with their long iron poles. Half in the water three litters, their corpses still roped on to them, awaited their turn. A mooning white cow was attempting to gain some sustenance from one, tugging and chewing at an end of rope. At a heap of cooled ashes from a long-extinguished pyre an old woman raked away with a twisted length of wood, suddenly stooping, pouncing and a moment later rising up with her prize, a metal bangle.

From a niche in the temple at the head of the steps a matted-haired naked sadhu jumped out, hurried on air-light bare feet down to a pyre one of the Doms had just left. He hunkered down, scrabbled up the cool ashes from the edge, smeared them over his body.

And, Ghote thought, perhaps I can use the place he has vacated. Somewhere to put myself to see what-all happens. One long careful scrutiny. Escape routes. Possible spots to meet Rick. Places where Mishra's two-rupee murderers may hide.

He made his way quickly over and settled down to

quarter systematically the whole long lines of the steps.

Parties of pilgrims on the prescribed round of the holy city's holiest places, blessedly footsore, were arriving to complete the ritual by bathing where so many lives had ended. But at midnight none of them would be here. To use as cover from Mishra's goondas.

But there, where that party making the pilgrimage by water is arriving, could I jump into one of those boats moored there? Cast off? Get away before some knife-wielding badmash gets to me?

Absorbed in such thoughts, oblivious of the shouts of boys, of the tang of the drifting smoke, of the hectoring ghatia priests, he hardly noticed an aged, yellow-clad sannyasin settle cross-legged on the stones just beside him.

Without any preliminary the old man began to talk.

'I have been here in holy Kashi for thirty-five years, never leaving. You know, I had just attained my fortieth year, and had been appointed headmaster of a new school when I felt the overwhelming urge to abandon all, wife, family – my two sons were old enough to support their mother – position, everything. I cannot now say why this urge should have come upon me, but I knew at once that I could not ignore it. I made my way to Banares – I come from the South, as perhaps you are able to recognize – and there I was able to take sannyas, to watch my body, in the form of a small wheaten image, being burnt according to the ritual, as you can see the bodies of the deceased burning there below, and to live here ever afterwards in perfect tranquillity and, as you may say, happiness.'

Ghote looked round to see if all this was being addressed to someone else near by. There was no one. The old man, a single breath taken, resumed. Implacably.

'It has been the greatest solace to me to be within the boundaries of Kashi, which, you understand, are by no means contiguous with the boundaries of Banares considered in the municipal sense. No, no. Kashi itself extends in a wide sweep, known by the name of the Panchkroshi Road. You may find it just this side of the Banares Hindu

University. Within that area I have been in no danger all these years, should death have overtaken me, of finding myself still chained to the endless cycle of birth and rebirth. Yes, even a mosquito, lucky enough to be killed by an idle slap inside Kashi's bounds, is assured of moksha, of eternal release.'

Till that moment the old man had been fluting his words out towards the river below, where a corpse whose mourners must have been unable to pay the Doms even for a stone to sink it was floating slowly past, pale humped back and buttocks. Now he turned and produced a toothless smile of radiant sweetness.

'But, I can see, my dear sir, you are disinclined to believe this. I assure you it is true.'

All Ghote had for a moment vehemently wished was that the mosquitoes making his life a misery at the Hotel Relax would, if he were ever quick enough to slap one to death, be consigned in their next lives to a yet lower place in the order of existence. But the old sannyasin was looking at him with evident enjoyment of his theological example. And in momentary silence.

An unexpected opportunity to shoot in a question that had come unbidden into his head.

'Tell me, please. The goondas and murderers they say infest this place itself at midnight, should they get killed, say in a police firing, will they also be relieved of the burden of their evil doings?'

What he hoped to hear in reply was an authoritative denial that any murderers, two-rupee or ten, lurked at the Manikarnika Ghat at night. But he was disappointed.

'Oh, my dear sir, certainly. Why, even a donkey will receive liberation here.'

'And an atheist?' doubting Ghote could not help putting in.

'Yes, an atheist, a Muslim, a Christian. Are they not, after all, of more worth than a donkey? When the Doms place woods on the body of an atheist who is believed to be a Hindu that gentleman will attain moksha as surely as the Dom himself. Even the greatest sinner will achieve this release dying inside Kashi. Do you know the story of the nefarious Durdhara?'

Ghote contemplated for a moment claiming that he did. But he strongly suspected it would make no difference to the determined old sannyasin.

Out in the wide, swirling river a vulture had settled on the floating corpse as it went past the flooded leaning temple upstream.

If I have to, Ghote thought, could I swim out to that temple, crouch on the far side, escape like that?

'The story of Durdhara,' he conceded.

'Durdhara,' the old man began, a light of pure joy in his eyes, 'was among the wickedest of mortals. He not only ate meat but he spent all his money upon it, together with alcoholic drink and loose women. He attempted to murder a brahmin. One small act alone stood out in this record of infamy. Durdhara had stolen into a garden and plucked some flowers for his lover, herself a prostitute. Chased, he leapt over the wall but in doing so dropped the flowers. "For God Shiva," he mischievously called out. But even uttering Shiva's name in this manner earned him some minutes in heaven before he was to be plunged into hell. Now, in that short time he encountered a heavenly damsel by name Menaka and became filled with remorse for his each and every sin. Menaka then fetched holy water from this city of Kashi and, by sprinkling it upon him, enabled him to enter within the city's bounds. As he was doing so the many sins emerging from his body in ghoulish shapes became burnt up by Kashi's fire. And it was, of course, that blue smoke rising up that is making the sky above us, up to then perhaps altogether without colour, into the blue you now can see.'

Ghote looked up. The sky was blue. But at midnight? What colour would it be then?

When it came to it H. K. Verma stood for almost an hour at the top of the great square bowl of the Serpent Well, his mind swaying this way and that. He stared, hardly seeing what was in front of his eyes, at the immense grey stone walls plunging downwards and the narrow stone steps creeping up their sides. At the bottom, far down, he contemplated the square of water, black in the dazzling sunlight, flower offerings dotting its surface in minute coloured specks. At its edge white-clad widows squatted in prayer, working through their last days in holy Kashi. A handful of pilgrims toiled up the steps on the opposite side cradling little glinting brass vessels filled with doubly sacred water from the well.

There he stood while the battle raged within. At times the forces of evil – yes, they are forces of evil, admit it – almost won. The idea that it was his right, that it was the right and only course for him, to send some of Krishna-kanta's wrestlers to the Hotel Relax and have this rat from Bombay put out of the way. For ever.

Then, at the last moment, the forces of good would fight back.

What has come upon me that I should even be contemplating such an act of wrong-doing? Myself, who from boyhood and always has striven and striven to do right? How can I even think of so much as going to talk to those goondas? Asking, in return for whatever sum they would demand, to have the policewalla blotted out? However necessary it may be.

But the battle was not decided there looking down far, far below to that black square of sacred water.

At last, moving almost as a sleep-walker, he made his way to the wrestling pit that had hovered in his mind, a vision of evil.

I am not committing myself to anything. Not even to speaking to one of those fellows. But it would be stupid, when I have come all this way, not at least to look. See what sort of goondas they are there. The sensible course. The right way to set about it.

I have not made up my mind. To do it. To . . .

Very well, say it. To add one more death to that death

109

I brought about in Bombay. But this would be a truly necessary death. If that little rat has got his teeth into the truth somehow, then he has to be made to let go. Even by blows.

And this is the way to make certain. To use one of these fellows. Krishnakanta has done it. I am sure of that, however much he will not say so out aloud. But strikers have been killed. In riotings, they were saying it in the papers. And if a striker, who is committing violence himself, has to be killed, why not equally a stinking little rat from Bombay?

He found himself standing just outside the pit, by a shrine to God Shiva. A conical lingam painted in stripes of ochre and red inside a barred cage. On the walls at either side crude paintings of devis, each with her long black hair reaching down to below her waist, red garment across one shoulder showing a full breast. Each with a bowl in one hand and in the other, raised high, a broad sword, its blade red with blood.

The blood I am about to pay to have shed?

Leaning up against the shrine, carelessly left, were half a dozen stout bamboo lathis. He saw them raised, descending, time and again. Blood on them. Brains. And a man left dead.

The face of the devi on the left was half-hidden by a spotted mirror in a battered frame, hung from a hammered-in nail. Reflected in it, he saw one of the wrestlers. A big muscular fellow, bare of body all but for a scanty pair of shorts, biceps bulging, shoulders wide, a mop of curling hair. He was sitting on a stone ledge, idly playing with a pair of heavy dumbbells.

His man? The one who would do it?

But did he want it done?

And perhaps that fellow would refuse. Every wrestler in Banares cannot be willing to . . .

He found he had moved round the shrine. To the pit itself.

Why? Was he really going to go up to somebody there?

Throw out some hints? Find one or more of the fellows ready to— Ready to take some money, half now, half later?

He looked at the muscular, oiled bodies in the sand of the pit. But which would it be best to approach? One of the youngsters sitting cross-legged at the edge watching the two engaged in a bout?

No. Too young. Too young. Surely boys like those could never . . .

Then the men fighting, sand clinging to their naked flesh and thin shorts? The shorts the man on top wore – he made out as he shifted to get a better hold – were a cheerful blue with little white flowers. Somehow they made the viciousness he was showing towards the man underneath all the more troubling.

Or should he go up to the fellow lying at the side of the pit? He was on his own, flat on his belly in the sand, evidently exhausted after a bout, his head resting on a forearm, his back still encrusted with sweat-soaked sand. It would be easy to go and stand just near him. There was a sad look on his face. He must have lost a bout. Would he be ready to earn a good sum another way? By going to the Hotel Relax tonight?

A good sum. A bad sum.

12

At the Hotel Relax Ghote sat waiting, counting the hours till he could set out from this safe haven for the Manikarnika Ghat and its incalculable dangers. They were hours passing with excruciating slowness. If, he thought, I have looked at my watch once, I have looked at it one thousand times.

He had returned from his long daylight vigil at the ghat feeling the sharp smoke of its fires engrained in his skin. The interminable soliloquy of the ancient sannyasin seemed still to be shrilly ringing in his ears.

'Such is the story of Durdhara. Now let me tell you the story of Mandapa.'

He could have said, *No, I do not wish to hear one other story.* But it would have offended that good old man. And, besides, there had been nothing else to do. Until midnight.

'I would like to hear.'

'Now, Mandapa, although he was the son of a man renowned for his piety, was himself both wild and wicked. With some friends he was drinking liquor and committing various crimes. He appeared to be, as you might say, an all-bad man. So sunk was he in his wickedness that, even when he and his co-riff-raffs had stolen gold from the maharaja, he then swindled those friends out of their share and hid himself in the house of a certain prostitute. Whereupon his father, learning the full extent of his wickedness, disowned him. Those riff-raffs, however, found Mandapa while he was walking out from that prostitute's place and beat him with great severity, leaving him for

112

dead on the bank of the River Asi, which is, as you may know, just within the border itself of Holy Kashi.'

Beat him with great severity. The old man's calmly trotted-out words came back to him now with a shiver of foreboding. Was he risking a beating of great severity himself? Once he had left the hotel? Risking even being left for dead? Death itself?

Once more he looked at his watch.

'When at last,' the old sannyasin had continued, 'this badmash Mandapa was recovering consciousness what should he see but a happy party on the Panchkroshi pilgrimage, the long walk round Kashi that takes, as you can tell from its name beginning *five*, five days and five nights to perform. Being at loose ends, wicked Mandapa thought to go along with these pilgrims. Now, even setting out on a pilgrimage with such good-seeking people had a somewhat transforming effect on Mandapa, and when they had reached to their next halting place he joined them in singing and dancing before the image there of God Shiva. And so it went on, day by day, night by night, till at last Mandapa was meditating upon Shiva with every step he was taking. Burning also with remorses, he neither ate nor drank. So they came at last to conclude the pilgrimage by bathing here at Manikarnika, just where we are sitting now. There his co-pilgrims were praising and proclaiming that Mandapa was now a sinless fellow, and, hearing so much, his father claimed him again as his son.'

The end of the story had come as something of a disappointment. Surely Mandapa, transformed so wholeheartedly from wrong-doer to right-doer, had merited some greater reward than that? He could, for example, have been given a maharaja's daughter in marriage. But, seeing the contented way the sannyasin's gummy mouth had closed, he had accorded the tale as much of a 'Wah, wah' of approval as he could rise to.

It had been a mistake. The old man had broken into speech again. A story about a Banares aghori, one of the renouncers going to the point of sleeping on graves,

113

drinking wine from split skulls, cooking their food on the embers of the funeral pyres.

He had done his best not to listen. What if at midnight he should encounter an aghori? Or worse?

Not all the minutes spent under the shower on his return had washed away the sound of that voice in his head or the smell of corpse smoke on his body. Nor had he been able to do much justice to the meal he had eaten, try as he might to time-waste over it.

Once more now he picked up that morning's copy of the local edition of the *Times of India*, although he thought he had read every scrap of its solid columns. News, rumblingly thunderous editorials, the That's Entertainment section, the Letters to the Editor, the sport pages, the business pages, even the classifieds – *Ravi Sharma wishes all Banares patrons and clients a very happy Bharat Milap and offers a selection of quality used cars (Bank Loan Possible)*.

Bharat Milap, was that the festival Mishra had told him about at some stage? The final night of the Ram Lila plays, one of which Mishra must be watching out at Ramnagar now? The last part, celebrated in the city itself, of the often-told story of Rama? Well, he would have left by the time that took place. If he did find out something at the Manikarnika Ghat in three hours' time – no, still almost four – then he would have gone back to Bombay with his culprit, whoever he was, handcuffed beside him. Some goonda, hired perhaps by H. K. Verma himself. But, much more likely, Rick's information proving so much nonsense, he would be going back to the Assistant Commissioner admitting Banares had been one wash-out only.

Ah, a little corner of tucked-away news items he had missed before.

And— And one small headline leaping out: *Murder Hunt Move*.

He seized on the few lines of smudgy print below. And, yes, as he had somehow known, the murder hunt was for the killer of Mrs Shoba Popatkar, famed freedom fighter.

The Bombay police, it said, had switched their investigation to Banares.

That and no more.

He dropped the paper, went to the hotel's battered old telephone and, not without frustration, got through to Inspector Wagh.

'It is Ghote. Ghote. Inspector Ghote. In Banares itself. But, Inspector, what is this-all I am reading in *Times of India*? Murder hunt is switching to here? Why is that? You are finding out something new?'

'No, no, Inspector. Just only complete dead-end here. So Assistant Commissioner, Crime Branch, is saying Banares is best bet. Up to you itself now.'

And at last it was time to go.

Midnight. The Manikarnika Ghat. And no sign of Rick. But in the strong, pinkish light of the full moon the ghat was by no means as deserted as he had imagined it would be. There were nothing like as many people about as there had been when he had sat in his niche in the temple wall with the talkative sannyasin beside him. But there were people, and they were hardly Mishra's two-rupee murderers. There was a bandarwalla with his performing monkeys, although he had failed to attract any onlookers and was sitting on one of the steps rhythmically caressing his two pets. There was a boy in a white kurta up on a stone plinth playing a shenai, an endless repetitive mournful fluting. Higher up on one of the platforms overlooking the unbroken waters of the Ganges half a dozen men were exercising even at this hour. Oiled bodies gleaming in the moonlight.

Good people. Simple people. Going about their lives as best they could. Nothing whatsoever under the Unlawful Activities (Prevention) Act. He felt a slow down-stepping of relief. The realization that his earlier fears had been self-created. Perhaps, after all, he would get back to the Hotel Relax without a bruise on his body.

Remember the proverb in Marathi: *Your own mind is your worst enemy*.

But he could do with seeing Rick.

He looked up at the moon softly shining in the star-set, cloudless sky. There was a ring round it. His mother always used to say a ring round the moon meant one of two things. A death, or a miracle. Well, death looked less likely now. But would there be a miracle? The boy Rick simply giving him without any trouble the name of the man from Banares who had killed Mrs Shoba Popatkar? The name, and hard evidence to prove it.

At the line of still burning pyres at the foot of the crumbling steps three or four Doms were poking at the remains of the corpses with their long rods. He saw one catch hold of an unburnt foot and twist the leg to get it consumed.

In the boats moored just beyond the steps the pinpoint orange glows of the cheap beedies the boatmen were smoking glinted like so many fireflies.

Rick, is he hidden somewhere, as I am myself? Waiting, too, to make sure the meeting is between ourselves alone? In one of the boats? Or ... Or disguised as that woman – one of the few to be seen – wrapped from head to foot in a pale-coloured sari, looking like a pillar only? Or has he, as he did near the hotel, taken up a position where he can make a getaway as soon as he has learnt what I have to tell about the drugs raid? Before he has produced any information himself?

Down by the river the leaping and sinking flames of the pyres, their light catching now one thing now another, the shadows coming and going, made nothing easy to see.

Murder Hunt Move. The little headline jumped out at H. K. Verma as, unable to make himself go to bed, he moodily turned the pages of the *Times of India*, neglected till this late hour and even now hardly read or remembered.

Murder. He read with desperate greediness the short piece under that headline.

Switched to Banares. The words came up at him like the cupped-hands splash of cold Ganges water which, waist-deep in the holy river, he threw on to his cheeks each morning. But they did not have the same sin-cleansing effect.

What had the police discovered down there in Bombay? Had that Bhojpuri-understanding fellow there suddenly remembered the man who had asked if he knew where Mrs Shoba Popatkar stayed? Had he gone to the police with a full description?

He jumped up from his chair, padded into the bedroom fast as he could make his heavy legs take him, flung himself in front of the mirror there. Deep-set eyes, heavily ringed round, sad-looking even. Large fleshy nose. Full lips, orator's lips they had been called, more than once. Solid cheeks descending into a neck that was almost fat. No, definitely fat. Complexion, wheatish. Hair plentiful, softly curling, and half-grey. Yes, a man it was easy to recognize.

But the Bombay mongoose had not so much as hinted at the likeness this morning, and if the switch to Banares was reported in the *Times of India* he should have known by then.

But what to do? What to do?

No. Face it with calmness. Show you know how to cope up with emergencies. The right way to treat them.

After all, it may be some other clue that has come to light in Bombay. A clue pointing to Banares but not at all to myself. Or, even, it may be just only that the Bombay investigation has got nowhere, and in desperation they are giving out that they have switched to Banares because that little rat has taken it into his head to come here.

That could be all. Calm. Calm. See what happens, and act accordingly. Do not do anything in a hurry. Think of that Ramayana saying, *There is no gain in strengthening the bund of the tank after the water has flown out.*

But, in any case, what evidence can the Bombay rat get? What possible evidence?

*

He saw Rick. Suddenly. The boy must have slipped out of the Dom Raja's house from somewhere in the deepest shadow. And now here he was, where the flooding moon-light made his white face and grease-clogged mop of yel-lowy hair stand out as if he was in some Filmi Nite spotlight.

Probably does not even know he was late coming. American watch long ago sold to feed his habit. Good-for-nothing.

He eased himself away from the wall where he had flattened himself in hiding and set off. An aged widow, little more than a bundle of white rags, sleeping in a corner woke briefly at the sound of his clacking shoes, cried out 'Baba' and lapsed into mumbling sleep again.

And then he was within two or three yards of the boy. What to do? Grab him? Or greet him?

'Rick. You have come.'

And the boy did not attempt to run.

He went up to him and without a word the fellow sat himself down on the broken step where he had been standing.

After a moment he decided he had better simply sit beside him. At least he could catch hold of him then if he tried to do what he had done on that compound wall.

'Okay. You got what I want to know?'

He turned a little till he was squarely facing the boy.

'But it is you who should be having what I am wanting to know.'

'Stand-off, I guess. But you're the one needs to know most.'

'No, I do not think so. The Dom Raja would be one hundred per cent pleased if you had cleared out all nef-arious substances before the time of this raid.'

'It's on then?'

Lie-telling begins here.

'Oh, yes. It is very very much on.'

'So when? Come on, give.'

'No, no. You first.'

'Heck, what I got for you's scads better than anything you can tell me. And how'm I to know what you're saying's the truth?'

'For that you would have to trust me. I am not at all a liar.'

'A cop, and not a liar. You gotta be joking.'

'No, no. I am not too much of a joke cutter.'

'I guess.'

He saw the boy's eyes coolly regarding him.

'All the same I reckon you're damn well capable of lying your ass off.'

Ghote wondered whether that was a compliment. Had the boy somehow recognized in him a narrow inner band of astuteness? It was a quality a police officer ought to have, the right way of going to work.

And, true, he was at this moment – what had Rick said? – lying his ass off.

'Well, whether I am liar or not, you would all the same have to trust.'

'Okay. But works the other way round, too. You gotta trust me.'

'A drug-taker? Living from what he is getting for selling brown sugar, isn't it? You say I must be trusting you.'

'Sure I do. You just can't do anything else.'

That was true. So hear from the boy whatever he had to say, and try afterwards to decide what of truth there was in it. If anything. And then give out his own pack of lies.

'Very well, I will tell you at the least something. But then I will be expecting the same from you only.'

'Go ahead, then.'

'Well, as I was telling, this raid is one hundred per cent planned.'

He waited, hoping that this might be enough. What he had invented, sitting there at the hotel in the hours before he had come across that little news item *Murder Hunt Move*, had been the best he could contrive. But, knowing nothing about the Banares police – Mishra had been more

119

eager to flood him with the glories of his time-battered city – he was by no means sure he had hit on bait Rick would swallow.

'Heck, you don't have to tell me a raid is planned. Don't you think we haven't seen those guys watching the house? Damn obvious.'

He grabbed at this piece of information.

'Yes, yes. But we are knowing you would see our fellows watching, sooner or later. So steps are being taken.'

'Right. Yeah. That's what we need to know. Just what steps. You tell me that, I'll give you the works about that H. K. Verma.'

The works about H. K. Verma. So has the boy really got something? About that man himself? Then I must, I must, learn what it is.

'No. I have already told one thing. Now it is for you to tell what is pointing to Mr. H. K. Verma.'

'You told me squat.'

But, the scent of success strong in his nostrils, time now – yes – to stop this ridiculous fencing.

He shot out a hand, clamped it on Rick's thin-worn wrist, jerked the arm up and twisted the boy round till his face was hard up against one of the broken steps higher up.

'Now, talk. Or you will find what bastards Indian police truly can be.'

He put a knee hard down on the boy's back.

Here, if he had to do it, he could give the boy enough of a dose to get him squealing. No one at the half-deserted ghat was going to come and intervene. Not the bandar-walla, asleep now like his monkeys. Not, nearer, two half-naked men, stuffed to their necks obviously with bhang, and dancing to music they alone could hear. Not, at the far end, the boy with the shaven head and dangling tuft of a brahmin who was sing-songing out Sanskrit scriptures to an intently listening friend.

He would damn well get out of this drug-fixated crea-ture underneath him whatever it was he knew.

'Talk,' he repeated, putting his mouth close to the

boy's dirt-encrusted ear. 'Talk, or . . .'

'Guy got himself flown down, Bombay,' came a tight-throated voice.

To Bombay? Flown? In some aircraft? But who was this? Was it H. K. Verma himself? Was that possible?

'More. Who it was who was flying?'

'Guy I said. Verma.'

'All right. But how was he flying? What Indian Airways flight? When? What time?'

'No. Got himself – private plane.'

'But when? When?'

'Hell, I don't know. When that Mrs What-you-call-her, one you talked about . . . Cantonment Station. When she was murdered. That's when.'

'How are you knowing? I am not at all believing.'

He gave the boy's arm a small upwards jerk.

A squeak of pain.

Not the pleasantest thing to be doing. But if he was learning the truth, even in part, about the murder of a person like Mrs Shoba Popatkar, something altogether right to do.

'Guy told me, is all.'

'What guy? I am less and less believing.'

'No, no. God's truth. Let me go.'

'What guy it is?'

'The goop Verma's grandson, or something. Guy called Vikki Verma.'

'Oh, yes? And why should he be telling you such things?'

'Feed him, don't I? He's loaded. Takes all the sugar I can get. He just let it out, is all.'

Ghote eased himself up a little. This needed thinking about. Was it likely? At least it was so unlikely as an invented story it must to some extent be true. So was H. K. Verma really—

But he had not been concentrating hard enough on the skeleton-thin body beneath him.

With a sudden sliding wrench the boy slipped sideways,

at the same time tugging his puny wrist free. In an instant he was rolling away down the steps towards the line of burning pyres.

Ghote scrambled up, cursing, and set off, bounding down the crumbling steps. The boy had managed to get to his feet in his turn. But he was close enough to him still.

It was the crumbling steps that defeated him. He felt his ankle twisting under him. And fell with bone-jarring heaviness.

He rolled down a step or two and ended on his back, looking up at the moon-radiant sky. Knowing that now he had lost his man for ever.

13

No. Each time he dashed Ganga jal from his cupped hands on to his face, standing there with the water swirling round his waist, he felt a stinging inside. As if it was acid he was splashing against his cheeks. No, from the moment he had put one foot into the sacred river it seemed as if he was being delivered a mighty rebuke. *You have done wrong.*

At least he had not added another death to the death that had come from his own throat-gripping hands. At least he had not hired those wrestlers not so many hours ago at the Nag Kuan pit. In the end, thank Bhagwan, he had not been able to bring himself to do it. He had turned away. Walked off, striding hard in the heat of the sun. Putting distance between himself and those muscular oiled bodies, ready to do whatever he was willing to pay for. At least he had had that much of respect for the man he had believed himself to be.

But his other crime stood there still. A mountain ready to fall. No amount of prayers facing the sun as it rose over the Sandbank made any difference.

Arise! Life's breath has returned.
Darkness has fled, light comes!
Dawn has opened the path for our lord, the Sun,
Now our days will stretch out before us.

Words only. Meaningless words. All that this ritual had ever meant to him had been wiped away like mist from a mirror. All of all the rituals' echoing of the order of everything, of the way the world should be. Gone. Stretching out in front now nothing but a desert of despair.

And just yesterday he had been filled with resolution to defy everyone, everything. He had been as determined even first thing today. He had jumped up from his bed, seized his fresh clothes, marched down to the ghat. Defying anyone to say all was not as usual with his life. The life of Shri H. K. Verma, party leader. He had been sure beyond the least trickle of doubt that this was the right thing to do. If he was being hunted, he would do whatever was necessary to outwit the hunters. It was his right to do it. His right for himself.

And then, at the moment his foot had felt the touch of the water, that familiar cool embrace he had daily delighted in, all that resolution had melted away. No, not even melted. It had suddenly not been there. A blank screen on the TV.

How could I have lived, for even that short time between when Jagmohanji made his announcement and now, feeling I was entitled to defend myself in any way I could? As if that— That business— No, that killing. As if that killing had not even happened.

But it has happened. It has. No, worse. It is not that it has happened, as if some machine only jerked into accidental action. It is that I myself with my own hands – say it, say it – killed Mrs Shoba Popatkar. My own hands strangled her.

Ghote was woken before dawn after a bare two hours of restless, ankle-throbbing sleep. The Hotel Relax roomboys felt it only proper to knock at the door of every sunrise-dipping guest with as much noise as possible.

Lying there cursing them, he realized he was still as confused as when he had limped away from the Manikarnika Ghat after losing Rick. Had the boy been telling him the truth at all? A drugs-ruled creature like that, was he capable even of knowing truth from fantasy?

Yet what he had said did make some sort of sense. H. K. Verma could have been flown to Bombay on the evening of Mrs Popatkar's death and then been back in time for his absence not to have been noted. If his grandson – what was he called? Vikki – was actually a pilot . . . If H. K. Verma even had a grandson Vikki, presumably Vikram.

But why would a respected party leader like H. K. Verma want to murder Mrs Popatkar? Yet on both occasions he had spoken with him the man had been plainly uneasy. All right, the questions he had put had been effectively enough brushed aside. But that had been when there had been no more to go on than the American junky's mere mention of his name.

So go and see him yet a third time? But what to ask? *Do you have a grandson known by the name of Vikki? Did you air-dash to Bombay on the night Mrs Shoba Popatkar was killed?* Ridiculous. Impossible.

No, first I must at least find out if this Vikki Verma is existing. So, before anything else, Inspector Mishra. Mishra will know everything about a prominent Banarasi like H. K. Verma.

If I hurry I may get to him before he sets out to have his day of masti at the Sandbank. Autorickshaw time, if not taxi itself.

Why? Why? Why had he done it? Oh, yes, she had had to be made to keep silent. And, true, there in that flat he had soon enough seen no amount of pleading and persuading was going to make her hold her tongue. But, when she had made it so clear that for her the truth, whatever it was, must always be brought to the light, then— Then he should have bowed his head and accepted.

That would have been right conduct.

He knew it now. He had deep down, hidden away somewhere, known it from the very moment that frail body had become a lifeless nothing in his hands.

He felt the heat of the sun drying the water on his chest.

So why had he not let her go blurting out the truth? Yes, the chance to be Minister for Social Upliftment would have vanished in that instant. But he would have kept his belief in the rightness of his life. Why, why, oh, why?

He picked up his fresh kurta, dazzlingly white in the early rays of the sun, slipped it over his head.

It was Mishra's little granddaughter, Rukmini, who blurted out the truth, for all that she had looked so shy, peeping round her mother's sari.

'Dada is doing his mal. You are not allowed to see.'

Her mother had blushed, broken into a fit of giggles.

'Oh, excuse me. Why must children always come out with such things?'

And at that moment Mishra himself appeared.

'Inspector Ghote, good morning, good morning. I am sorry. I should have answered when you were ringing at the door. But I was under the shower itself.'

Ghote suppressed half a dozen answers that came to mind.

'I was hoping you had not left already for the Sandbank,' he said.

'Well, I was going soon. But if you are wanting to take recourse to my help . . .'

'It is just only a few things I am needing to know.'

'We could go to the Sandbank together? I am almost ready. I could tell you what you are wanting, and you could fully sample our Banarasi life. Before, you were hardly there.'

'No, no. If you are able to tell me what I am wanting to know, I would have to go and see—'

Mother and daughter were still there. Little Rukmini with ears sharp as a squirrel's.

'I would have to go at once to see a certain person, if indeed he is existing.'

*

126

Krishnakanta himself came into the office downstairs. H. K. Verma thought immediately that he had not seen his son inside the house for years.

Then a snicker of cold ran through him.

Something must be wrong. Krishnakanta must have heard something. From Delhi perhaps. His contactmen. But why should the first whispers about the imminent arrest of one H. K. Verma be the gossip of distant Delhi? Impossible. But then . . . Well, what could Krishnakanta be wanting?

He pushed himself up from his chair, totally forgetting he had been listening to the chairman of the panchayat at a village near the old family home. Some long, complicated tale about the landlord and the ownership of some fields.

'Let's go up.'

Krishnakanta followed him. He felt as if each loud step on the stone stairs behind him – Why does he have to be suited and booted always? What is wrong with good Indian kurtas, chappals? – was a separate stroke on the bell at a temple of Yama, God of Death.

Krishnakanta turned as soon as he had come in and shut the door firmly.

'No one can hear outside?' he asked.

'You know that. You know the servants do not hear what is said inside this room. This was your home for twenty years.'

He had not meant to let anger spill from his voice. But he was too caught up with anxiety.

'All right, all right. But what I have got to say must be kept secret-secret.'

So his worst fears were coming true.

'Then say it. Speak.'

'It is Vikki.'

Vikram. Then after all nothing to worry?

'The boy is in some troubles? You should not spoil him the way you have. Giving so much. Car. Lessons in flying. Flying, it is ridic—'

Then he remembered.

'But what is the problem? I can help?'

'Oh, yes. You can very much help, Pitaji. A man as much respected as yourself.'

Not so encouraging. If Krishnakanta is talking about my status, they are going to call on me to use influence. To get something done. Something that should not be done.

'Listen, my boy, I have told before. You cannot always be coming to me when you have put yourself in some awkward position. It is up to you always not to go too far.'

'Yes, Pitaji. You have said. But I am your son only. And Vikki is your grandson. The last having the family name.'

'Well, well. So what has he done now?'

'Oh, not too much. But there are problems.'

'Tell me.'

'The other day in his car he was running down some student, a girl. Hospital matter. I think I was mentioning before. Well, it should all have been okay. Five hundred, a thousand chips to the parents, and no more heard of matter. But the father is being difficult. He is a school-master, not altogether one of the poors, and he has some bee in bonnet that if his daughter is knocked down driver should be prosecuted.'

'Quite right. There are too many such hooligans and hoodlums driving cars.'

'Even if the hooligan is your grandson?'

He drew himself up.

'Yes. Justice must be done. Whether it is Vikram or some other young man with more of money than sense. He has done wrong: he should take his medicine.'

'And you, Pitaji. What if you have done wrong?'

'What— What is this?'

'I have been talking with Vikki. He was telling me he was flying you to Bombay one night.'

So it is known . . . But, no, all may not be lost yet.

'Well, what of that? I had some business there. Confidential. With Jagmohan Nagpal.'

'With Jagmohanji, when he was seeing you itself here

two–three days later? No, Pitaji, I am able to put two and
two together, even if that know-nothing Vikki was not.
He flew you to Bombay in secret the night Mrs Shoba
Popatkar was murdered.'

He felt suddenly hollow. As if whatever was inside his
body – stomach, lungs, everything – had in an instant
been replaced with air. Anything could blow him away, a
scrap of dirty paper caught up in the wind before the
monsoons.

Krishnakanta knows. He knows something. And, if Krishnakanta, who else?

'What— What it is you are saying?'

'Altogether simple, Pitaji. Vikki is knowing now, when
I have explained, why you must have needed to get to
that woman Shoba Popatkar before she was opening her
mouth. Hundred per cent truth-teller. It is all over Delhi
she succeeded to read KK's *Recollections*. Something
there you would not at all like to become public, yes?'

He knows almost all. What will he do? Will he . . . No,
he cannot.

'But, of course, Pitaji, if any police inquiries are made
Vikki would not let you down. How could he? You are
his grandfather.'

Then what . . . What does Krishnakanta want? He is
wanting something. It is there in every inch of his face.

'And Vikki is your grandson also. He is hoping— He
is knowing-knowing you would not let him down.'

'What must I do?'

No point in pretending. Vikki is holding a gun to my
head. Whatever Krishnakanta – my own son, my own son
– wants to be done for Vikki, I will have to do it.

'Not too much of difficulty. You see, we are needing to
show Vikki is too young to be prosecuted in a full court.
Sixteen years of age only. Then it is a juvenile offence
matter. No possibility to go to jail. Fine only. No problem
to pay.'

'But— But— The boy is eighteen, nineteen even.'

'Yes, Pitaji, we are all knowing that. But what we must

have is signed and sealed statement he is sixteen itself.'

'But I cannot— Will anyone believe it?'

'Oh yes, when it is coming from someone as much respected as H. K. Verma. It has been done before, you know. People are willing to turn one blind eye without daring to investigate further when an influential man is making statement. And I have made somewhat more sure. I have told the *Gandiva* you will shortly be taken into Government.'

'But— But—'

'Oh yes, Pitaji, I am knowing damn well it is not so. Half Delhi knows also. But for some days Banarasis will believe you are truly a man of influence. Soon to be a Minister. That is all we are needing. Write that statement. We will produce it. All will be okay.'

H. K. Verma sighed, deep as the Serpent Well itself.

14

So, Ghote thought, Rick was right to this extent at least.
H. K. Verma has a grandson, by the name of Vikram,
known as Vikki, aged eighteen-nineteen. And this Vikki
is a flying club member. He could have flown H. K. Verma
to Bombay and assisted him even to kill Mrs Popatkar.
After all, the boy has been in troubles many times already.
Court case just coming also. Some girl badly injured by
his car.

All kudos to Mishra for knowing so much about holy
Banares and its foremost citizens.

His autorickshaw came to a halt.

'You are here, sahib.'

Yes, there on the gate-post was a painted board *Mr K.
P. Verma – K. P. Verma (Private) Ltd.*

He paid the man, took a long look at the house.

Mr K. P. Verma, very well-off. Big place. Surrounding
wall freshly whitewashed. Garden inside altogether well
looked after. Two-car garage at the side, doors open, one
car gone, one car left. Open top, heavy dent in wing.

So Mr K. P. Verma at office at this time of morning,
and the owner of the imported sports car at home. Young
Vikki Verma, accessory to murder perhaps.

Go altogether carefully.

He pushed open the close-railed iron gate, went up to
the wide door of the house, rang at the bell beside it.

A servant.

'I am wishing to see Mr Vikram Verma.'

'Sahib, too soon.'

'Too soon? Too soon? What is this?'

'Chota sahib still sleeping, sahib.'

'Sleeping? At this hour? Wake him now only. It is police. Inspector Ghote, Bombay CID.'

The servant scuttled away.

Ghote sat himself on an ornate bench in the hallway. He looked around.

Wide wooden staircase, shining with polish. On the walls brightly decorated tribal masks. Well-watered palms growing lushly in big brass pots. Glittering chandelier, red and white glass. Directly behind, when he twisted round to look, a very large framed photo. Of some posh-looking new factory.

Time passed.

Was the boy never coming? Or . . . Or has he gone by some back way?

Well, all right. If he is truly absconding, it will make plain his guilt. Then I can call for the full help of the Senior Superintendent. Even Central Bureau of Investigation can be brought in from Delhi itself. The fellow will be found quickly enough.

The sound of steps from above.

Coming down the stairs a young man wearing blue jeans, very clean-looking, a shirt bright with red stripes gold-edged, heavy gold chain at its open neck. Air of idleness, betrayed as forced by the rigid way he holds his head. Beside him a dog, a German Shepherd, restrained by a hand loosely gripping its collar, looking at this intruder with no air of idleness whatsoever.

'You must be the chap.'

Obliged to look up to the boy on the stairs, he gave him a hard-faced glare.

'If you are meaning I am Inspector Ghote from Crime Branch in Bombay, then yes, I am. And you are Mr Vikram Verma?'

'Yes. Well, yes.'

Already a little subdued. Fine.

'So, what can I do for you, Inspector?' Then a little

perking up. 'I haven't much time. Must be on my way.'

'First of all, you can come down so that I can see.'

'Oh. Oh, very well. Though perhaps I should warn you, though, Demon here is not always friendly.'

Clattering descent of the last few stairs. Demon padding after. Defiant stand at their foot by man and dog. Murderer and attacker?

'Well, what now?'

'Some questions only.'

'And— And if I won't answer?'

Aha, you have given yourself away now, young man. You have been half-expecting a Bombay police officer to come. You did go there then.

But what did you do? You and your grandfather?

'If you do not reply, I can arrest under Section 179 of Indian Penal Code, *refusing to answer a public servant authorized to question*.'

Momentary battle of wills.

Demon, sensing his master's hostility, gave a low growl. Hackles rising.

'Oh, for heaven's sake then, ask your damn questions.'

The hairs on Demon's neck ceasing to bristle.

'Thank you. Number One, are you in possession of a licence to fly aircraft?'

'Good God, have you come all the way from Bombay to check on whether I have a licence to fly?'

Demon allowed, or encouraged, to growl again.

But the boy's answer tells something. He is to some extent confident. So . . .? So, surely, he cannot be wondering if I am in possession of evidences that he was strangling Mrs Popatkar. Or even was abiding and abetting. No, he has something to hide. But it is looking as if it is not that.

But it is near it. Give him the full fist-blow.

'No, I have not come to check on any licences. I am here to investigate murder in Bombay of one Mrs Shoba Popatkar.'

Plain to see. The quiver of the boy's right eyelid.

'Afraid I don't know who you're talking about.'

Oh, yes, you do.

'No? Yet Mrs Popatkar is a famous lady in the history of Independence struggle.'

Heavy sigh. Not a little of filmi in it. Too much of filmi.

'I dare say she was a tremendous heroine and all that, Inspector. And I dare say it all means a lot to you. But to me it's past history. Very exciting, very noble. But nothing to do with me.'

He resisted the temptation to give a lesson in history.

'Nevertheless, I must ask if you flew in an aircraft belonging to your flying club from Banares to Bombay on the evening of October the sixth last, the night Mrs Popatkar was murdered.'

'Have you been out to the club, asking your damn questions?'

The boy gave Demon's collar a quick tap. The dog lurched forward where he stood and gave another growl.

'It was my bounden duty.'

Or, it will be my duty unless I am getting plenty of good answers here and now.

'Well, what if I did fly down there? Nothing criminal in that.'

Ah, young man. Backing down somewhat. You are not so tough as you would like.

'No, that is not at all criminal. In itself. But now I must ask: what did you do in the time that you were in Bombay. Some hours only, yes?'

What reply will I get? If the boy at least went with H. K. Verma to Dadar, he will lie and lie. But perhaps he was doing no more than fly him down. All the same he is knowing what happened there. I have seen and heard enough now to be sure of same.

'In Bombay? Very simple, Inspector. I visited a friend. The film star, Miss Dainty Daruvalla, as a matter of fact.'

One sudden lift of confidence. No doubt I would find this Miss Dainty – never heard of her, some junior only – will confirm his story, even with witnesses.

So Vikram here did not go to Dadar with his grand-father. If his grandfather did go there. But he flew him to Bombay. That I know now, as if the boy had taken the dust from my feet and confessed to it word for word.

'Very well. Now, who was the passenger who was flying with you?'

'Passenger, Inspector?'

Too much of a look of blank not understanding.

But now something else. Quarter-smile of insolent pleasure. Very much like what I have sometimes had from some anti-social in the slums thinking he has found some clever way out of his troubles.

'Well, I suppose, Inspector, you could say my passenger's name was Demon.'

The boy smiled, delighted with the smart answer.

'Very well, you took this dog with you to Bombay. Now, who else were you taking?'

'Why, no one, Inspector. No one at all. I can't believe they told you at the club I had a passenger with me. They can't have seen anybody. Absolutely not.'

H. K. Verma had not gone back down to his petitioners after his son had left. Instead he had told Raman to send them away.

'They may come tomorrow. Or not at all. Not at all.'

He thumped down into his chair. The interlaced bamboo strands of its seat and back creaking out in protest.

So that idler Vikram has been told at last why I was asking him to fly to Bombay. So he knows what I have done. Krishnakanta also.

Oh, they would not betray me. I have paid even to make sure of that. Paid with my good name. When at the Civil Court they are looking at this statement I have just signed for Krishnakanta they will smile to themselves, damn well knowing it is lies and lies only. Yes, they will accept. They will not think it worthwhile to get into a battle with H. K. Verma. But in their eyes I will begin to sink down. Down to being one of those who pay to get nomination to a seat, Legislative Assembly in Lucknow or Lok Sabha in Delhi itself, for whatsoever they can make in bribes after.

And I am not such. I was not such. I disdained to take bribes. Even the *Gandiva* once was calling me as 'our Banares Mr Clean'. And I was. I was. Perhaps not altogether perfect. Who is in this world? But I was a good man. A good man.

And now I am not. Now, very soon, they will be whispering in the Banares Officers' Club, in the PNU Club, in the Kashi Club, that HKV is no better than anybody else. And I am not, now. I am a liar. One who would do anything disgraceful to squeeze and squirm out of his troubles.

But what they do not know is how much worse than that I am. Worse, worse, worse. I am – say the word, if in my head only – I am a murderer.

And it will not be in just only my head that 'murderer' will be said. It will be said, if in altogether hushed voices, within the family. By Krishnakanta, my son I have so often rebuked. By Vikram, that idle goodfor-nothing. And soon enough he will be whispering it as a fine secret to his good friends. A boy like that can hardly be trusted to keep such a thing locked away and locked away inside his head.

So will they get to me through him? Oh, not just now. Just now, if that Bombay mongoose should somehow reach to Vikram, the boy will keep to his side of the bargain. He will say nothing and nothing. And then that Ghote inspector will have to give up.

So am I safe? Safe for some time?

Time. Time is all I am wanting. Time to think. Time to decide. Time to look at myself and see where I could go.

Bhagwan, grant me some time only.

I could escape. Go abroad. The Gulf. America. But what should I do in America? How should I live my life there? Oh, yes, I could have enough of money. Krishna-

136

kanta at least would see to that. But what would I do? I cannot sit idle. All my life I have been active. Active in doing good. Yes, in doing good so far as I was able. I cannot go to any such place, America, Gulf, and sit in the sun only.

And then I would be outside Banares. Outside Holy Kashi. If I died in such a place, in my next life my crime would take me to be the lowliest of the low. To one of the 84,000 lower forms. A rat. A snake. A mosquito.

No, I must stay here inside Kashi itself. I will never leave. I will resign from Lok Sabha, and nevermore go to Delhi. I will at least live out my days in this holy city.

Or should I give myself up also? That idea has been before me. I have not always wriggled and run. I could seek out this Ghote, and just only make one clean breast of all.

I might do that. I have wanted to do it. I want to do it. The right thing. But . . .

But could I bring myself to do it? To go to that man, to anyone, and admit. Oh, yes, some damn goonda could glory in such an act. But I could not. I have been a good man. Some wrestler from the pits could laugh and say he had killed dozens with his own hands. One of the ones I saw there. How many like that are there? Many? All? A few only? Men who care for nothing. One of the ones I was nearly using.

Oh God, God, what have I done?

Wait. I could do what I was almost doing before, when I went to Collector Swami. Take sannyas. As KK was doing after he had set down that retraction in his *Recollections*. He was altogether another man after sannyas. Without his former name, without his caste. Without his sins. Yes. Yes, I, too, could do that. Leave this world. Lose my name. Renounce everything. Cut away each and every tie. See my symbolic body, a little wheat-flour image on its leaf, crackling to nothing from the flames of the nest of sticks under it. I could be as if reborn. Krishnakanta no longer my son. Vikram forgotten.

But I cannot decide now. Time. I must have time. I must keep them off just only long enough.

A knocking at the door.

It must have been going on and on. Tap. Tap, tap. In the back of my mind I was hearing something. It must be Raman, knocking and knocking. And he is not daring to come in. He knows what a shelling he would get.

Leave him to knock till he is tired?

No, it must be something important-important. He would not come up unless he could not help it. Cowardly scoundrel.

But must I answer?

I must. Life must go on a little more. I must try to go about in the usual way. For no one to suspect. While I have a little time.

'Yes? What it is? What it is? Come in, damn you.'

Raman's one-eyed face poking in. Looking altogether scared.

'Sir, it is Bombay inspector. Sir, he is just here only.'

15

Ghote stepped into the now familiar big room in the old house under the shadow of the Golden Temple. Once again he took in the blue-painted walls, the red rexine-covered sofas, the table with the telephone and the television set under its embroidered dust-cover, the curious patches of red, green and violet light thrown by the coloured panes of the narrow ventilators up near the ceiling. And he wished he could have found any other way ahead besides questioning H. K. Verma.

But he had got no further with Vikki Verma, for all that he kept pressing and pressing him for almost an hour. The boy simply repeated, time and again, that he had taken no one with him on his flight to Bombay.

Leaving him at last, he had gone straight out to the Flying Club. But, however much he interrogated everybody he could find there, he discovered nothing to contradict Vikki Verma's claim. Yes, a plane had been fuelled for him that evening. Yes, he had had his dog with him. Yes, he was qualified to fly solo. Yes, a flight plan for Bombay had been filed. But, no, no one had seen any other passenger.

Yet he was still convinced H. K. Verma had been in the plane. Rick, there in the darkness of the Manikarnika Ghat, his arm jerked painfully upwards, had no reason to squeal out anything but the truth. Even if he had wanted to produce some fantastic lie there was nothing to have made him hit on just that story. No, H. K. Verma had been flown to Bombay by his grandson. Vikki's blank-faced hostility had made it all the more certain. He had flown his grandfather to Bombay and left him to go to Dadar while he himself had seized the opportunity to visit the film star, Dainty Daruvalla.

Two telephone calls to Bombay had confirmed even this. Calls he had not much wanted to make. First to the Gossip Editor of the only Bombay filmi magazine he could remember the name of. *Miss Dainty Daruvalla, you are asking if she is a film star? If, if. Inspector Whoever-you-are, she has been on our cover itself. In two-three weeks her first film is premiering.* And the call to this as yet unseen, but apparently fully famous, star had been even more unpleasant.

'I don't care a jot if you're the Commissioner of Police himself. I'm giving a lunch party. Here. Now. Can't you understand that?'

'Yes, yes, madam. Sorry to disturb. But it is hundred per cent necessary I am knowing if one Mr Vikram Verma was with you on the evening of October the sixth last.'

'October the sixth? That's my birthday, you know. Why in God's name are you talking about that, you insufferable little man?'

'Madam, it is concerning your friend Mr Vikram Verma. If he is your friend only.'

'Vikki. But of course he's a friend. Sweet guy.'

'Then, madam, can you be telling, please, where he was on said evening, October sixth?'

'But he was here, of course. Flew all the way from boring old Banares, just to see me. I'll say one thing for Vikki. He knows how to do things right.'

'Madam, thank you.'

He had been wet with sweat when he had replaced the receiver of the Hotel Relax's battered old telephone. Then at once sweat had broken out all over him again when he had realized there was nothing else to do now but tackle H. K. Verma. With no more real ammunition than he had had before.

The party leader was sitting in the same tall, spreading-backed peacock chair. But something about him was different.

What it is? Perhaps just only the way he is having his hands, one clasping the other, instead of resting like a statue's only on the broad arms of that chair. But – do not jump to conclusion – that may be for one hundred and one reasons nothing to do with the death of Mrs Shoba Popatkar. He may have had any sort of bad news. Or be not cent per cent well. Some fever, a bad stomach. Anything.

'What— What is it now, Inspector? Why do you come bothering and bothering?'

He braced himself. The moment had come. He flung in at once the one piece of half-evidence he did have.

'Sir, it has come to my notice that one Mr Vikram Verma, your grandson, flew in a private aircraft from Banares to Bombay on the night that Mrs Shoba Popatkar was murdered.'

No response in words. But was there a tiny stiffening in that heavy body almost slumped in the chair? Surely yes.

'Sir, you have some comment to make?'

'No. No, Inspector. No, I do not see that there is any comment I can make. Vikram is my grandson, yes. And, yes, he is able to fly a plane. It is his hobby, one that I do not at all— But never mind that. Yes, I suppose the boy may have flown to Bombay when you say he did. Or to Calcutta. To anywhere.'

'Sir, it is not a question of anywhere. He was flying to Bombay. From here. His plane was in Bombay at the time Mrs Popatkar was strangled. It is that I am asking you to comment on.'

'I— I have no comment. Why should— Wait, yes. Yes, are you attempting to claim that Vikram is the man you believe came from Banares and— And killed Mrs Popatkar?'

'No, sir. No, I am not. I am satisfied that Mr Vikram Verma just only saw a certain film star by the name of Miss Dainty Daruvalla during the time he was in Bombay.'

'Then— Then your inquiries must be at an end, Inspector.'

The slumped figure in the big chair heaved forward as if to get up, to usher out this visitor. The sweat that had flushed on to his heavy cheeks plain now to see.

'No, sir,' Ghote barked out. 'Inquiries are not at an end. For simple reason it is not yet known who was the evil man who committed that callous deed. The murder, sir, of a figure of light in our Indian history. A lady who up to the day of her pointless death was doing nothing but good.'

Again no immediate response.

'Oh, yes, Inspector,' the dragged-out words came at last. 'Of course I am wishing such a— Of course, I am wishing the culprit will be found. But— But—'

Silence once more.

'Sir, what *but* it is?'

In the big chair H. K. Verma stirred. Once.

'Inspector,' he brought out at last with a sudden bang. 'Do you have a daughter?'

'A daughter, sir? What— No, sir. No, I am having just only one son. By the name of Ved.'

H. K. Verma seemed to be pondering this, dark eyes clouded.

'Very well. But I suppose you can imagine yourself to have a daughter? Daughters even?'

'Yes, sir.'

He had imagined it. Very often in the early days of his marriage. He had pictured how good he would be to a steadily growing, ever more pretty girl. Lively, innocent. He would have helped her. Pulled out the thorns from the hem of her breezes-flying kameez. The thorns of life. But it had not come about.

'Now, Inspector, what if one day, coming home, you had found your daughter, a girl you had believed to be good as a decent Hindu girl should be, if you had found that she had run off with some Muslim badmash? That she was living with him in sin?'

142

'Well, sir . . .'

'No. Imagine it, Inspector. And then . . . Then if you had gone and struck that girl to the heart, would you not feel that you had been right? Right to do it?'

'No, sir. No. Sir, as investigating officer, I have dealt with such cases, many times even. And, sir, no. Such an act is always wrong. Wrong.'

'Wrong, Inspector? To punish sin? To punish wrong-doing?'

He felt a sharply growing unease under this sudden pounding. Was it too battering? What was H. K. Verma trying to do? What was he trying to bulldoze him into agreeing to?

And was what he had answered really true to his own feelings?

'Sir,' he replied at last, moving almost from syllable to syllable, 'I am not all saying that such a wrong act must be condoned. I think, if I had had a daughter and this had happened to me, I would want in myself to forgive her altogether only. But, sir, I understand that would not be right. There would have to be some mark of dis-approval. But, sir, not the taking of a girl's life. Not even a father has the right to do that.'

H. K. Verma licked once at his full underlip.

'Very well, shall we take another example?'

The heavy body leaning an inch further forward. Hands gripping hard at the chair's canework arms.

But it was some seconds before words followed.

'Inspector, please understand this. What I am putting to you is one hypothetical case only. We are not speaking now of the death of Mrs Popatkar itself. But I am wishing for you to show me you are able to see the whole of a question. I am wishing you, Inspector, to be more than a police officer: I am wishing you to be a full human being.'

What is the man getting at? Why ask me now to be a full human being? Mrs Popatkar, he has given out her name at last even with denials. So is he beginning to tell me something? Despite that *hypothetical* of his?

A gulp of apprehension moved in his throat.

He saw he was being watched intently as a snake eyeing its prey before the moment of striking.

'Inspector, consider these circumstances. For some reason it has come to your knowledge, you as a human being, not at all as a police officer, that some person is altogether evil. And, more, that this evil man is imminently proposing to commit some wicked act. Very well, he can be denounced to the police, to one such as yourself, my good friend. But there may be circumstances where that is not possible. Say, this evil man is on the very point of committing this deed, or some other reason prevents you disclosing the facts to the proper authorities. Surely then it is your duty, a good act, the very best of acts, to take the life of that evil man?'

'Well, sir . . .'

H. K. Verma pounced on the note of doubt.

'Come, Inspector, you can hardly say it would be good conduct, right conduct, to let this evil man carry out his wicked intentions.'

'No, sir. No.'

He felt a flush of oily sweat springing up.

Why am I being put under such pressures? It must be because he is hoping to convince me. Of something. But what? What?

'Sir, if I may say it, you are putting one most extreme case. Sir, it is a case in real life not at all likely.'

'No? Well, perhaps not. But, let me assure from my experiences over many years, that life – what you are pleased to be calling real life – can bring about circumstances one would not have dreamt of until they were occurring, face to face.'

Now is he getting near what has happened to him itself? To what perhaps he has done? All this *from my own experiences*. What experiences? And *circumstances one would not have dreamt of until they were occurring*. And then that final *face to face*. Very much of personal there.

But too late. Fellow rushing on once more.

'Then . . . Then take another instance, Inspector, perhaps more likely, though still, of course, altogether hypothetical. There is a person, shall we say, who has somehow become possessed with speaking the truth. Always, always. Excellent behaviour, it is seeming.'

Ha, chance now to be showing hundred per cent agreement. Wherever this sudden forgetting of complaints about *bothering and bothering* may be leading, what he is saying can only give me some useful clues. However hard to untwist. So any encouragement is right to offer . . .

He murmured a 'Yes, sir'.

'Excellent behaviour, one might say, Inspector. At first. But, Inspector, you and I are men who have lived in this world. We know the way life is truly conducted. We know, you and I, that there are in this world some truths which are better kept out of the light.'

You and I. H. K. Verma, party leader, man of influence, and one Ganesh Ghote, just only inspector of police. Something very very fishy beginning to show here.

It was at once plain he had failed to keep that doubt well enough hidden.

'Oh, yes. Come, Inspector, do not be playing the soul of goodness with me. Ask. Ask yourself how many times here in Banares, holy city itself, you have already not told the whole truth to one and all. Have you, for instance, confided everything to that retired fellow who is assisting you? I think you said you had not.'

H. K. Verma flung himself back now in his chair. A mighty sitar sweep of creakings under him.

'Ah, Inspector, best of motives only. That I am well understanding. But all the same here was one truth you were keeping in dark, yes?'

Fellow has hit home all right. But why is he needing to do it? For softening up? And what, when softening process is fully ended, will I be asked to do? And why is he needing to ask?

'Very well, sir, yes. Yes, I agree duty is insisting on occasion that a truth be concealed.'

'Very good, very good. So now, Inspector, let me put

this to you. Say, there was a person who was—'

He hesitated, pursed his orator's lips in thought.

What is coming now? What person is he thinking of? Mrs Popatkar? She was very much against any concealings of truth. So . . .?

'Say, there was a person who had somehow learnt some truth, one of those truths which we are both agreeing must not be told to all and sundry. Yes?'

'Yes, sir.'

Where is he going? And am I being taken with him, whether I am willing or not?

'Then let us say, Inspector, that this truth, were it to come out, would do untold harm to many, many innocent people.'

'Yes, sir?'

'Well, now, Inspector, can you not see – I am asking you, remember, to answer not as a police officer but as a simple human being only – can you not see that in such a case a murder might be, as I have suggested, a good act?'

A case, long stuffed away behind banked-up memories, came back into Ghote's head. It had been not so different from this hypothetical one H. K. Verma had at last arrived at.

He wished once more, yet more fervently, he had been able to avoid this meeting.

Plainly H. K. Verma must see he was by no means as strong in opposition now as he had been.

'Inspector,' came the shot-out question, 'have you considered what might be the motive for Mrs Popatkar's murder?'

Oh, before I am getting into this swamp any more deeply, I can at least fall back on police procedures.

'Yes, sir. Naturally I have considered what motive there might be. We do not need to prove motive in a Section 302 offence, that is to say murder. But it can be most helpful to an investigator to learn what is behind any crime.'

'Well, Inspector . . .?'

'Well, sir?'

'What conclusion have you come to? What do you believe was the motive for the murder of Mrs Shoba Popatkar?'

'Sir, I have not at all been able to find out same.'

True. Altogether too true. Why should anyone have gone to Bombay from Banares just to kill such a woman as Mrs Popatkar? Why, in particular, should H. K. Verma have gone? But he was in Bombay that night. I am sure of that.

So if he did go to Dadar, commit that act of wrong-doing, why was it? Until I know that, I cannot risk charging this man. This man of influence. This figure, after all, in India's national life.

'No? So, on the question of motive you are having an open mind, yes?'

'Yes, sir. I am supposing so.'

'Very well then, let me put to you yet one more hypothetical case. Shall we say . . . Yes, shall we say that Mrs Popatkar was threatening to expose some particular individual. Not an individual who had done some wicked thing. We know Mrs Popatkar has many times exposed such individuals. It is a great credit to her. But let us suppose in this instance – it is, of course, just only something I am imagining – let us suppose Mrs Popatkar out of some unthinking love of the truth at any price was about to expose a secret, no matter what, that would do nothing but harm, grave harm, to some very good cause. Would you continue to say then that the murderer was a callous and evil man? I think you were using some such words.'

So step by step, surely, getting nearer and nearer. Now he is saying, almost plainly, the motive for Mrs Popatkar's death is that she was in possession of a secret that would harm many, many people. But what secret? What secret could it possibly be? And is it a secret that H. K. Verma alone would wish to keep dark? Or is he just only shielding some other person?

He felt an overwhelming need for an uninterrupted time to think.

H. K. Verma – it is all too clear – is attempting and trying to manoeuvre me into condoning Mrs Popatkar's murder. And he has something of a good case. A murder in the circumstances he has put forward could perhaps be justified. It would be somewhat like the killings in a war. If the murderer was as good a man as Mrs Shoba Popatkar was a good woman. In such a case I might feel some deep unwillingness to make an arrest.

But . . .

But is this case of his so hypothetical? Is he, in fact, putting the case for himself? And is he such a good man? Should I be agreeing now that investigation need not be pursued?

And, another thing, should I be making some answer that will bring from this heavy figure in front of me a full and complete confession?

'Well, Inspector?'

H. K. Verma's turn now to await with impatience a reply long in coming.

Ghote squared his shoulders.

'Sir,' he said, 'it is the bounden duty of an investigating officer to bring to justice whatsoever person has committed a crime, no matter how much of good intention such a person might or might not have.'

'Oh, the police officer's duty. Duty, the excuse down the ages of the man who does not dare to think. It was General Dyer ordering the Amritsar massacre. *It was my simple duty.* It was the British clinging on to power in India. *Our solemn duty to the Empire.* No, Inspector, that is simply not good enough.'

'But, sir, murder is murder. The taking of a life. It is the act of the man without anything whatsoever of scruples.'

H. K. Verma's face suffused with dark rage.

'And do you not know, Inspector Ghote, that life after life is being taken in India today, and not one scruple is heard? Men and women have been starved to death. They are being starved at this moment itself. And where are your Section-this charges, your Section-that?'

There must be an answer to that. Find it, find it.

And, yes . . .

'Sir, with respect, I am believing you are not comparing one thing with another. Oh, yes, sir, I know that the lot of the downtrodden in this country is sometimes very bad, that people are, yes, dying when they should not. But that, wrong as it is, sir, is not murder. Cold-blooded murder.'

'It is not, Inspector? What then do you think I and my party have been fighting for during so many years? That the murderers of the downtrodden and the starving shall not be allowed to go on with their evil work. When I am Minis— Well, never mind that. Am I making you understand what I am saying?'

He gritted his teeth.

'Yes, sir, I am very well understanding. A police officer who has to enter the worst slums of Bombay and the pavement dwellers' jhopadpaddies cannot but understand that.'

'Good. Good. So now, answer this. If Mrs Popatkar was standing in the way of saving the lives of hundreds of such dalits, of the downtrodden, of thousands, even of lakhs of them, would not her own death be a good act?'

Why is he asking and asking this? He must be attempting to persuade that the murder of Mrs Popatkar is a purely good act. And that it should not at all be investigated. He must be.

What should I say?

An answer that at least put off any final decision rose to his mind.

'Sir, nevertheless, what you are saying is not at all what has happened. You were stating hypothetical case only, yes? Mrs Popatkar was not standing in the way of so many lives being saved. I do not know what it was that made whoever was killing her do what he did but it cannot have been that.'

'No, Inspector?'

149

'No, sir.'

For several long seconds H. K. Verma sat brooding.

'Look, Inspector,' he said at last. 'Consider this. Can you truly say ending the life of one person whose continued existence is a threat to the general well-being is different from ending the lives, in a manner equally violent, of six–eight–ten people on the grounds that they are somehow anti-social?'

And now a thick spurt of rage.

'And you know who is doing that? You policewallas. Yes, you police are doing it, time and again. Any week you can read in the papers *Five Die in Police Firing*, *Ten Die in Police Firing*. And what they are calling *Lock-up Deaths* also, they are so common they get just one small headline. If they receive any mention whatsoever.'

Under this redoubled battering he was beginning to feel like some broken-winged, feathers-torn kite attacked by a mob of noisy, darting crows.

He shook his head.

'Sir, I will not say that each and every death in the lock-ups has not somewhat of unjustified brutality in it. Or on every occasion Armed Police are using their rifles it is one hundred per cent correct. We in the police are human also. Mistakes are made.'

He heaved his head out of the mass of cawing, pecking attackers. Yes, here was the answer.

'But, sir, what I will state is that such deaths are never the same as murder. Sir, let me be definite. Such deaths, however wrong, are not the deliberate, self-decided act of one single human being making up his mind to kill another. They are not Indian Penal Code, Section 302, offences. And it is those, sir, that must be tracked down to the last vestige.'

H. K. Verma glared back at him with sullen hostility.

What more was to come?

But abruptly the party leader shrugged his ponderous shoulders. Gleaming white kurta rising and falling like a huge ocean wave.

150

'Well, let it be. Let it be.'

The heavily fleshed face set in a mould of chill inflexibility. The orator's lips, so full only moments before, tightened to a hard line.

16

H. K. Verma sat where he was when at last the Bombay mongoose had taken his departure.

Very well, the little rat had shown no understanding of— Of what had happened. Well then, no way out there. No chance of being given some time. The time needed. To think. To decide.

Then let him do his damnedest while he can. He will find he is up against a man who can still fight. Better also than a jumped-up detective from Bombay-side. A man who knows what to do. Who knows the right way to go about things.

And I am entitled to some freedom. I have earned it. By all I have done and striven for since I became leader of the party, and even before. From all I have done in my life. Who is this Bombay fellow to deprive me of that?

And peace. Suddenly he longed for a stretch of peace. A time of not having to think. Of quiet. Of being without the insistent hammerings from every direction that seemed to be beating down at him.

He felt the need dragging at every inch of his body now, as if to each point of his flesh a sticky tugging line had become attached and all together were pulling, pulling him down. A sucking lassitude that threatened to remove from him even the ability to get up out of his chair. He tried to struggle against it.

Think. I must think. I must think of everything that Bombay fellow said. How much does he know? Is he

keeping back some evidence he has got? Is there anywhere I should act to check him? To secure myself that
stretch of time?

All right, the fellow has somehow got on to Vikram
and the flight to Bombay. Bad enough. But, plainly,
Vikram has stuck to the bargain Krishnakanta made.
He has kept his mouth shut. And, clearly again, the
Bombay mongoose cannot have found any witness that
I got into that plane. Or he would have faced me with
that.

But he could not have found out anything there at the
Flying Club. Vikram was clever. Give him that. The way
he taxied the machine to the edge of the field, opened
the door on the far side from the clubhouse for me. And
when I had pushed away that dog, all I had to do was
crouch in my seat, head down, till we were safely in the
air. And at the Bombay end the boy was as clever. No,
all should be well there, despite the setback.

Plainly, too, this Ghote fellow did not have any news
from Bombay. Beyond that, so it seems, they have confirmed Vikram visited some junior film star during the
time we were there. Nothing from the airfield there. No
new evidence from that damned Bhojpuri speaker.

So that was what the boy was doing while I was away.
Seeing that film star. And more than seeing? No
behaviour for a grandson of mine ... But ... Well, good
luck to him. After all, young blood is young blood. A
man is needing that from time to time.

Usha.

The thought burst in his mind like a star shell. And
with it the burden of lassitude was lifted away. Why should
he not go, now even, to Dal Mandi? Find Usha and gain
with her at least some peace? She knew how to give him
that. None better. Lost in her lively arms.

Ghote, emerging from the house, took automatically the
turning leading down towards the Ganges. It was not that
he hoped to gain a new access of strength at the ghats.

153

He wanted, simply but passionately, not to have to go anywhere.

He wanted to think.

His mind was full of half-realized impressions. Time. He must have a little time to sort them out. To discard the mere imaginings. To examine the more substantial hints. Search for the hidden meanings, and the half-hidden ones.

He came to a halt just round the corner where a faded, red-painted wall slogan read *Please to Vote for Communist Party (Marxist)*. It was hardly the quiet spot he would have wished for. There seemed to be more people in this holy city even than in Bombay. The narrow lanes to either side were two boiling torrents of humanity, pilgrims of every shade and hue, every garb and headwear under the Indian sun going to the ghats or returning from them, priests, vendors, beggars, shoppers, all-but-naked sadhus, tourists. And everybody talking or shouting out at the tops of their voices. Nor were many of the words he caught what might be expected from people whose ears must be full of the tonk-tonk-tonk of the hanging bells jangled as worshippers entered temples, large and small, and of the singing of holy bhajans emerging from doorway upon doorway or distantly wowing from the loudspeakers down at the river. 'How much it was?' 'I have been three times cheated.' 'We must take one of those paans to eat, bed-smashers only.' 'You have paid twice too much, you fool.'

What a city.

Something brushed against his legs. He looked quickly down, suspecting a pickpocket. It was a bent-double widow, another one, white sari draped over gaunt limbs, fuzz of grey hair on shaven head, hobbling past with the aid of a staff. She must be the hundredth at least he had seen. The patient attenders on death in death-loving Banares. Eking out the barest of existences, until the end came. The last minutes with Ganges water washing over some part of them, then the flames.

But none of that. Think. Think.

What did I learn in that talk? Number One: that I am not up to outfacing a man like H. K. Verma. Well, let that pass. Number Two: that H. K. Verma is at least a very, very worried man. One moment shifting in his chair, the next holding himself rigidly still. Sweat, too, on his face. You could smell sweat on him also, the sweat of earlier hours on his body.

But what exactly was causing him worry? Because he had been that night to Mrs Popatkar's flat? Or is it, after all, for some altogether lesser reason? Something to do with politics even? It could be that. In the *Times of India* yesterday there was a lot of comment on how Government had only just now got out of some difficulties. How they might have needed to make concessions to one of the smaller parties to keep their majority but in the end had contrived to placate a faction inside the party itself. They could have wanted the votes H. K. Verma controlled, however few. Have even offered the man himself some post. He had said something, half-said it. It had sounded like *When I am Minister* ... Perhaps he had been offered seat in Cabinet, and at the last moment offer had been withdrawn. That would be enough to have made him worried.

Or would it?

And, Number Three: that famous hypothetical case. Was he truly speaking about himself? Sounding me out to see if I would call off investigation? If he was saying he had committed murder but for some good reason, then he might have thought I would listen.

And if he had come out with it fully, would I have given way? To the plea of a good man? Should I have given way?

No. No, murder is murder. Let the judges look at mercy. That is their duty. I have mine. And it is no more than to find who was killing Mrs Shoba—

Wait. Look, there. H. K. Verma himself. At the corner. And seeming in one hell of a hurry.

Is he escaping only? Did what I was saying, what I was refusing to say, make him ...

But never mind *Is he* and *Did what*. After him.

He pushed his way against the stream of people rounding the corner. Yes, there, already some distance away, was the broad back in the white kurta he had just glimpsed. He forged after it. Almost at once a ribby white cow, slewed right across the narrow galli, blocked his way. He squeezed to the side, put a hand on one of its horns, swung round, pressed on. A beggar thrust a dirty hand almost into his face, then up to his own mouth, beseeching.

'Maaf karo.'

Forgive me. And on. No hope of running. Not in this narrow lane, three abreast at most between the tall, sky-seeking buildings. But at least the bulky shape ahead in dazzlingly clean white could go no faster.

A young man paddling his way along on a bicycle, dabbing at the paving stones, ran over his foot. Looking up in fury, he saw H. K. Verma had succeeded in hailing a cycle rickshaw.

Was he going to lose him?

He flung himself forward, careless now of any damage he might do, squirming and sliding sideways, ducking and weaving.

On a grey-white wall a bright painting of a tiger almost pouncing on a long-horned deer, red mouth ready to sink into soft flesh. Would the tiger he was ever get as near to his prey?

He got within twenty yards. Pointless to call out 'Halt' in this bedlam of noise. And H. K. Verma, haggling ended, was clambering heavily on to the rickshaw's narrow double-seat. At once the rickshaw walla, an old grey-haired veteran, sunken chested but wiry in every limb, set off.

But at no great speed. Hardly possible in the jam of people to go any faster than a sharp walking pace.

Plunge on then.

But soon the old rickshaw walla was contriving to go at a better speed. H. K. Verma, leaning forward, urging him on.

Where was he making for? The Cantonment Station and a train? A train to anywhere. Or was he aiming to get just far enough out of the lanes to pick up a taxi to the airport? But he would hardly get a flight at a moment's notice. To the Flying Club then. But there he would need his grandson to pilot him. So, to his son's place, and Vikki Verma's sports car in the garage there?

Ah. The unmistakable black hood of an autorickshaw. Not much further ahead. H. K. Verma had passed it, evidently not thinking it worth switching to the faster vehicle.

Push forward.

Let no one take it. Please God.

No one had.

Hardly able to speak for shortness of breath, he gasped, 'Cycle rickshaw. There. Man in white-white kurta. Follow.'

'Ji haan, sahib.'

The driver, young and shining-eyed, seemed delighted to have been set on a chase. But, jerk his engine from the usual puttering to a frenzied clatter though he might, shout at people blocking him, hoot hoot hoot on his horn, the way in front was still so crowded there was no question yet of overtaking the hard-pedalling, bell-ringing cycle rickshaw walla ahead.

Then, as the lane broke out into a wider road, they began at last to gain ground. But not much, even though, motorized vehicle versus pedalling legs, they were heading sharply uphill now. Far too much traffic for any real progress. Pedestrians walking happily in the roadway. Hawkers at the kerb pushing carts and trays out into the passing stream. A pack of donkeys trotting in the opposite direction and spilling all over the road. Scooters, other autorickshaws, long unwieldy handcarts, horse-drawn ekkas, trucks.

But the road was becoming steeper and steeper. Noisy

two-stroke began to gain faster on bare feet straining at pedals.

Now, what to do? Can I arrest him? Arrest H. K. Verma? Hardly. Still no proof he has committed his crime. So just only bring his rickshaw to a halt? Confront him? Escape unexpectedly stopped, will he break down? Blab out something, anything, making it clear what he has done?

Then, crossing straight in front of them, came a long procession of sadhus, naked bodies ash-smeared, striding out, eyes fixed at some point in the far distance, in blank silence. Only an occasional clashing jangle when one of their tridents struck another. And going on for ever.

At last they were out of the way. And, ahead, no sign at all of the broad back in the dazzling white kurta.

'Where has he gone?' Ghote shouted. More a cry of despair than a question expecting an answer.

But in his driver the heat of the chase was running hard.

'He would have turned off, sahib. Not many places to go. We would find.'

He set off again, briskly as the traffic would allow, glancing at every narrow turning.

Ghote did not see their quarry. But the driver did.

'There. There. Into Dal Mandi itself.'

The frail vehicle swung round, careless of whatever was coming on behind, just scraping an immense sacred bull lying contentedly in the roadway. *Beware of whores, bulls* . . . Its purply-black sides much scarred by less skilful drivers of car or rickshaw.

Dal Mandi, Ghote thought. The prostitute quarter. So was . . .

They plunged into the new area of tight-packed gallis. The crowds here were different. Almost half the passers-by were chuklas. Everywhere there were bare arms clinking with heavy bangles, large glinting glass jewels in noses, ears dragged down by showy earrings. Eyes deeply ringed with kohl looked at this autorickshaw passenger speculatively. Lips glaringly red from chewed paans mouthed invitations, insults. Predatory men moved among them, assessing, jostling, spouting out crude jokes.

And, plain to see ahead, there was the cycle rickshaw moving onwards, the broad white back.

It came to a halt beside the ruins of an ancient temple. H. K. Verma got down, looked round once, waddled determinedly towards a house opposite.

Ghote noted the doorway he went in at, paid off his driver – a gratefully generous tip – and settled down to wait.

H. K. Verma, stumbling at last out of the house, told himself that this must be the last time. He was too old, had seen and done too much, had lived his married life, had taken his wife to the burning ghat. It was no longer right to be doing that. Oh, yes, Lord Krishna had had his loving gopis. But he had been then a young man, not married.

And coming to Usha as he had today, coated black in misery, cushioned away at last from all his cares had he in sheer relief talked too much?

What had he said? No, he was too tired, too battered by everything, now to remember it all. Oh, he had told her about Jagmohan Nagpal and the honey jar of high office that had been smashed at his feet. But Usha, for all her crooning sympathy, would have hardly understood. But there had been something else – Was it when I was . . . The second time? – something that had come from the seat of all his troubles.

From that.

But what exactly had he said? Or done there with Usha? Or was it something he had tried to do? Had it been anything definite? Anything too definite? Because that was a part of life she would know about. She would not let anything she had heard about those hours in Bombay glide over her.

So, if . . . If, as was hardly possible in the worst of nightmares . . . If somebody, that Bombay detective, cornered her and asked what he had said, would she be able to pass on anything, something, that would finally betray his secret?

Would she? Would she?

But it was impossible that should ever happen.

Altogether impossible.

17

Darkness was beginning to descend on the holy city. Ghote was still perched on the ledge where he had been keeping observation on the house H. K. Verma had gone into almost three hours before. He was doing his best to pretend to be listening to a pair of street musicians who had settled just beside him with their battered old harmonium and tasselled drum. Then he saw his man come out.

At once he dropped into a sitting position where he would be concealed by the little crowd watching the entertainers. No point in confronting his man now, when he knew he had not been absconding.

He had had a better idea.

Waiting there, it had been an inescapable life-size wall-drawing opposite that had put the notion into his head. A crude sketch of a man with an aggressive moustache standing upright in the plain act of intercourse with a woman, round-breasted as any stone carving from ancient days. Why not see if the prostitute H. K. Verma had been with for such a long time had learnt anything from him? She might even know something to lead him to the hard evidence he needed.

The old sannyasin's story of the wicked Mandapa came back to him. How he had hidden from his fellow goondas in the house of a prostitute and, after he had been beaten almost to death, had repented and become as much of a doer of right as he had been a wrongdoer before. H. K. Verma, might he have repented? Be no longer wicked as

Mandapa? Be ready, presented with just one more fact telling against him, to confess?

He sat crouched where he was. The raucous singing of the harmonium player still deafening in his ears. At last he calculated H. K. Verma must have turned in the other direction to find a rickshaw to take him home.

Then, not at all liking what he had to do but pushed on by a sense of duty – *You are going to Banares, beware of whores* – he went slowly along towards the house H. K. Verma had come out of. Mishra's boast, the first time they had talked, about Banares whores being 'most tickling in all India' came back into his mind. What lay ahead?

Just inside the door of the house some sort of a goonda was sitting on a lopsided cane stool. A thick cudgel lay across his knees.

He stepped up to him.

'A good friend was telling me this is a very fine place.'

The man gave him a grin, half in complicity, half in warning.

'Go in, go in. See Rukmini Auntie.'

A gesture down a narrow, littered passageway to a room at the back.

Cautiously he went along, past a blue plastic shopping basket, a bicycle frame without wheels, a large empty tin that had once contained mango jam, a child's kite with one of its spars broken.

Rukmini, he thought. Odd chance that this brothel madam should have the same name as Mishra's bright little granddaughter. This Rukmini must once, too, have been a three-year-old with no notions in her head other than, like Mishra's little Rukmini, to do what was good, not to make mistakes in her reading or counting. How then had – he saw in the dim orangey light ahead a hugely fat woman in a gaudy sari, legs up on an old wooden chair, buttocks spilling over – how then had some little girl, wholly innocent, become this creature, plying this trade?

But no time for such speculations now. Difficult negotiations ahead.

He entered the room.

'I have been told by a friend there is a girl here who is very-very exceptional.'

'All my girls.' The flat statement.

'This girl ... Tell me, are you knowing one Mr H. K. Verma?'

A grunt of acknowledgement. One that could, if need be, appear as pure denial.

'My good friend H. K. was telling me there is one special girl he is very much liking.'

'When was he telling? Just now?'

'No, no. It was one week, two weeks past.'

'Well, Usha is just only free. Rupees one hundred. Half an hour.'

He paid.

The money would have to come out of his own pocket, but if it led to the murderer of Mrs Popatkar ... And, should it by some wonderful piece of luck do so, then, by God, he would claim it as some other sort of expenses. Small dishonesty.

'Usha,' the madam called in a loud croak, harsh as a crow's.

In a few moments the girl appeared.

With a certain lightening of his spirits, he saw she was at least a better class of chukla than those he had seen parading up and down during his long wait outside. She must be, he thought, perhaps thirty. Still, despite the life she must have led, with a good complexion, lively eyes, upright body.

She was looking at him now in frank assessment.

What will she be thinking, he asked himself. *Is this one a quick come-and-go fellow? Will he want something strange? Will he be gentle? Brutal? Will he insist on talk?*

Well, that he would do. And he had a notion that Usha would not be impatient of talk. She looked – and why, he thought, should she not? – distinctly intelligent.

'Come then,' she said. 'Or is it that you are shy only?'

There was a twinkle in her eyes.

Following her up a narrow, very dark staircase, he felt

that this was going to be someone he might like for herself as a person. Perhaps he really would stand a chance of learning something from her.

As soon as he had entered the room she led him to – bare walls, green painted, ceiling fan slowly whirring, broad old bed with ornately carved legs, silky red shawl scantily covering it – he told her he had not come to her for the usual purpose. It was a risk, but, right from the moment he had seen her, he guessed she might be someone he could say that to.

'You have paid. I am happy if you want to sit only. But one half-hour, mind, no more.'

She looked at him, head a little cocked to one side, a hint of a smile.

'Though I have an idea you are wanting a little more than sit.'

'That is very clever of you.'

'So you want to talk and talk. Is it, *Why did you take up this bad-bad life?*'

'So why did you?'

He had wondered how to wind into what he wanted to know. This seemed as good a start as any.

Usha smiled.

'One old story. My parents were poor. My father was a Second Division clerk, and by the time I was eleven or twelve he had altogether lost his health also. At last one evening when he had just returned from work he went out, as was his habit, to fill the buckets of water from the outside tap. But he was a long time returning. And then—Then when we were going out he was there lying dead, buckets spilt beside him. So we became very much poorer, and I also had no brothers and there were my younger sisters to feed and educate so far as possible. Then I got to know a woman older than myself, who seemed to take pity on me, and after some time she suggested I could make money by this work I am doing now. At first I was very much troubled by what she had said. But she told me that the work was nice once you had begun. So bit by bit she got me to agree. Of course, at first I did not find it nice. But now ... Now I sometimes like it, when the man is in any way decent.'

Now, he thought. Can I ask now if she found H. K. Verma in any way decent?

But take it slowly.

'And you find many of the men who come decent?'

'Decent?' she said sharply. 'It is depending what you are meaning by decent. To me it means the ones who do not make too much trouble. But are they truly decent? No. No.'

Damn. Heading fast away from H. K. Verma.

'But some ...?'

'No. It is immoral what they are doing. It is immoral also what I am doing. I know it. But how many women are also as immoral? Working in some office and pleasing the boss, in whatever way it is done, that also is immoral. Having boyfriends, as some young girls are doing nowadays, even in holy Banares, and exploiting them. That is again immoral.'

All perhaps true. But going even further from H. K. Verma.

'And Mr H. K. Verma,' he plunged in with sudden recklessness. 'How immoral was he? Was he one of the decent ones? You know who I am meaning by Mr H. K. Verma?'

She looked at him, alert eyes hard now.

'So that is why you have come? What it is you are? Private detective? I have yet to meet one of that sort. But there is something about you that says you are the breed.'

A double risk.

'No, I am not a private detective. But your guess is not too bad. I am a police detective. From Bombay.'

Hard now to read what was in those eyes. Suspicion certainly. And anger? Anger at having been a little tricked?

No, he did not think so.

165

'And, Mr Detective, you are knowing, isn't it, Mr H. K. Verma was here this afternoon itself?'

'Yes. Yes, I was following him. I waited till he had gone. He was here very much more than one half hour.'

'He paid for that. You may also, if you are wanting to stay so long. But I would not waste your money. However long you are staying, you will not hear one word about Mr Verma.'

'No? But why?'

'Because I am doing my work as it should be done. I am giving the men who come what they are wanting, and I am doing nothing more. They know their secrets are safe with me. That is what they come for, some of them, the ones who say truth is at the bottom of a well and there also I am. So they are finding truth of what they are wanting in sex matters. And, if they are wishing it, they can tell me the truth about their all lives, and know that truth will stay with me here at the bottom of my well.'

'Shabash,' he exclaimed.

Well done. All right, this was a prostitute. One they called 'worn as a temple stair', the lowest of the low. But she was doing what she did in a hundred per cent the right way. And he could not but admire that.

'You have found your duty in this life,' he said, slowly unravelling the thoughts in his mind, 'and you are following it. That is good. Yes, good. I mean it.'

'Yes,' Usha came back at him, eyes bright suddenly, 'you are right, I must have been born to this life. I must have been quite bad in my former janma.'

A sharper twinkle in her eyes suddenly.

'Yes, I may have been even a CIDwalla.'

He grinned.

'So,' he said, 'however bad it is to be a CIDwalla, I must all the same work out the duty of the janma I have been given. Perhaps for being a prostitute in my former life. And it is the task of a CIDwalla to ask questions.'

'And for a prostitute not to answer.'

'But if I tell you that I am almost certain Mr H. K.

166

Verma has done something that will make him in his next life a donkey or a rat or even a mosquito?'

An abrupt look of understanding.

'So that was why he was saying he will never, never leave holy Banares. He is hoping to die here and gain moksha despite any sins. No more lives, donkey, rat or mosquito.'

'And you are happy if he escapes from what he has done in that way?'

She thought for a moment, sitting there on the edge of the big, shawl-covered bed, looking up at him.

'Ah,' she said eventually. 'Yes, that is something to think. If I am paying now for misdeeds in a former life, why should he not pay for his?'

'So, what else, besides wanting to die within the bounds of Banares, was he saying?'

'Shall I tell you?'

'Oh yes,' he said, suddenly sure. 'You will tell me.'

For a little she was silent.

'There is not so much to tell.'

'But all the same tell.'

'He was talking. Much more today than he has done before, and much different.'

'What different?'

'Oh, he was saying about his politics-follitics. But I was not paying so much of attention.'

'But he was saying more?'

'Yes.'

She frowned in concentration.

'He was talking – it was when he was almost asleep – about going to Bombay. Is there also somewhere there called Dadar?'

A bright light shining in the distance.

'Yes, yes. What did he say about Dadar?'

'No, it was not anything. It came when he was trying the second time. And, half asleep, not much able to do it.'

'And . . .?'

'First of all, it was Bombay, Dadar, Bombay, Dadar.

And then when he tried to begin again ... Then he was different. Always before he has been one of the easy ones. He was never wanting very much. Some comfort only. But today ...'

'Yes, today?'

'Suddenly then I was having to push him away. He was putting his hands to my throat. At first I thought it was love juices beginning at last to flow fast. But then I began to think he might press in his thumbs altogether too hard. And as he was doing that he was saying also, *Stop, stop, damn you. Stop. I will not let you speak.*'

'And he said more? A name? Was there a name?'

'No, no. I was pushing him off then. And soon he was becoming quiet, and after we were chatting this-and-that only.'

'What this-and-that? Bombay talk? Dadar?'

'No, no. Banares only. Ram Lila plays. Had I been to Ramnagar to watch? He had not been this year. He was not quite knowing why. Did not feel like. That is all.'

But, yes, he thought. Yes. it may well be enough.

18

A bar of greenish light slanting in from one of the high
ventilators, alive with twirling motes in the bright morning
light, stretched like a barrier between them. It was a little
after nine o'clock.

Too strong a barrier?

Ghote had decided it would be best to wait till the next
day to go to H. K. Verma. He needed as much time as
he dared take to think out how, with evidence as shaky
as he had, he could go about his interrogation. Because
it was as an interrogation now, rather than an interview,
that he thought of the encounter.

To go to the Senior Superintendent and ask for H. K.
Verma to be brought in for a fully formal interrogation,
he had immediately realized, was simply not practical. He
could almost hear the Senior Superintendent's very
words: *Inspector, what possible motive could a Banares
citizen of Mr H. K. Verma's standing have for killing a
lady like Mrs Shoba Popatkar?*

And he would have had no proper answer. Yes, it
looked likely that Mrs Popatkar had been strangled by a
man with a Bhojpuri flavour to his Hindi who shortly
before her death had asked where she lived. It was fair,
too, to assume her murder was connected with her visit
to Banares and her forcing Mr Srivastava to let her see
Krishnan Kalgutkar's *Recollections*, of which as leader of
his party H. K. Verma happened to be the guardian. But
H. K. Verma had done no more than enforce the ban
Krishnan Kalgutkar had stipulated. What could there be

in the *Recollections* to have given him an overriding need to kill Mrs Popatkar?

Nevertheless he had felt almost to a certainty that, when he confronted the party leader, he would be face-to-face with Mrs Popatkar's killer. Because of Vikki Verma's obstinate silence. Because of what Usha had said. Because of that strange plea on behalf of 'the good murderer' H. K. Verma himself had made.

But he knew he would have to tread very carefully.

'Sir,' he began. 'I have come again because I am not one hundred per cent happy with what you were saying in this room itself yesterday.'

He saw H. K. Verma's heavy face freeze into a glare of chill rage.

'Inspector, if you are happy or not happy, that is no concern of mine.'

'Oh, yes, sir. Excuse me, but it is your own answers I am doubting.'

'I answered you, as I recall, with very great fullness.'

'Sir, what you said gave me much to think. But, sir, speculations as to whether a murder can be a good deed are not my duty to consider. It is just only for me to seek simple answers, yes or no, to simple questions.'

'But what if there are no simple answers?'

'No, sir. There are things which are not at all matters for rumination and philosophizing. To matters of fact just only one straight answer can be given.'

'So you say, Inspector. So you say.'

H. K. Verma's heavy shoulders moved up and down in a massive shrug.

'Sir, I do say. Let me ask one such question only.'

Silence on the far side of the slanting bar of greenish light.

'Sir, did you on the night of October the sixth travel to Bombay in a plane flown by your grandson, Mr Vikram Verma?'

No immediate answer.

What was the fellow going to reply? Could this be it

already, the moment of breaking? Had this one direct, inescapable question brought in a single leap the end of his task?

'No, Inspector. No. I did not go to Bombay that night.'

Liar. Liar. I know that you were going. That denial has just only confirmed it.

Right. Make him feel to the full what it is he is doing. Lying. Denying. Wriggling to save his skin itself.

'Mr Verma, let me ask you one more time. Did you fly to Bombay in a plane piloted by your grandson?'

'No. No, Inspector, I did not.'

'No, sir? But let me remind you, Mr Vikram Verma has admitted he flew there.'

'And has he stated that I accompanied him?'

'No, sir. He would not say you were there also.'

'Then, Inspector, you must take his word for it. And mine also. I did not go to Bombay. What makes you believe I did?'

I can hardly say it was, in the end, because a prostitute told me what you had muttered during failed sexual intercourse.

But at least, with that extra question, I have an opening that a flatly repeated denial would have blocked.

'Sir, I was unable to believe what Mr Vikram Verma was telling.'

Leave it at that? Or go on to say I expect – as I do not for one moment – young Vikram to break down under further questioning? Watch the effect of that jump of falsehood?

He hesitated. And found the hesitation had been enough.

'How dare you accuse a grandson of mine of lying and lying. I shall take this to the highest authorities. I am not without friends at the Centre. At the top. The very top.'

Altogether too much. Too much shouting. Too much bluster. Nothing less than another admission.

And I know, by God, how to make the most of it.

'Sir, you are welcome to go to whatsoever top you are

wishing. Would you like to make some telephones now this instant?'

He settled his glance firmly on the smart, cream-coloured instrument on the table beside the shrouded TV set.

H. K. Verma simply sat and glowered.

'Well then, sir, let me now ask this: where were you itself on October the sixth, from – shall I say? – the afternoon onwards?'

Again a pause. A give-away pause. Plain that the big man in the peacock chair, that bar of greenish light just touching the outermost pure white folds of his dhoti, is not simply sorting out in his head where exactly he was. He is busy inventing. Something not too detailed, but all the same likely.

He is. He is. I am sure of it.

'Inspector, this was some time ago. How can—'

Cut sharply in.

'Sir, it was six days ago only.'

He is on the hook. Keep the line hard-tugging.

'Yes. Six days ago. Thank you for pointing it out. It helps me to bring it back to mind.'

'So, sir, where were you?'

Do not let him have one second more of thinking time. Let him make every sort of mistake in the inventions he is producing. Let him tangle himself more and more.

'I was— Let me see. I was, of course, here. In the house. But I work in this room and down in the office also. One or the other. Impossible to say where at any one moment.'

'Very good. I am taking it there are people who could confirm same. The clerks in your office? Your peon?'

'Yes, yes. The clerks see me coming and going, though they may not know whether I was there on one day rather than the next. Or I could call Raman some time later.'

Yes. After you have had a quick, secret word. I know that one-eyed Raman. The type who is scared, scared for his job and ready to lie till he drops down dead to keep same.

172

'Then, sir, you were in the house. But for how long? Did you leave it at all that day, just six days ago? You must be able to remember.'

This is pressing him. Pressing hard. If he flew with his grandson to Bombay – as he did, as he did – then at some time he must have left the house. Can he be sure now someone will not remember, for some chance reason only even, seeing him go?

But, no, damn it, perhaps I should have insisted to see Raman straight away. Catch that one-eyed liar before he is having a chance to be taught his answer.

Change tactic, even now?

No – damn, damn, damn – he is beginning to answer. And this might be where he is slipping up. Listen. Concentrate.

'Oh, but, yes, Inspector, you do not expect me to remain captive in my own house all night?'

Never mind answering that sort of pleading. Ask a question myself. One with some dagger in it.

'So, sir, at what time precisely were you leaving?'

Short pause again. Another tiny drop of admission. But now...

'Really, Inspector, you are demanding too much. Who keeps time to that extent in our easy-going Banares? I can tell you the exact hour I leave the house every morning because I take a holy sunrise dip. But after that, who knows?'

Damn. Should never let him take the chance to dodge, and he has taken it. To the full. Sunrise dip. Holy Ganges. *I am a good man. How can you think I could ever stoop to murder?* All that stuff and nonsense.

Well, try to get back.

'Very well, sir. I am understanding it is not always possible to say to one minute where one is, especially after some days.'

Ha, yes. Fellow is relaxing. A little, little pause now. Yes. And pounce.

'But you can at least remember where you went.'

Yes. Got him. Hundred per cent confused.

But not for long. The brain must be working fast.

'But, yes, Inspector, I can easily remember what I did six days ago. We were then at the fourth Ram Lila night. I, of course, went out to Ramnagar to watch that play.'

Clever, clever devil. Something he would hardly be able to produce a witness to if he went on his own. No doubt a huge crowd there. Ram Lila just outside Banares is famous. Second only to Delhi itself. There would be onlookers by the thousand, by the lakh. And all taking place in darkness. For the fireworks that come after.

What night of the ten that the plays happen would this have been? What would have been enacted? Ask him. Catch him out? Not a chance. He will have seen them year after—

No, wait. Usha said he had not gone this year. Something they chit-chatted about.

But can I challenge him with her? Never. He will deny he was ever with her. He will say, if I tell him I saw him leave here and traced him to that house in Dal Mandi, I was altogether mistaken. That I followed someone else.

But all the same it is evidence once again. He was not in Banares that night. He was in Bombay. In Dadar.

He is leaning forward now, smiling. One damned oily smile.

'But, alas, Inspector, I can produce no witness. The Maharajah of Banares, of course, was there. He presides each night. But I do not think he saw myself.'

Smile at the joke? Laugh even? Never. Never.

'That is all very well, sir. But I want definite proof you were here in Banares and not flying to Bombay.'

Sharp frown on the wide brow under those greying curls of hair.

'Inspector, I tell you again. I very much resent your attitude. Wherever Vikram was, I was not with him. I cannot make myself clearer than that. Now, if you please, I have work to do.'

'No, sir. I have questions still to ask.'

'Inspector, I have told you where I was that evening. It is a matter of regret I did not happen to see anyone I know. And that this year I did not go to Ramnagar with a party of friends.'

As you could not have done, you liar. Because you were flying to Bombay. You were. You were. And somehow I will trick you into admitting.

'But, Inspector, as it is, you will have to take my word for it. As you should. I am not without a certain reputation for truth-telling. Even when truth-telling has kept me out of Government for many, many years.'

Try that, will you? The man of good deeds. No. The man of one evil, evil deed.

At him again. At him.

'Very well, sir, let us assume you have—' Make one small pause here, show I have not believed one word he has said – 'remembered correctly what you did that night. But the Ram Lila episodes do not last too long. So what were you doing after?'

Yes, that tiny eye-flick of dismay. Grabbing for one more lie.

Press hard. Press harder.

'Did you come home, sir? What time did you come home? To within one hour, let us say? I know you Banarasis do not go in for the clocks and the watches.'

But the smile back on those bloody orator's lips.

'No, Inspector, we do not consult our watches at each and every moment like you hustle-bustle Bombayites. And on the nights of the Ram Lila itself we are even worse.'

What is he going to try now? What of difference can Ram Lila nights make?

'Those plays are there, Inspector, to teach us. And I, for one, take what I have seen to heart. After the play that night I walked about asking and asking myself had I kept up to my resolutions to do good and to be good.'

Utter hypocrite.

Ah, but try this.

'Sir, while you were walking and pondering also did you perhaps stop and buy a paan? I am knowing you Banarasis are so much liking to munch your India-famed paans. Sir, you are one well-known figure in this city. Will some paanwalla have recognized?'

He is considering.

Will he fall for it? Is he thinking whether he knows some fellow he can bribe? Will he dare try that?

'Inspector, after watching that play I was altogether too concerned with the state of my soul to go buying paans.'

The state of your soul. Black, black, black. Too black to be washed white by all the water in Ganges itself.

'Then, sir, you were, after however much of pondering, you were returning at last here?'

Moment of caution. But answer coming quickly enough.

'Of course I came back home. What else should you think I would do? I came back. I went to my lonely bed. You know my wife was expiring some years past? And in the morning I rose up and went, as always, to Mother Ganga.'

Pleased enough with himself now. Must be damn sure none of that can be disproved against him. But keep trying.

'And you cannot say, at all, when it was you were returning here?'

He is even daring to laugh now.

'Not at all, Inspector. Not one least little bit.'

'But someone will have seen you come in, no? You have servants, isn't it?'

'All sound asleep by that time. Whenever it was.'

'You do not keep a watchman?'

'Why, yes I do. Or rather I did. A fellow by the name of Karim, something of a rogue. A Pathan. But, I am sorry to say, the fellow has vanished. Some articles missing. Nothing of value.'

Vanished. Or sent away? Could I get hold of this Pathan? This Karim?

'Vanished, sir? You mean he is absconding altogether?'

'Yes. Exactly, Inspector.'

'But you have an address for him in his native place? That is the procedure police are recommending to all with servants in Bombay.'

'But here, Inspector, with Nepal not so far distant there is no point in keeping such details.'

Check.

Some other way to force him finally into the corner? His link with Mrs Popatkar? I cannot at all see what it is. I cannot. And without it I will never be able to go to the Senior Superintendent, request full back-up for an arrest.

All right, he has denied knowing her at all. But I can anyhow ask once more. Better also make it easy for him to admit. Before he has grasped what it may mean.

'Mr Verma, you have stated you have never met Mrs Shoba Popatkar. But, if you would search your memory, I believe you must find some occasion. She came here, a ticket examiner was telling me, many times over the past years.'

'Inspector, how often must I repeat? When I make a statement I tell the truth. That and nothing more. It is my lifelong habit.'

'And you are telling the truth itself now when you are saying you have never, not once even, met Mrs Popatkar?'

And – what is this? – no immediate reply. No angry *Inspector, I have told you the truth. Why must you keep asking and asking?*

Now a sudden, sharp lurch forward in his chair. Cane-work creaking.

'Inspector, I have told you the truth itself. Why must you keep asking and asking?'

Well, there is the answer. Almost to the word as I had imagined. But why did it take so long to come? Why?

Cannot think of any possible reason. Checkmate now after all?

The slanting ray of green light, all dancing with motes,

had moved round a little with the slow-moving sun outside. But it was no less broad.

Checkmate? No, by God, I will not let it be. Think. Think.

Yes, one more move I can make. On same line – not very much of cunning – but all that is left to me. May threaten his raja. With some luck, just may.

'Mr Verma, the first time I came to see you it was to make one simple request. It was to take your permission, as chief trustee, to read the *Recollections* of the late Krishnan Kalgutkar.'

Blank face opposite. Heavy cheeks weighted with flabbiness.

But go on.

'Sir, I was informing you then I required to see the said *Recollections* in view of the fact that Mrs Popatkar had read same shortly before she was murdered. Mr Verma, I am now repeating that request.'

Sudden look of stony opposition. Enough. Enough to tell me, yes, that whatever refusal he will bluster out that last frail arrow I had, against all odds, has struck home.

For a tiny flash of time Inspector Ghote saw himself as wielding the bow of legendary Arjuna in the *Mahabharata*, victor at the great battle of Kurukshetra.

19

A bar of greenish light slanting in from one of the high ventilators, alive with twirling motes in the bright morning light, stretched like a barrier between them. It was a little after nine o'clock.

Too weak a barrier?

H. K. Verma wondered once again whether he could have refused to see the Bombay mongoose. There were too many gaping holes in his air-puffy defences. Too many questions he would find hard to answer. And, always at the back of his mind, there was the temptation. To surrender. There like a hanging cloud before the start of the monsoon, hovering, rain-thick.

Or, more, it seemed at moments like a bed. A bed ready waiting as, hammered down with fatigue, he approached. Softness, repose, comfort. How easy to fall down on to it. How easy not to go on fighting. To say suddenly, for no reason, *Inspector, I cannot keep on lying and lying. I am not the man to do it. Inspector, yes, I did kill Mrs Shoba Popatkar.*

But if I had refused to see him now, he thought, the fellow would probably have gone to the Senior Superintendent of Police and asked to have me arrested. They would not like to do that out there at Cornwallis Lines, but they might think they had no choice.

No, best to hear the worst.

And to fight. To fight and fight and fight. If it is only for time to decide where my life should go. Now that this has happened. Now I am a murderer.

'Sir,' the fellow was beginning now, 'I have come again because I am not one hundred per cent happy with what you were saying in this room itself yesterday.'

Rat. Rat. Rat. How dare he . . .

At once he could feel the rage making his face, his whole body, into one heat-frozen pillar of hatred. All the more icily bitter because what the rat had said was right. He should not have been happy with the lies I had to tell, the dodgings and evasions I had to make.

'Inspector,' he managed to bring out at last in answer, 'if you are happy or not happy, that is no concern of mine.'

Not the best thing to have said. It will just only antagonize the little rat even more. But all I could find to say.

'Oh, yes, sir. Excuse me, but it is your own answers I am doubting.'

And you think I also did not have doubts about those answers?

'I answered you, as I recall, with very great fullness.'

And I did. In the fullest truth I did. I put my case to this man. I made him my judge even. I touched his feet.

And what is he saying now?

'What you said gave me much to think. But, sir, speculations as to whether a murder can be a good deed are not my duty to consider.'

There. Not bending one inch towards me. Not for all his pretending, then or now. All his *gave me much to think* . . .

'It is just only for me to seek simple answers, yes or no, to simple questions.'

But, no. No. The answers cannot be simple. The questions I put up were not simple. Was I right when I choked the words in that woman's throat? I was. I was. How much harm, to so many, she would have brought. But also I was not in the right. No. Killing her. Taking her life.

'But what if there are no simple answers?'

All I can say. It is not much. But, to say all I would like, I would have to begin with a confession. A full confession to what I actually did. And, no, I cannot do it. Not now. Not just now.

'No, sir, there are things that are not at all matters for rumination and philosophizing.'

Wrong, Mr Inspector. Wrong. And you must know it. Always everything is a matter, not for the pointless *rumination and philosophizing* you are trying to make them out to be, but for weighing up. For weighing the right and the wrong. You know it. I know it. And I must be given time to make that weighing.

'To matters of fact just only one straight answer can be given.'

What is he saying? Oh, hopeless to try to convince the stupid donkey.

'So you say, Inspector. So you say.'

Drop it. Drop it. Let it go.

'Sir, I do say. Let me ask one such question only.'

Now it is coming. Now. And this one question may be the one that goes, like an arrow, through some thin place in the wall I have built round me. That weak wall of air only. An arrow going to the heart of it. To my heart.

But I will not make it easy for him. Not a word. Not a word in answer. Till I must.

'Sir, did you on the night of October the sixth travel to Bombay in a plane flown by your grandson, Mr Vikram Verma?'

Answer *Yes. Yes, I did*? Finish it now? Take rest? Let what will happen happen?

No. No, he will have to fight harder than that. He will have to fight me. Me. For my life itself.

'No, Inspector. No, I did not go to Bombay that night.'

There. It is told. The direct lie. I have done it. Myself, the man proud, yes, proud, always to have told the truth.

'Mr Verma, let me ask one more time. Did you fly to Bombay in a plane piloted by your grandson?'

He knows I am lying. He stands there in front of me and asks me, like a master at a school, to repeat to him what he knows I have got wrong. Just as Masterji, taunting, did to me in those days, and more than once. And I will have to do it. No matter what extra of punishment it will bring.

'No. No, Inspector, I did not.'

'No, sir? But let me remind you, Mr Vikram Verma has admitted he flew there.'

Ah, it is trying tricks now, is it? You have come down from Masterji to bully in the classroom when the lesson is over. Well, I can answer you now in the way you should be answered.

'And has he stated that I accompanied him?'

Now, will you lie to me? Will you go on with your too easy trick?

'No, sir. He would not say you were there also.'

So, no more trickery. Good. And keep to saying that, Vikram, my boy. Keep to it. Remember, I have lied for your sake. One flagrant lie. *Sixteen years of age.* So, lie now, and for ever. For me.

And let me lie, boldly and well, for him. For myself.

'Then, Inspector, you must take his word for it. And mine also. I did not go to Bombay. What makes you believe I did?'

Carry the fight into the enemy camp. Rush in with torches blazing. Let him see he is not the only one who can fight.

'Sir, I was unable to believe what Mr Vikram Verma was telling.'

So that is the best you can do? No, you are not being so clever, Mr Inspector. And I see you hesitating now. Thinking where you can possibly go, is it?

Very well. One blast from my gun.

'How dare you accuse a grandson of mine of lying and lying. I shall take this to the highest authorities.'

Yes, let it rip. Blast him to pieces only.

'Let me tell you, Inspector Ghote, I am not without friends at the Centre. At the top. The very top.'

Hah. Now we would see.

'Sir, you are welcome to go to whatsoever top you are wishing.'

No. No. I went too far. I have opened once more some wide gap for him to come through.

'Would you like to make some telephones now this instant?'

And he has the cheek only to look at my telephone there. To dare me to go to it. And he knows damn well I cannot. That if I were to try it even, I would be laying myself open to a hundred more difficulties in explaining to Jagmohan Nagpal. To whoever I could think of.

How I would like to take this rat and shake him to death. Yes, to death.

Now he is coming at me once more.

'Well then, sir, let me now ask this: where were you itself on October the sixth, from – shall I say? – the afternoon onwards?'

What to answer? What to answer? I was still, the day after I had heard from Srivastava, running round this way and that. To Vikram. To the Flying Club. To the bank for money. Just so as to get to Bombay before that woman's slow, slow train reached. And how can I say that?

Why, why, did I not take time to think? I should have guessed this question could come, even though I did not think the little rat would dare to put. I could have thought out some answer when he was saying only that he could not believe Vikram. He was hesitating then. Thinking. And I, too, could have been thinking.

But what can I say now? What?

'Inspector, this was some time ago. How can—'

'Sir, it was six days ago only.'

Damn it, he is right. Damn him, damn him.

'Yes. Yes, six days ago.'

Spin it out. And think. Think, think, think.

'Thank you for pointing it out, Inspector. It helps me to bring it back to mind.'

To bring back what? What, for God's sake? What?

'So, sir, where were you?'

Where? What can I say? Where could I have been that he cannot prove I was not?

'I was— Let me see . . .'

Ah. Yes. Yes, yes, yes.

'I was, of course, here. In the house.'

Yes, this will do. I believe I can get away with it.

'But it is my custom to work in this room and down in the office also. One or the other.'

Yes, yes. This is good. The right, right answer, surely. The proper way to do it.

'Impossible to say where at any one moment.'

'Very good. I am taking it there are people who could confirm same.'

Ah, yes. You are as much as saying you know this is something that can hardly be fully confirmed, one way or the other. I have hit on it. Definitely. The right answer.

'There are clerks in your office? Your peon?'

Raman? Yes, mongoose is getting near to one small weak place. That good-for-nothing, Raman. He would like to say whatever will please the policewalla. But, damn him, he will say whatever pleases me also. And in the end he is owing me more than he could ever owe anybody from the police. Bombay police especially.

But try to hide Raman somewhat if I can. One danger place.

'Yes, yes. I expect the clerks see me coming and going, though they may not know whether I was there on one day rather than the next.'

Enough? No, I see him ready to pounce on Raman. He will have seen what sort of a fellow he is. Give the mongoose that much of credit.

'Or I could call Raman some time later.'

Give him the idea that I know Raman is out, taking a message or getting me a paan to chew. Not very good. But perhaps it will do. So long as I can get to Raman first. I will need one word only. One look.

And it seems to be enough. He is not insisting on seeing Raman now at this moment.

'Then, sir, you were in the house. But for how long? Did you leave at all that day, just six days ago? You must be able to remember.'

Oh, yes, I can remember. I can remember every minute

of all that time, from the moment old Srivastava spoke those words, *Perhaps you are not knowing Mrs Popatkar. Sir, she is not a person it is possible to refuse*, to the moment my hands went round her throat.

But what to claim that I remem— Hah, got it. Got it. Got it.

'Oh, but, yes, Inspector, you do not expect me to remain captive in my own house all night?'

Yes, this will do excellently. Could not be better.

'So, sir, at what time precisely were you leaving?'

Ah, that is a little problem. The time I was leaving? When to say? Be careful. Tell him nothing that will allow him to trap me.

'Really, Inspector, you are demanding too much. Who keeps time to that extent in our easy-going Banares?'

Ah, yes, this is good. Remind the fellow where he is. In Banares. Where truth itself should reign.

'Yes, I can tell you the exact hour I leave the house every morning because I take a holy sunrise dip. But after that, who knows?'

Yes. Make him think. *Is this, after all, a man of truth, of right-doing? Perhaps he is not in the end a liar.*

'Very well, sir. I am understanding it is not always possible to say to one minute where one is, especially after some days.'

Yes. Plain to see. He is wavering. Doubting himself and that belief of his. Yes, I am coming out of it all now.

'But you can at least remember where you went.'

No. A leap like a panther.

But I am ready for him. Altogether ready.

'But, yes, Inspector, I can easily remember what I did six days ago. We were then at the fourth Ram Lila night. I, of course, went out to Ramnagar to watch that play.'

There. Try to catch me out in that. All the crowds out there at Ramnagar. A lakh of people, more. And in the darkness. How could anybody have seen me there? Or not seen me?

And if he tries asking what I was seeing, why I can

remember from last year that day in the cycle. Or from the same day the year before, and ten, twenty, thirty, forty years before that. Going with my father as a child hardly old enough to understand.

Yes, I begin to think I am at the end of it now. What a piece of luck to have found such an alibi. One he cannot disprove if he is questioning-questioning all the rest of the day.

In the darkness moving slowly towards home. Riding on my father's shoulders. My hands clutching the thick, oil-smelling hair of his head. And my mind full of the noble deeds of Rama. My soul flooded with the urge to be good. As good as the man Sage Narada described when the poet Valkmini asked, *O venerable rishi! Tell me is there a perfect man in this world who is virtuous, brave, dutiful, truthful, noble, kind to all beings?* To be as good, as brave as Rama himself.

Now. Shall I do it now? Be Rama. Throw away everything. Say at last, *Inspector, no, I cannot keep on lying and lying. Yes, I did kill Mrs Shoba Popatkar?*

But no. No, this is not that moment. Not when I am so much winning. Winning for myself what I most need. What I must have. Time. Time to decide what I will do, when I will do it.

So smile a little. Show confidence.

'But, alas, Inspector, I can produce no witness.'

Oh, and add to it. Shine with confidence. The confidence of a man who knows he has done no wrong.

'The Maharajah of Banares, of course, was there. He presides each night. But I do not think he saw myself.'

Will he smile at my joke? If he does, it will be a sign. A sign he cannot help believing, in spite of all, I am a good man. I am not possibly a murderer.

'That is all very well, sir.'

No, not a hint of smile.

'But I want definite proof you were here in Banares and not flying to Bombay.'

No. No, not the smallest going-back on what he so plainly believes.

'Inspector, I tell you again. I very much resent your attitude. Wherever Vikram was, I was not with him. I cannot make myself clearer than that. Now, if you please, I have work to do.'

But he will not go. The mongoose. I know it.

'No, sir. I have questions still to ask.'

Yes. And what questions? I should not have given myself even that one firefly glimmer of hope.

But try once more. Once more.

'Inspector, I have told you where I was that evening. It is a matter of regret I did not happen to see anyone I know. And that this year I did not go to Ramnagar with a party of friends.'

Thank goodness, I had not even arranged to do that. Because – and this hurts – because I thought in a few days I would be a Minister in Delhi itself and I should be careful what company I was keeping. But some use coming out of it. At least I have this alibi. And it will take more than a Bombay rat to break it.

'But, Inspector, as it is, you will have to take my word for it. As you should. I am not without a certain reputation for truth-telling. Even when truth-telling has kept me out of Government for many, many years.'

More bonus coming out of that act of treachery of Nagpal's. But I can see the mongoose glint in that man's eye there. Unchanged. Unchanging.

'Very well, sir, let us assume you have remembered correctly . . .'

What weight of mockery he put on that *remembered*. He might as well be pointing his finger and proclaiming me as a liar.

'. . . what you did that night. But the Ram Lila episodes do not last too long. So what were you doing after?'

What can I say? What is it likely I would have been doing? What would have kept me away from any witness?

'Did you come home, sir? What time did you come home? To within one hour, let us say? I know you Banarasis do not go in for the clocks and the watches.'

So now even he is accusing me because I am a Banarasi.

The little gnawing Bombay rat. Well, tell him. Give it to him, hot and strong.

'No, Inspector, we do not consult our watches at each and every moment like your hustle-bustle Bombayites. And on the nights of the Rama Lila itself we are even worse.'

Yes, keep to the Ram Lila. It is my certificate of goodness. If I can make him believe in my following Lord Rama's teachings. If I can lie enough, despite those teachings. Lie about doing right.

'Those plays are there, Inspector, to teach us. And I, for one, take what I have seen to heart. After the play that night I walked about asking and asking myself had I kept up to my resolutions to do good and to be good.'

And next year? Next year if I am here to see the play that night, what will I be able to say of the year past? That during it I committed one murder? That I told lie upon lie to stop myself being found out? That I contemplated having this little rat here made away with? Even that I was forced into making the most ridiculous false statement about the age of my own grandson?

But if I had not told these lies, told the lies I am telling even now, then I would not be here to see the Ram Lila once more. I would have been hanged as a murderer. Hanged outside of Holy Banares. With my next life destined to be as the lowest and vilest of the low.

No. I cannot endure that.

Lies it must be. Lies and lies and lies. Till at last lying saves me, the truth-telling man that used to be.

Oh, and are you coming at me again, sharp-toothed mongoose?

'Sir, while you were walking and pondering also did you perhaps stop and buy a paan? I am knowing you Banarasis are so much liking to munch your India-famed paans...'

What is he saying? What is this-all about paans? Am I going mad? Has he driven me mad with his questions-this and his questions-that?

188

But listen to him. Listen. Beware of some trap, even in paans. *India-famed paans.* He is trying something with his flatteries.

'. . . Sir, you are one well-known figure in this city. Will some paanwalla have recognized?'

Ah, does he hope I will find some paanwalla, bribe him? And then does he think he could break the fellow down? Well, I am not so easy to catch, Mr Inspector.

'Inspector, after watching that play I was altogether too concerned with the state of my soul to go buying paans.'

Oh, I am too old to be caught by such a schoolboy trap. You must do better than that, my fine inspector.

'Then, sir, after however much of pondering, you were returning at last here?'

Quickly, think. No, must be safe to say I came back here. But keep it vague. Vague.

'Of course I came back home. What else should you think I would do? I came back. I went to my lonely bed. You know my wife was expiring some years past? And in the morning I rose up and went, as always, to Mother Ganga.'

Who has lost the power to bring me, cleansed of sin, to the new day. Yes, admit that.

But not to him. Not to that rat. For him the look of calm and confidence. As if I had indeed just stepped from Ganga Ma, renewed.

'And you cannot say, at all, when it was you were returning here?'

The best you can do, little mongoose? You are losing the scent itself.

'Not at all, Inspector. Not one least little bit.'

'But someone will have seen you come in, no? You have servants, isn't it?'

Yes. And, thank God, they go to bed early. I can speak the plain truth here.

'All sound asleep by that time. Whenever it was.'

Unless one of them was up, knew I was not in my bed. But they cannot have done. They would not dare come into my room. No. No, I am safe here. Safe.

So where will he go poking-poking next? Or is it over? No, do not hope. Wait. Be ready.

'You do not keep a watchman?'

Ha. Karim. So, thank goodness, I was getting rid of him. They will never find him now, not however far they are looking.

'Why, yes, I do. Or rather I did. A fellow by the name of Karim, something of a rogue. A Pathan. But, I am sorry to say, the fellow has vanished. Some articles missing. Nothing of value.'

That should do it altogether nicely. Tie up the whole business. No ends left to be picked at.

'Vanished, sir? You mean he is absconding altogether?'

'Yes. Exactly, Inspector.'

How right I was to chase that blackmailer out. And no sign of him since. You will not get anywhere in this line, mongoose.

'But you have an address for him in his native place? That is the procedure police are recommending to all with servants in Bombay.'

This will get you nowhere, my little friend. Nowhere at all. Why don't you go home to your Bombay and its procedures-procedures?

'But here, Inspector, with Nepal not so far distant there is no point in keeping such details.'

So your way blocked, I think, my friend. Gaps in the defences filled. If only with more and more puffings of airy lies.

But he is going to try something more, I see. Well, try. Try, little mongoose.

'Mr Verma, you have stated you have never met Mrs Shoba Popatkar.'

Well, he has chosen a good place. Give him that. If there is anywhere I am truly weak, it is with her. If Srivastava should ever tell him that when I telephoned he reported to me that she had read the *Recollections* and that at once I was furious, then he will begin to guess perhaps why I— Why I had to do what I did. Perhaps then he would be able to go to the High Court, or to somewhere, and get legal permission for the hundred-and-one year ban to be broken.

Thank God, he has no idea that it was I myself who was imposing that.

'But, if you would search your memory, I believe you must find some occasion when you were meeting her. She came here, so a ticket examiner was telling me, many times over the past years.'

Hah. On the wrong trail now, mongoose. Sniff, sniff, sniff.

'Inspector, how many times must I repeat? When I make a statement I tell the truth. That and nothing more. It is my lifelong habit.'

Cannot tell him that too often. Why cannot he believe it? And get out of here?

'And now when you are saying you have never, not once even, met Mrs Popatkar you are telling the truth itself?'

Oh, you have struck hard there. You may have been repeating only one damn question, but you have showed me to myself. *I tell the truth. That and nothing more. It is my lifelong habit.* It was my habit. Once. Or almost my habit. I did try. I wanted to be a truth-teller. And I was. I was. For the greater part. Yes. For the greater part I was.

But now . . . Now I must give out one full lie. About the truth itself.

Lean towards him. Put as much of force into it as I can.

'Inspector, I have told you the truth itself. Why must you keep asking and asking?'

Is it enough? Have I done it? Will he leave me alone now at last?

No. He is thinking. I can see it. What is he going to find to ask now? Something new altogether?

'Mr Verma, the first time I came to see you it was to make one simple request.'

What is this? He came to ask to go through the *Recollections*. He cannot have learnt now what is in them. Have come to know why I dare not let them be read. Why I had to stop Mrs Popatkar telling the world KK had ceased to believe all his party still stands for.

This is the worst I had to fear. The very worst. And, now when I had begun to think it was all over, it has come.

What is he going to say? Listen. Listen.

'It was to take your permission, as chief trustee, to read the *Recollections* of the late Krishnan Kalgutkar.'

Go on. Go on, damn you. Come out with what you know. What you have known all along. If it can be.

No. No, no, no. That cannot be. He cannot have found out. He cannot.

'Sir, I was informing you then I required to see the said *Recollections* in view of the fact that Mrs Popatkar had read same shortly before she was murdered. Mr Verma, I am now repeating that request.'

Nothing.

I feel nothing. I have nothing to say. There is nothing for me to do any more now.

I suppose I must answer. Somehow. Say something. Say, *Read then, read. Find out everything. Arrest me. Take me out of Holy Banares. Hang me. Condemn me to a hundred thousand more lives to be lived*? Or say No? No, you may not see those *Recollections*?

And what will he do then? He will only get permission some other way.

'Inspector Ghote, I must tell you again. A ban is a ban. No one can read those *Recollections* for one hundred and one years. No one. No one.'

But— But, yes, there is a chance for me here. A tiny chance. I send him packing now, and then, fast as I can go, to Srivastava's library. Get hold of the *Recollections*. Burn them. Destroy them. Then let them suspect whatsoever they like. They will not have proof.

Yes. Yes, that is the thing to do.

20

Just only one thing more to do, Ghote thought. Since I did not get the confession I was hoping for I must find one thing more to go with to the Senior Superintendent and make out a hundred per cent good case for an arrest.

And that must lie in those *Recollections*. So, to the BHU and Mr Srivastava. Persuade him just to let me look. A matter of perhaps one hour only. Or should I march in like Mrs Popatkar herself and demand to see? I could do that. Mr Srivastava is not the fellow to oppose me with fisticuffs if I am seizing whatever keys he has. But . . .

But I would not like it to come to that.

And, if it did, there would still be problems. How would what I did affect the case when it is coming to court?

No, better to try first the soft approach. And – yes – it would be a damn good thing to have Mishra by my side. He would know some Banarasi way perhaps to get round Srivastava. Or to persuade him to turn a Nelson's eye to what I am doing.

H. K. Verma did not leave it long after the Bombay inspector had left. He gave him just enough time to get clear of the immediate area – *I would not put it past that mongoose to follow me* – and then he heaved himself from his big chair, padded into his bedroom, took the matches – Cheetah Fight brand – that always stood by a candle there in case of a power cut, picked his stoutest pair of chappals from the almirah and set out.

He found he was possessed of a sense of burning urgency. No need for it, he kept telling himself. Why should that Bombay rat go out to Srivastava at this very moment? As likely as not the fellow would not even try to see the *Recollections* at all. He would feel the one-hundred-and-one years ban is not so easily got past. Oh yes, he could try to get legal permission to break the trust. But that would take him months. Even years. So no danger there.

Yet he could not stop himself counting every second.

Hurrying and pushing through the narrow galli leading from the house. Thrusting aside pilgrims, their faces dazed with bliss. Barging past the less holy, making Banares one stop on a sight-seeing visit to north India, wide-eyed, looking this way and that, pointing out the most ridiculous things to one another – 'Look, that painter is putting an elephant on the wall there', 'Yes, look, Maharajah himself in the howdah' – kicking a goat out of his path, almost knocking down a man strolling towards him reading a newspaper, its pages held wide. Pushing on, pressing on.

On along Bengali Tola where already down at the ghat the dhobis must be busy slapping and slapping at the garments they were washing.

Push on. Press on.

And at last a taxi.

Shout out. Catch the taxiwalla's eye.

Yes, thank Bhagwan. He has seen me.

'To the BHU.'

'Ji haan, sahib. Ninversity.'

'Yes, yes. But BHU, mind. I do not want to find myself at Sanskrit University.'

'Nai, nai. BHU.'

But the traffic was appalling. Every few yards, it seemed, they were brought to a halt.

A handcart loaded with baskets of flowers had some-how been tipped over. The baskets had rolled all over the roadway. Tight-crammed marigolds still in place, circles of blazing orange. Looser flowers blowing to and fro, brilliant red and pink petals everywhere. And the man taking them to the flower market at the Chowk running here and there, wailing in despair, stopping to dab up a handful, running back to his cart trying to heave it upright once more, running out again to snatch at another tumbling ball of brilliant petals.

H. K. Verma sat fuming. Should he at least get out of the taxi and push a ten-rupee note into the man's hand? An act of charity.

'Drive on, drive on,' he shouted to the taxiwalla. 'Go past those people. Get up on the pavement.'

'I am going as fast as I can, sahib. Will the world end in ten minutes only?'

'Drive on, I say.'

And at last they got going again.

Soon to be stopped by a long camel train, paying no attention to any other traffic, the tall, swollen-bellied animals, with their burdens swinging down at either side, indifferent to whether they were moving flat-footed over the sands of Rajasthan or working their way along a Banares road. And then, as indifferent, it was a 'rolling' sadhu, making his way to some sacred destination, some particular one among the city's two thousand temples fixed on weeks or months ago as the only right aim in life. Painfully slowly he measured his length on the dusty roadway, got to his feet, carefully stood exactly at the point his hands had reached, lay down again, scrabbling a mark on the road surface with his fingers, got to his feet once more.

But too holy a man for any taxi driver to pass, unable as he was to make a wide enough detour.

'Go on, man. Go on.'

'Sahib, I cannot.'

'Yes, you can. Go past him. You need not touch one hair of his head.'

'Sahib, no.'

'Five rupees if you start this second.'

'Oh, sahib, how cruel you are to a poor man.'

'Go. Go.'

And they went.

Did one of the wheels run over that hand, flat there on the road?

H. K. Verma refused to let himself think about the tiny bump he thought he had noticed. It might have been anything, he told himself. Anything. A stone. A stick. A piece of jackfruit husk. Anything.

Well, I could come back this way, see if he is still making his way along. Look at his hand. Do the needful.

Another halt.

He peered ahead to see what the trouble was. A big, shiny tourist bus, *Super De Luxe Colour Video* boldly on its side, white faces under a variety of bright cotton hats at every big glinting window. It was manoeuvring with difficulty into the narrower road leading down to the Harishchandra burning ghat where the guide would, no doubt, tell the story of how Raja Harishchandra, lover of truth to the very core, in order to keep to his vow had beggared himself to the point of having to act as a funeral-pyre attendant.

What for do tourists like that want to come here? What of benefit to their souls, if they have them, can there be in Banares? They are wishing to stare and smear only. To make fun even of our Hindu legends and customs. *You know they burn your body when you're dead? And they put corpses in the Ganges. Total pollution.* No. No, I must not be bitter. They do have souls. They may not be Hindus, but they are men and women. They are capable of leading good lives. They need whatsoever of help they can get to do so. And if the sights of Holy Banares are assisting them, let them take the help.

At last, after three or four more manoeuvrings back and forth the glittering bus disappeared. *Horn Please* painted in elaborate multi-coloured letters under its big rounded back window.

They advanced a little further. But the tangle of traffic caused by the tourist bus, jammed trucks, cars, autorickshaws, scooters, cycles – each and every one hooting and ringing, ringing and hooting – had extended for a quarter of a mile or more beyond. All too soon they were forced to a halt once more.

He managed now to contain his fury. No use shouting at this fellow driving. He has done his best. It is his duty to push his vehicle along as fast as it is proper to take it, and that duty he has done.

Nevertheless he could not prevent himself sending rage-hot glances out at the houses and shops to either side.

The *Be Good and Do Good Typing And Xerox Centre*. Two typists in its open front, heads down, pounding away at their big old machines. Their duty to type. *Cute and Crisp Copies in Secs*. Good work.

But . . . Be good? Do good? Had he himself done what was his duty?

Perhaps, after all, he had. After all. If it had been his duty to become Minister for Social Upliftment . . . If that was what this life of his had been destined for at the last . . . And, then, Mrs Shoba Popatkar with her obsession with the mere telling of the truth, with her wholly self-centred passion, had stood in the way. So, if that was right – if it was – it was the good thing he had done. The good action.

No fault of his, in that case, if the jockeyings of Delhi politics had prevented him becoming Minister. That can have had no bearing on what had happened.

But was that what had happened? Or had he simply given way to rage then? As just now he had done in telling this fellow here at the wheel to drive over that rolling sadhu? If it was his hand they had driven over . . .

Ah, moving again at last.

And now Asi Road straight ahead. In a minute or two, surely, they would come to the bridge across the little River Asi just before it joined with the Ganges. And then it would not be so long till they reached the BHU campus, just over the Panchkroshi Road. And once inside the campus with its radiating semi-circle of clear wide roads it would take no time at all to reach the library, Mr Srivastava and the *Recollections*.

Ghote hammered on Inspector Mishra's door. What if he had already left for the Sandbank?

For some reason, for no reason, he had abruptly been overwhelmed by a notion that he had to get to Mr Srivastava's library with all possible speed. He had tried to fight the feeling down. Such causeless hurry-scurry was not the right way to go about any investigation. What would the great Dr Hans Gross, author of the famous *Criminal Investigation*, his guide for years past, have said?

But it was with a surge of joyous relief that, when the door was opened, he saw Mishra.

'Ah, Inspector Ghote. Today I have already dealt with the matter of my natural functions.'

He grinned.

Ghote grinned back.

He would have liked to have asked after little featherlight, chatter-box Rukmini. But the inner urgency was too strong.

'Please,' he burst out, 'I am wanting your help at the library of Mr Srivastava at the BHU. Can you come at once? I have a taxi waiting only.'

'Yes, yes. Why not? Sandbank would still be there.'

Restraining himself with difficulty, he allowed Mishra to call out to his daughter-in-law to say where he was going. Getting back into the taxi he shouted, 'To the BHU, fast as you can.'

'One moment,' Mishra broke in. 'Bhai sahib, go round by parts of the Panchkroshi Road.'

'Sahib, it would be longer-longer.'

'But quicker also.'

Mishra turned to Ghote.

'Altogether less of traffic. Take my word. If there is truly so much of hurry.'

'Yes, yes, there is. Panchkroshi Road, driver.'

The way Mishra had chosen was a great deal less traffic-thick than the road leading to Dal Mandi where his eager autorickshaw walla had followed H. K. Verma. But it was clearly a long way round. In places, too, it became scarcely more than a dusty track. And the tourist-guide commentary Mishra at once embarked on soon became intolerably irksome, however much he told himself it could not in fact be delaying them.

'Yes, Inspector, the Panchkroshi Road is the route taken over perhaps two thousand years by pilgrims in Banares, though of course, you understand, we are now going over just only some parts of it, and in the opposite direction from the pilgrimage itself, as laid down. In ancient days, so it is said, they took a string and set one end at the Mahakaleshvara Temple, then the centremost point of Banares, and drew a circle. Everything within that circle, on this side of Mother Ganga, constitutes Holy Kashi. And the circumference of that circle, which has a radius of five kroshis, is the Panchkroshi pilgrimage, though of course the road no more takes an exact circle. Do you know that the kroshi, the Sanskrit measure of distance, is about two miles in length?'

Two miles, Ghote thought. And *panch*, five, kroshas. So a ten-mile radius. How long does that mean this Panchkroshi Road is? Even if we are going along only part of it? It will take us altogether too long.

'There are no fewer than one hundred and eight stopping places for a pilgrim on the route,' Mishra continued with happy implacability. 'They include Shiva temples, Devi temples as well as numerous shrines of Ganesh, of lesser gods and of bhairavas, those figures of terror such as Dandapani, the god I was calling as the Police Officer of Kashi when we were in the Vishvanatha Lane running after that junky fellow.'

He broke off.

'By the way did you catch sight of the chap ever?'

Ghote felt himself in a dilemma. If he told Mishra he had been accosted by Rick that night near the Hotel

Relax he would have to go on to say he had gone to the Manikarnika Ghat at midnight, and without taking this Banares-knowing colleague with him. It would give Mishra good reason to feel slighted. On the other hand, perhaps he ought to confide in a fellow officer, even if retired, who was also on the case. Neither course seemed altogether right.

He snatched at the sight of an autorickshaw going towards the city on a main road crossing their path. Tied to its flimsy roof was a long stretcher, with on it under a white shroud a corpse.

'Look at that. Tell me, do bodies sometimes fall off? That rickshaw walla was going at a fine rate.'

'Yes, yes, it happens,' Mishra said, in quick dismissal. 'But I was telling you about this Panchkroshi pilgrimage.'

'Yes, yes. Kindly go on.'

But speed it up: that will somehow speed up the journey.

'Rightly seen,' Mishra said, eagerly taking up the invitation, half-hearted as it must have sounded, 'Holy Kashi is a well-laid out mandala, with each of its temples having its proper place in the radius of five kroshas. Of course, you cannot see this nowadays, and perhaps it was never so except in the theory. Nowadays, as you must have found, Banares is one fearful jumble only. But kindly remember what it ought to be.'

But Ghote was in no mood to remember any such thing.

What if H. K. Verma, he thought with thudding impatience, takes it into his head just now to warn Mr Srivastava on no account to let me see the *Recollections*.

'Look, look,' Mishra said urgently. 'Look, that temple there, to the right. That is Kapiladhara, the building near by is the last of the four dharmashalas on the route. It is where the pilgrims to spend the last night. The pilgrimage is taking five days, you know. The pilgrims must set out very much before dawn each day, and they must reach the halting place by midday.'

Why *must*, Ghote wondered. Banares seemed netted

down with thousands of sets of rules that had to be obeyed. One only way to do everything. If it is not these pilgrims having to start so early just to finish by noon itself, it is the pandas down by the Ganges giving it left and right to anyone sitting before them. *Put a flower in the pot. Rub in a circle. Sprinkle Ganga water.* On and on. Do this, do that. Do not do this, do not do that.

'But, of course,' Mishra went on, apparently oblivious of how little progress they seemed to be making, 'you do not need to make this pilgrimage to gain the blessings that accompany it. You may go also to the Panchkroshi Temple where there are one hundred and eight carvings on the walls, each one representing a station on this road. If you stop at each of those it is the same as coming round by the road here.'

'Oh, yes,' Ghote said.

Another widow, he thought, staring at a party of trudging pilgrims with an old, old, bent-backed woman hobbling along on her staff in the rear.

How much longer would they be?

'Now,' Mishra was churning on, 'have you heard the story of Mandapa, the wild and wicked, and how he by chance made this pilgrimage?'

'No, I have not heard,' Ghote answered, scarcely listening.

But at once he realized he had heard the story. The unstoppably talkative sannyasin at the Manikarnika Ghat had recounted it, in full detail. Tell Mishra? It would save him from another recital. But it would mean, too, admitting he had gone to the ghat, saying why he had, saying how he had met Rick there at midnight and how, in a manner he was a little ashamed of, he had got more information out of the boy.

He held his tongue.

Mishra embarked on the story. Once more Ghote heard how Mandapa had been so wicked as to drink liquor, how his father had disowned him, how he had cheated his friends over what they had stolen, how he had been beaten up after leaving the prostitute's house. Was that at Dal Mandi? Was that quarter just the same all those years ago? In Banares nothing was more likely. Till at last Mishra reached the moment where the wicked youth, recovering on the bank of the River Asi, joined the pilgrimage along the Panchkroshi Road and became totally good.

But when would they themselves get to the Asi? And the BHU lying just beyond?

21

H. K. Verma found Mr Srivastava sitting at his battered old table, carefully altering an entry in a huge, handwritten ledger, face intent, spectacles slipping down his thin nose.

The old man half-rose from his chair.

'It is Mr Verma. Sir, this is an honour. We do not often have distinguished visitors. Or, to tell the truth, any visitor whatsoever. Nobody, in fact, since that police officer from Bombay I had to send to you when he was asking to examine the *Recollections* of the late Shri Krishnan Kalgutkar.'

'Which I also wish to examine now.'

Mr Srivastava looked up, his face stamped with complete dismay.

'To examine? The *Recollections*?'

'Yes, yes. Why else should I have come?'

'I— I do not know.'

Mr Srivastava seemed to be puzzling over his question, endlessly.

'Well? Are you going to find them for me?'

The Adam's-apple in Mr Srivastava's stringy neck moved up and down. Once.

'Well?'

'But, Mr Verma, you must surely know that is impossible.'

'Impossible? What are you saying? Am I not the chief trustee? Was I not the person responsible for depositing the *Recollections* under your care when the late Krishnan Kalgutkar was taking sannyas?'

Mr Srivastava nodded quavering agreement, but produced no reply.

'So, if I am the chief trustee, do I not have the full right to examine the *Recollections*?'

'Sir . . . Mr Verma, you know the fact of the matter is that no one has a right to see the *Recollections*. That was the condition made, passed on to me by you yourself, sir, when the papers were deposited here. Under a ban of one hundred and one years.'

'But it was I myself—' He bit back the *you fool* he had been on the verge of adding. 'I myself who made that stipulation. I must have the right to override it.'

Mr Srivastava considered.

'Of course, Mr Verma, I was not at all understanding at the time the *Recollections* were placed under my care that it was you who had imposed the one-hundred-and-one year ban yourself.'

He looked up once more.

'However,' he said, 'I cannot consider that this fact may alter the situation. A ban was imposed. A ban stating that no one was to see the *Recollections*. I do not believe I am entitled to make any exception.'

H. K. Verma felt the rage swelling up inside him till it was almost cracking open his whole body.

'But— But, you fool, you were allowing that woman Mrs Shoba Popatkar full access. Full access. So why in God's name are you refusing it to me?'

'But— Oh, sir . . . Mr Verma. But Mrs Popatkar I was not able to prevent. I was explaining per telephone. She is not a person it is possible to prevent.'

'And am I any different? Let me see those *Recollections* this instant.'

'No, sir. No. I have been deficient in my duty once. I will not be so again.'

'Let me see the *Recollections*.'

He thrust his face into the old librarian's.

Inside, frustrated anger boiled and bubbled. So near. So near. Almost with the damned *Recollections* in his hand. Almost able to take the Cheetah Fight matches from his pocket, strike one, put the flame to the corner of the thick wad of paper. And burn it. Burn every damn word of it. Burn away the truth. That truth that could finish him.

Barely six inches away, Mr Srivastava's face was shiny now with sweat. Shiny forehead. Shiny, drawn cheeks. Shiny nose, thin and twitching just noticeably at one side, spectacles canting over. Shiny chin. Mouth, hanging open. Teeth, old, loose-looking. Breath smelling of cardomum.

'Where are they itself? Where? Where?'

'They are under lock and key. After what Mrs Popatkar was doing I felt it my duty to take such security measures as were appropriate.'

But the old man had been unable to prevent himself giving one quick sideways glance towards a tall green metal filing cabinet.

So they are there. Almost under my hand. Key. There must be a key to that cabinet. Where will he have it? In one of the pockets of his kurta. Must be. On some key-bunch? Yes. That must be it. So what to do? Take hold of him? Pull him up to his feet? Push my hand into his pockets? I could. I could. Or will it be enough just only to demand?

'Give me the key to that cabinet. Now. This instant.'

'No.'

It was a squawk. Like a kicked cat only.

'Give it to me.'

'No. No, it is my duty. It is what I have to do. The right course. Correct. Correct procedure.'

'Give me that key.'

'No, Mr Verma. No, sir.'

The old man put both his hands flat on the table.

'Mr Verma.' His voice was strained with the burden of what he must be feeling. 'Mr Verma, I do not know why it is that we are born – we are all born – with this need to do the right thing deeply implanted within us. But we are so born. We are.'

He looked up again.

'I know what it is right for me to do now, and I will do it. I cannot do anything else without being false to what in the core of my heart I feel to be the one and only right thing.'

The words struck home. He stepped back. Almost staggered back.

'But what exactly do you want from Mr Srivastava?' Mishra said, abandoning at last his interminable history lesson.

Ghote, not knowing where they were, felt a little jump of pleasure. If the Banarasi had begun to think what the object of their dash to the BHU might be, they could not be too far away.

'It is this,' he answered. 'It is this. I cannot think of any reason why some person—' He baulked at saying H. K. Verma. 'Why some person should have come to Bombay from Banares and murdered Mrs Shoba Popatkar unless it was because of what she had done here in the city itself on that one day she was here. And what she was doing, all that she was doing, was to go through the *Recollections* of Krishnan Kalgutkar. So, unless I can go through them also, I will not know what possible motive that murderer could have. But when I do know, I will be able to chargesheet that fellow straightaway.'

Mishra gave him a sharp glance.

'So you are knowing who it is?'

Damn. Did not mean to let that out. However . . .

'Yes. Yes, I am knowing. Almost to a certainty. But I must find out why he was needing to kill Mrs Popatkar. What there is in those *Recollections* that is so dangerous for him.'

'Yes, I see. But what are you going to do? The *Recollections*, you were telling me, are under a one-hundred-and-one year ban.'

'I know. But that is why I was asking you to come with me to the BHU. I am going to persuade that fellow Srivastava to let me see them. Somehow. Perhaps I have only to demand. But, if he is making difficulties, as I suspect he will, then I am counting on you to get round him. At least to persuade him to turn the Nelson's eye.'

He looked over at Mishra.

Mishra did not look at all happy.

'Yes, Srivastava sahib, you are quite right,' H. K. Verma said. 'You must forgive me. I was altogether in the wrong.'

He smiled down at the old librarian.

Smile of cunning, he asked himself. Or smile of truth? A question he found he could not answer.

'Let me explain. You know, of course, that Mrs Popatkar was murdered in Bombay almost as soon as she had reached home after leaving here. After leaving you here itself, having read the *Recollections*.'

Mr Srivastava straightened himself up, pulled a handkerchief from the sleeve of his kurta, dabbed at his forehead, his cheeks, his mouth.

'Yes, that Bombay inspector was telling me.'

'Of course, of course. But do you know what he was saying to me also? It seems police inquiries down there elicited the fact that some Banarasi fellow near where Mrs Popatkar has her home was asked by a stranger, whose Bhojpuri Hindi he later recognized, the way to her flat. Now, at the time I paid little attention to that. But I have subsequently come to give it some thought. One wants, of course, the perpetrator of such a brutal killing to be brought to justice. If at all possible. Now, it seems to me that some indication of who that Bhojpuri-speaking fellow must be could lie in the *Recollections*.'

He paused, looking to see whether Mr Srivastava had followed.

'Why, yes, Verma sahib. I am not at all an expert in detective work, but that appears to me to be not unlikely.'

'So now you see, my dear Srivastava, why it is important that I see the *Recollections*.'

But that conclusion plainly came as a surprise to the librarian.

He blinked rapidly, adjusted his spectacles, looked

down at the ledger still open in front of him.

Did he expect to find the right answer there among those meticulous pages?

'Yes, yes. I understand all that. However, I am not sure that in any circumstances—'

He must cut in quickly as he could.

'No, no, my dear fellow, I would not for one moment suggest you should be derelict in your duty. Not for one moment. On the other hand, however, you must see it can only be to the good that the *Recollections* are examined.'

'Well . . .'

'Now, it seems to me there is one way out of the dilemma which unfortunately I have had to place you in. I believe, you know, that there is a right way through any of life's thickets, if we only look hard enough— No, work hard enough. If only we work hard enough to find it.'

'Yes . . .'

He let the tension drain away from his whole hot body.

'Suppose, my dear fellow, you are needing to answer a call of nature?'

'But I am not. I—'

'No, no, you misunderstand. Let us merely suppose such to be the case. And let us also suppose that you find keeping a heavy key-bunch in your pocket somewhat irksome. So what could be more natural, more right even, but that you should place the key-bunch on your table while you were out of the room? Out of the room for barely two or three minutes?'

'We are nearly there?' Ghote asked.

'Yes, yes. Five minutes only. Or ten. We are now in University Road itself. You can see the BHU campus to your right, and just here the Panchkroshi Road rejoins once again. So we are really on that pilgrimage once more. But in reverse direction.'

Mishra smiled happily at the notion.

'Then why ten minutes more?'

'Oh, it may not be so long. We have only to go round

208

as far as the BHU gate, and then there is usually not much traffic inside the campus.'

Ghote looked at the long wall of the university. What a huge place it was. What a seat of learning. What a triumph. Into his mind there flicked one of the innumerable pieces of information Mishra had tumbled out on to him. Pandit Malaviya, the founder of the BHU, and how he had refused to enter the safety of Holy Kashi at the end of his days because he wanted another life to go on with his work.

And he himself? Would he like another life as a CID-walla? Yes. Yes, perhaps he would. Better anyhow than coming back as a buffalo, or worse.

'Inspector,' Mishra said abruptly.

'Yes?'

'Inspector, you know, I do not altogether see how I can persuade that fellow Srivastava to turn the Nelson's eye. I suppose you Bombay CID chaps are different. But I was never liking to employ trickery in my work. It is somehow not right.'

Ghote sat straighter.

Was he being judged? Being found wanting?

'But if the object is right, you should not have too much of scruple,' he answered, with more firmness than he felt.

Mishra gave him a look of mournful unhappiness.

'Well, I suppose . . . If it is right . . .'

H. K. Verma snatched up the keys almost before Mr Srivastava had closed the door behind him.

Damn the fellow. Just leaving the bunch where he was dropping it. No indication which key to use.

What seemed like minutes of fumbling. Then at last the smallest key slid into the little round lock.

He twisted it back.

Immovable.

He pulled the key out, compared it to the others. No, none quite as small.

He thrust it back into the lock. Not the least resistance.

It must be the one. It must.

He wriggled it furiously. And suddenly, twisting it forwards, he heard the tumblers click round.

He had locked it. Locked it. The damn cabinet had been open all along.

Unlock it. One turn of the key. Tug out the top drawer.

And there. There it was. In the drawer, empty of all other documents. The thick bundle of paper fastened together with two long brass paperclips. A sheet of buff card on top with, in large sprawling capitals slanting slightly to the right, the one word.

Recollections.

A match to it now? No, no. Srivastava will be back at any second. Say two–three minutes to that fellow, and not one second more than three minutes it would be.

He pushed the thick wad up under his kurta, gripped it with his arm, wondered for a moment whether the sweat in his armpit would do it harm, thought how ridiculous that was.

And at a waddling run left the room.

What will Srivastava think when he returns and finds no one, the keys dangling in the cabinet, the *Recollections* gone? Never mind what Srivastava thinks. Too late for any objections from him now. Let him keep his mouth shut. He will not dare do anything else.

But the thing is I have got them. The *Recollections*. And in just a few minutes, as soon as I can find some quiet corner, they will be no more than one heap of charred paper. That admission of despair KK was making will never be known to anyone.

There will be no hint of what motive I had to kill Mrs Popatkar. Oh, yes, little Bombay mongoose will have his suspicions. But now he will be able to do nothing. Nothing.

And I have gained time. Time to look at myself. Time to ask am I a justified murderer, or not? Time to decide. And then to act. To take whatever path I know to be right. To the end. Whatever end it may be.

22

'Stop!'

The shout, almost a scream, burst from Ghote's lips. Their taxi came to a slewing, side-skidding halt.

Within a foot of its front wheels the overturned motorcycle lay on its side. Its engine still wildly racketed. Its rear wheel spun furiously. The youngster who had been riding it, and had moments before overtaken them at full speed, had been flung right across the road when his machine had collided with the man in its path. He was, however, already scrambling to his feet, apparently hardly injured. But the man lay now an inert, blood-pumping mass in the roadway.

'Mishra, look, look,' Ghote jabbered out, heart still racing. 'Look who it is. It is H. K. Verma himself. It is him.'

He pushed open the taxi door, tumbled out.

There had been a number of spectators of the accident, people who had been waiting to cross the road. Already half a dozen of them were crowding round the injured man. As many again, Ghote took in, had decided their duty lay in running over to the young motor-cycle rider to shower him with abuse.

While he and Mishra hovered, looking to see what help they could provide, the men round H. K. Verma began to hoist him up.

'Hospital,' an old gentleman waving a badly furled black umbrella cackled out. 'Hospital is just only here. What a mercy of God.'

The men who had lifted H. K. Verma turned in the direction of the great bulk of the BHU Hospital and set off with their heavy burden, dipping and ducking awkwardly.

Ghote, starting to follow beside Mishra, saw that H. K. Verma was at least still alive. Blood was dripping on to the dusty ground below as he was carried along. But it seemed to be pumping out at a horrible rate, and the chances of survival looked appallingly slim.

Then he glimpsed something out the corner of his eye, lying a few inches inside the road. He turned back without quite knowing why, thinking vaguely that the road must often be very busy and the object might be run over. In a moment he saw what it was. A thick bundle of papers, bound up together. He darted over, picked it up, read the single word on the buff outer cover.

Recollections.

In sudden understanding he smiled to himself, turned back, caught up with Mishra. The old man with the black umbrella came skittering along beside them.

'What a mercy of God, what a mercy of God,' he kept repeating. 'BHU Hospital, best in all India. BHU Hospital, the best, the very best.'

Then, suddenly, his high cacklings seemed to penetrate to the inert bulk being lugged towards the hospital.

'Hospital,' Ghote heard H. K. Verma pronounce in a deep interior groan.

Perhaps, he thought in a lightning-flash of hope, forgetting everything he knew about the man, he will survive after all.

'BHU,' H. K. Verma uttered then in a muffled, wild-sounding shout. 'No. No.'

With a tremendous roll of his bulky body, he tipped himself out of the hands of the men carrying him and stood swaying as if storm-rocked.

He turned at last in the direction they had come from and began a lunging, staggering walk back towards the road.

'Kashi, Kashi, Kashi,' he seemed to vomit out with each lumbering step.

Mishra moved as if to halt him and allow his helpers to take him to the hospital and its waiting medical staff.

'No,' Ghote said. 'No, Mishra, let him be.'

'Let him— But why?'

'Kashi. Holy Kashi. Do you not see? He is wanting to die within the bounds of Holy Kashi.'

Mishra took a step back.

'Yes,' he said. 'Yes. He must be . . . But, Ghote, if he is the one do you think we should allow . . . ?'

'I do not know,' Ghote answered. 'I do not at all know.'

But, as if statue-struck, he stood and watched H. K. Verma's blood-pumping, staggering progress.

At the back of his mind he realized, too, that he was not alone in his indecisiveness. Both Mishra now and all the others seemed equally unable to move. Only the umbrella man was still feebly cackling, 'BHU Hospital, best in India . . . Best in all . . .'

H. K. Verma reached the edge of the road. University Road according to the municipal map. The Panchkroshi Road of old, according to religious precept, border between Kashi, City of Light, and the outer darkness.

Ghote took one horrified look to left and right. Traffic? Speeding cars? Thundering trucks? Heedlessly swishing tourist buses?

But there was nothing.

H. K. Verma put one foot into the roadway, plunged forward almost to the ground, heaved his whole weighty body back up, took another wavering step forward.

Will he make it, Ghote asked himself. And do I want him to make it? Should he make it? He is a murderer. I know it. Beyond any doubt whatsoever. So should he be allowed to escape justice? If that is what he is doing. Escaping the ordained justice of the ages, escaping from the interminable cycle of birth and rebirth, gradual gaining of merit, sudden lapses, painful grappling upwards once more. Until at last moksha. Release. But should

H. K. Verma, the man who strangled Mrs Shoba Popatkar, be allowed to cheat on this ages-long travail by setting foot in Holy Kashi?

If such release was really possible. If the long, long scrabble from life to life really existed.

He took a couple of running strides forward in the direction of the bending, blood-spattered figure in the once-white kurta and dhoti. And then halted.

In the roadway H. K. Verma had taken three or four more onward steps. But now he came to a stop. Stood swaying there, almost on the point of toppling sideways.

Ghote, transfixed, simply watched.

Mishra, he saw, and all the others were as dumbstruck. Even the old man with the umbrella seemed now to have realized what was happening and had fallen silent.

Now H. K. Verma had brought himself to go forward once more. Each single step a huge exercise of will. One. Two. Three. Four. And a halt again.

Stay up, stay upright, Ghote found he was willing the bulky, blood-splashed figure. All doubts about what he really wanted for him gone. Walk. Move. Yes, go on. Go on.

And, as if receiving a jolt of transmitted willpower, H. K. Verma suddenly lurched into motion again. Now he was halfway across.

'Mishra,' Ghote begged, his voice coming from he did not know where. 'What is the boundary itself? Exactly? Do you know? Where? Where is it?'

'It— It— I think it must be just as soon as the road is crossed. Should I— Should I help him only?'

'No,' Ghote said, at once sure of his answer. 'No, he must do it himself. Or it will not ...'

He was by no means sure what it would not. But he felt through and through that it must be somehow right to leave the battered, wounded man, the battered wounded murderer, to make this long crossing entirely through the force of his own will.

Behind him the thought that had occurred to Mishra

214

seemed to have infected the other onlookers. They made a concerted move forwards.

'No,' Ghote repeated, filled with authority. 'Leave him be.'

The little crowd halted. As if mercifully relieved of a difficult duty.

In the roadway H. K. Verma had come to a stop again. And had, almost visibly, forced himself to go on once more.

Five more yards to go. Four. Three.

A rocking sway to left and right.

'No,' Ghote heard himself murmur aloud. 'No.'

And on again. Two yards. A yard.

The heavy figure fell forward.

Feet clear of the roadway. In Holy Kashi.

As if released from some supernatural bondage everyone there, Ghote, Mishra, the helpers, the onlookers, the old gentleman with the black, bulgy umbrella, surged forward.

If there had been any traffic there would have been a massacre. No one looked. In less than a minute they were on the far side, surrounding the unmoving bulk, face buried in the roadside dust.

Ghote knelt beside him, felt for a pulse.

Nothing.

Ghote stood on one of the higher steps at the Manikarnika Ghat watching in the fast fading light the body of H. K. Verma burn. H. K. Verma, whose motive for killing Mrs Shoba Popatkar he now knew. A rapid reading of the *Recollections* before he had solemnly handed them back to Mr Srivastava had been enough. If Mrs Popatkar had ever told the world that the unbending figure of the great KK had in his last days renounced his firmest beliefs, then the party that had upheld his stern view of what was right and what wrong over so many years would in a moment have been laughed into oblivion.

Below, silhouetted from time to time against the

215

brightly licking flames, Verma's son, Krishnakanta, head shaved, dressed in seamless white, looking thoroughly sulky, stood with that spoilt brat Vikram, other male members of the family and a gathering of Banares notables, all properly barefoot, white-clad.

Led by the priest conducting the ceremony, as bullying a pandit as any in Banares – the mourners had been rebuked for dipping too deeply in the pot of Ganges water before scattering it on the unlit pyre – Krishnakanta had managed to carry out the rituals. He had poured more Ganges water into the mouth of the dead man. He had gone five times counter-clockwise round the pyre, prodded on by numerous nudges and hissed commands. And then he had put the torch of holy kusha grass twigs, lit at the ever-burning fire kept up by the Doms, to the three hundred kilos of high-piled, ghee-smeared wood. And the flames had leapt up.

No question H. K. Verma is being conducted to the afterlife in the fully correct manner, Ghote thought. If, having died inside Holy Kashi, he is needing any conducting.

It was a knotty little theological point he had put to Inspector Mishra the evening before. Why, he had asked, if by dying within the boundaries of Kashi as H. K. Verma had done you immediately attained moksha, was it necessary to have a funeral conducted according to a ritual designed to pass you without danger into your next life?

Mishra had seemed a little embarrassed.

'Always as well to be safe than sorry,' he had offered.

'But surely that is indicating not much of faith in the merit of dying inside Kashi?'

'Well, it is the way it is done. The way they are saying is correct. The right way.'

He had thought it best then not to pursue it.

In any case conversation had been difficult. They had been talking jammed tightly side by side in the middle of an enormous crowd. At Mishra's invitation he had gone, to occupy the time till his evidence about H. K. Verma's accident had been given and he was free to return to Bombay, to watch the final play in the Ram Lila story. The Bharat Milap, held by tradition in the short time between daylight and night in Banares itself, at Nat Imli near the Sanskrit University, had been about to begin.

The Maharajah of Banares, small, dumpy, dressed in cloth-of-gold, under a huge white umbrella, riding high on the back of a stately, much-caparisoned elephant, had arrived. Now there was a sudden stillness in the huge throng that had been slowly gathering over the past two hours and more, a jam-packed mass of humanity in clothes of every colour, threaded through with the khaki of the police.

'Sometimes up to fifty thousand onlookers,' Mishra had murmured.

Up on the flat, red-silk adorned roof of a small temple the twelve-year-old boy enacting Bharat, brother of hero Rama, who had guarded his kingdom for all the fourteen years of Rama's forced exile in the dangerous forest, sat, solemn in yellow robe. An elaborately tall golden taj crowned his head. The innocent youthfulness of his face was still manifest under the hours-long make-up of paints and plastered-on sequins. Quietly he awaited the return of Rama, reunited at last, after tremendous warfare, with his wife the faithful Sita, and accompanied as always by his brother Laxman, companion in exile.

Then at last the longed-for moment came. The three twelve-year-olds playing Rama, Sita and Laxman appeared. 'In olden days,' Mishra said, 'they would have by now been fed a poisoned meal. They were altogether too holy to be allowed to go back to ordinary life.' Slow step by slow step they advanced towards the temple. Beside them the brahmin regulating the ceremony hovered and darted, obsessed with getting every last detail right. Then suddenly the three broke into a joyous, unrestrained run, on and up to the temple roof and the brotherly embrace that ends the long, long years of exile and danger.

At that moment Ghote, for all that he had not gone through the dangers and the fears of the Ram Lila plays as they had been enacted out at Ramnagar, felt the tears come to his eyes. Tears of joy.

Rama and Bharat embraced. Each proclaimed, voices high and fluting, the words of greeting. Garlands were exchanged. It was over, the long struggle of the perfect man to do right whatever adversities befell. From the immense crowd there had come a huge shout of wondering triumph, repeated and repeated to the now star-bright sky, 'Rama ki jai, Bharatabhai ki jai.' Right, the long story has told them, must triumph, must be served.

Ghote, standing now at the Manikarnika Ghat watching the sharp flames eat into the weighty body of the murderer he had seen die, acknowledged to himself that at that moment of the Bharat Milap the evening before he had sighed, deeply sighed.

Sighed for what? For a world where right did triumph? Or for the world where right so seldom seemed to triumph? Or for his own failure to nourish enough in himself the ineradicable urge to do right he knew to be there?

He could not say.

Down where the pyre had consumed by more than half H. K. Verma's body Krishnakanta was performing his final duties. Handed by the brahmin a stout length of bamboo, he stepped forward and struck the now fleshless skull one single hard blow. With a dull pop of an explosion the fragile, calcified bone broke open, freeing the spirit within. Then, taking between his two hands a large clay vessel of Ganga water, Krishnakanta turned his back and threw it over his left shoulder to shatter on the pyre. With a great hiss of rising steam the flames were doused to a solid core of red heat. Finally he walked away without, as the ritual dictated, looking back.

The other mourners had already begun to move away, down to the river, in accord with custom, however little they had gone near the corpse, to wash themselves once more pure.

Soon they had all left. Only a single Dom, his long iron pole resting on his shoulder, stood guard over the smouldering mass that had been H. K. Verma.

Ghote stayed where he was.

Over the still waters of the river the sun was setting in a wide swath of fading red. The lonely figure of a widow, the very last of the light catching her thin white sari, crept, bent double, between him and the mound of smoking ash.

Protima, he thought. Will one day she be a widow here in this city of death? If I should die before her, be taken to the electric crematorium back in Bombay . . . Or even if, as perhaps H. K. Verma contemplated, I had had my mouth shut for ever here in Banares as he shut Mrs Shoba Popatkar's in Dadar, Protima might very well decide this was where to end her days.

And perhaps, even at this moment, some tiny inner event has occurred in my own body that is the beginning of my end.

My life may be in its last stage. This life, if they are right, the pandits and the pandas, this life in the long, long cycle of life upon life we are condemned to.

Well, but how have I lived that life? Will I come back as a pandit myself, or as a maharajah to ride on an elephant? Or – he looked out across the wide Ganges to where the light of the sinking sun had turned the Sandbank into one long sullen black hump – will it be as a donkey?

Have I done enough of the right in my life? Have I?